She loved her job, and that was all that mattered, wasn't it?

Rory's end of the line was silent. He cleared his throat. "I understand. So, should I get in touch with you if…if something happens?"

A sickening grumble went through Elle's stomach. Something happening meant that Kate had died. She didn't know how to respond. It angered her to think he may be using it as a way to make her feel guilty.

"Why would you say something like that? Are you trying to guilt me into coming back?"

"Is that the only reason you would?"

"You idiot. Why are you even involved? If I want to see my aunt, I will and it won't be from an invitation from you."

"Elle, I'm not trying to start a fight. I'm just being realistic. She isn't well and I thought you might want to be in the loop." Rory continued, "How do I contact you over there?"

Elle couldn't keep thinking about Kate being gone. She numbly gave Rory the main number at the news desk in Washington as a contact.

Rory returned to his formalness. "Well, since I won't be seeing you, have a happy holiday."

Elle just sighed, annoyed and irritable.

"And Elle…" He paused.

"Yes?" she asked sharply.

"You be careful over there."

Elle huffed.

He gave a small laugh, which irritated her even more. "Maybe I'll see you when you get home."

She hung up the phone and took a seat on the sofa. Home, she thought looking around the apartment. Why did it all of a sudden seem so cold and impersonal? She sat up straight and shook herself back to reality. *What is it with me lately?*

Elle took the handle of the suitcase and reminded herself of the awesome assignment she'd been given and the daunting task of saving her job. She was about to take an adventure. Even though she had been alone for years, it was the first time the loneliness of being alone hit her.

Home. The word rang out in her head. She walked out the door and closed it behind her. She put the key in the door to lock up the apartment, and as she turned the bolt, she thought about how little was in there that she'd actually miss if it were stolen.

When aggressive television network news producer, Elle McCord, is assigned to Iraq at the beginning of the Gulf War, she feels her career is beginning to take off. But when her mother informs her that her elderly and ill aunt is about to give away the family farm to a mysterious stranger, Elle takes a detour to try and stop the man who is at the heart of it all.

On the rural Pennsylvania farm, Elle's horrific childhood memories surface, and what she learns about the mysterious stranger who is swindling her aunt is nothing like what she expected.

Elle finally leaves for Iraq, but when she arrives, she meets Faiza, her translator, who teaches her about the sacrifices of family and love and what home really means.

Critical Praise for *Like Ravens in Winter*

"Unexpected twists and one really creepy turn." ~ Debbie Worten, KUTV

"Expertly told story about this crazy news business is a story about us all." ~ Alex Cabrero, KSL TV

"Riveting! A real page turner!" ~ Tracie Potts, NBC News

"From Washington, DC, to the streets of Baghdad, to a Pennsylvania farm, a story-driven journalist discovers herself crossing personal and professional boundaries— boundaries she thought she had buried with her nightmare-causing past. What a ride!" ~ Todd Blackinton, KPVI TV, Idaho

"Hooked from the very sentence! I was fascinated with the dichotomy with Elle's life; her drive to find the real story juxtaposed with discovering her own 'real' story. I not only related to Elle as a journalist, but as a woman. This is a fantastic book club book. Everyone should grab a glass of 'chilled' red wine and read it." ~ Mary Sturgill, KBMT TV, Texas

ACKNOWLEDGMENTS

I want to thank all the journalists who I've worked with and watched over the years, who have taught and inspired me in ways they can't even imagine.

LIKE RAVENS IN WINTER

BRENDA STANLEY

A Black Opal Books Publication

GENRE: ROMANTIC SUSPENSE/ROMANTIC THRILLER

This is a work of fiction. Names, places, characters and incidents are either the product of the author's imagination or are used fictitiously, and any resemblance to any actual persons, living or dead, businesses, organizations, events or locales is entirely coincidental. All trademarks, service marks, registered trademarks, and registered service marks are the property of their respective owners and are used herein for identification purposes only. The publisher does not have any control over or assume any responsibility for author or third-party websites or their contents.

DEDICATION

"For David"

CHAPTER 1

August, 1990:

There were few sad situations in life that compared to a grown daughter who hated going home. For Elle McCord, it was a yearly challenge, and a creative drain that began the night after New Year's Eve and lasted until the night before Christmas the following year. This year was especially taxing. Maybe it was the stress of the recent police action breaking out in the Persian Gulf, or maybe she had just burned out.

"Two minutes to air!" the director yelled, as the studio lights burned down upon the set. It was early September in Washington, DC, and the muggy summer of 1990 was slowly coming to an end. Iraqi dictator, Saddam Hussein, had invaded Kuwait just a week before and the tension was building, as the United Nations demanded his withdrawal.

Elle knew that the possibility of a war in the prime of her career was a dream come true. She had covered murders, political fraud, and scandals by the dozens, but nothing compared to the emotional and sensational im-

pact of a war, except maybe the assassination of a president. A war would give her that rush she needed. It was
the reason she went into news. It was what made her life
full and exciting. For ten years she had covered everything from extreme horror, to terrible sadness, to incredible love, and when it was over, she flew back home to her
apartment and moved on to the next story.

Elle had just returned from a short trip to North Car-
olina, where a large number of troops headed to the Persian Gulf. It was a quick but productive trip that only
piqued her interest in the impending hostilities overseas.
She sat winding the telephone cord around her finger and
tried to bring her conversation back to a quieter tone.

"Mother, I can't make it this Christmas, because I've
got too much to do with the stuff breaking out in the
Gulf."

Going to her mother's home in San Diego was
smothering and usually humiliating. Elle had left home
after high school and over the last decade hadn't spent
more than a week each year with her mother. When she
did visit, she ended up leaving after just a few days and
wondering why she had ever agreed to go in the first
place. Did she really think her mother would stop goad-
ing her about her weight, her inability to apply eyeliner,
or her lack of a husband? Not since junior high did Elle
remember a conversation with her mother that didn't focus on her falling short of her mother's ideals.

During the last couple years, she hadn't made the trip
at all. It gave her a twinge of guilt knowing she was all
her mother had left, but she had become an expert in ra-
tionalization. The weekly phone calls were enough to
keep her from feeling guilty enough to succumb.

Elle was an only child. But that wasn't always the
case. When she was young, her sister Suzanne was killed
on the family farm. It was a tragedy that hit the family so

hard and unexpectedly that her father left the farm too. Elle didn't know if it was the pressure or overwhelming sadness that made him leave. She was so young herself at the time, all she knew was she lost both a sister and a father in the same blow.

Now as she was nearly thirty, she still felt pressure each fall when her mother asked what her plans were for the holidays. Elle loved her mother, but disliked being around her. She loved the sound of Rose's voice, as long as it came from the other end of a phone line. Her weekly phone calls home were like clockwork and seemed to satisfy both women. But being in her mother's presence was a different story.

Ted Malone took his seat at the desk. Elle admired his calm style and never tired of watching him adjust his coat and prepare to greet the masses. Holly Rand followed like a royal servant, making last minute touch-ups on his hair and make-up. She winked at Elle and made a chatty motion with her hand, knowing Rose was on the other end of the line.

"Are you going to wave at me, honey?" Rose asked during mid-gripe.

"Mother, I've told you for years, I can't wave at you."

"Then do that hair flip thing. Come on. It's the only chance I ever get to see you." This really meant, "If you did something with your hair and makeup, maybe you'd be in front of the camera instead of behind it." No matter how many awards Elle won for her writing, in Rose's eyes, it was still a step below being the one who was on TV.

As the opening music for "Nightline" boomed through the studio, Elle leaned back and stroked a piece of hair behind her ear.

Rose giggled with delight, knowing the blurred figure at the desk behind Mr. Malone was her daughter "waving" at her. "Hi, honey!" she yelled into the receiver.

"Hi, Mom," Elle mumbled, playing along.

"Is that the sweater I sent you?"

"Yes," Elle replied, actually pleased at the sappiness of it. But she clicked her nails nervously, wanting to end the conversation before it turned into the usual argument about Elle's lack of consideration and attention paid to her mother.

"Elle, I need you to do me a favor."

Elle continued to click as she waited to hear the request.

"Your Aunt Kate isn't doing too well. I need you to visit her."

Elle sat up straight as if she didn't quite hear Rose correctly. "Aunt Kate. Visit. I barely remember her. Why?"

"Because she's family."

"But I don't even know her."

"Sure you do. You called her Auntie K.K."

Elle put her hand over her eyes, frustrated at her lack of memory. "Mom, that was over two decades ago."

"I showed you pictures. She was holding you, remember?" Rose continued to ramble on. "My second cousin Dodie's daughter called. She says Kate is trying to change her will. She's giving the land to…well, to someone else. It's horrible."

"What land?" asked Elle, trying to type and listen at the same time.

"Your Grandpa Elmer's farm, it's been in our family for years. Kate's been living there, but now I hear she's trying to give it away."

"So what's the big deal? You don't have any need for it."

Rose paused and cleared her throat. "But it's worth

some money and she's giving it to a…younger man."

Elle couldn't help but let a small burst of laughter erupt quietly into the receiver. "Like how much younger? For someone who's Aunt Kate's age, younger doesn't mean young. I think you're jealous."

"Don't be ridiculous. It's not what you think and it's not funny, Elle. She's giving away everything Daddy worked for to some gold digging kid."

Elle enjoyed the comical aspects of her mother's predicament. "So what do you expect me to do?"

"Harrisburg is only two hours from Washington. You can do it this weekend."

"That's tomorrow. I can't just up and go to Pennsylvania tomorrow."

"Why not? You aren't dating Kevin Marcus anymore, and you need to get away from work once in a while, besides the family is counting on you."

"For years you've been talking about how you have no family. Now all of a sudden we have family and they're counting on me."

Rose paused, trying to pick her words. "They wouldn't have called me if it wasn't urgent. They know that you're an investigative reporter and will be able to get to the bottom of all this."

"Mother, I'm a field producer. Get to the bottom of what? What did you tell them?"

"Elle, your relatives are simple people. Most haven't even finished high school. They want someone to come and talk to Kate and find out if she really knows what she's doing. They think she may be a little…demented."

"So why don't *they* talk to her?"

"They can't just talk to her."

"Why? You call her. She's your sister."

"You don't understand, Elle. Kate's…well, different. We were never close. She's been causing trouble like this ever since…" Rose hesitated. "She's stubborn and, well, I couldn't stand being around all of it."

"You've always said you left Pennsylvania because you hated living on a farm," Elle said, annoyed.

"I did. I couldn't stand Pennsylvania. I hated living in the middle of nowhere. I wanted a career. That's why I moved to California."

Elle pondered what Rose had gained from moving to LA. Five husbands later, she was a condo-dwelling divorcee, with a dozen vain friends, whose only joy in life was outdoing each other with stories about their exes.

"The family in Pennsylvania is very reserved. They don't talk about anything that could cause a conflict. They know that, with you being from the big city, it's okay for you to be more…"

"What, nosey?" Elle interrupted.

"You don't understand, Elle. They are horrified by the thought of Kate and this guy. They don't want to see the land go to someone other than family."

"But I thought you said there wasn't any other family alive but Kate."

"Yes."

"Then who are all these people you keep calling family?"

"They are mostly distant cousins from your grandpa's sisters."

"So, you want the land so you can just sell it."

"Well, it is a lot of money…about two million, but it's not just the money. Dodie's daughter Cynthia and her husband Jonathan want to expand their restaurant there. Your grandpa used to raise chickens, and they want to build a little diner that serves chicken, that way it can stay in the family."

"You're going to sell it to this Dodie person. Is she the closest relative to Kate, besides us?"

"Yes, she is the granddaughter of your grandpa's sister. They will be so excited to see you."

"I didn't agree to do this, and I still don't understand what you want from me. What makes you think she'll even speak to me? You certainly don't think that I'll be able to change her mind about the will."

"No, but maybe if this guy sees that the family is checking things out, he'll back off. If he doesn't, then we can do something, maybe through an attorney. She has no one to protect her, and I'm so far out here."

"How long ago did grandpa die?"

"It's been over twenty years now."

"And you've never been back?"

"No."

"Well," Elle said smiling to herself. "This ought to be interesting. I guess I need to go check out the hunk who has my aunt all a-quiver."

"Don't talk like that. The cousins have planned a brunch for you at Cynthia's house. She'll call you tonight with directions."

"Figuring I've never had any cousins, this ought to be interesting. I hope you know I will have completely done my 'duty to family' thing for a lifetime with this one."

Rose scoffed. "You always make it seem like work when it comes to helping me. You should want to help your family."

Elle held her tongue at the hypocrisy of her mother, and began to contemplate her visit with the cousins.

❧❧❧

Holly picked through Elle's clothes. "So you've never met any of these people before?"

Elle threw toiletries and shoes into a bag. "We left

when I was about eight. I remember some things, but not much. I know I've never had a desire to go back,"

Holly pulled out a pair of shoes with thin heels. "You're going to the country. You need jeans and boots. You act as though you're trying to impress the hayseeds."

Elle smiled and slicked her blonde hair back into a tight ponytail. "I'm not trying to impress anyone, but I'm not planning on plodding around in a barn. It's a lunch."

"So, do you know anything about these people? Imagine you, the queen of Type A related to a bunch of farmers. They're probably nervous about meeting their big city cousin."

Elle shrugged. "I've barely had any family and don't know how to act when we meet. Do I act as though we're old friends? Mom says they are conservative. What if I offend them?"

Holly laughed and propped herself up at Elle's vanity and began to experiment with a new shade of lipstick. "Trust me, you'll offend them, but they'll all say, 'She's from the city.' And then everyone will nod and their ideas about us urbanites will be confirmed and everyone will go home happy. You'll come back to work on Monday with great stories about how warm and endearing they all are, and that will be the end of it."

"You're probably right," Elle said, clicking her perfectly sculptured nails.

Holly grabbed a sweater. "Wear the red. It screams out bold and sassy. Oh, and don't forget the World Network News jacket. I have to wear mine to all the relative things. You'll make Rose proud."

Elle grimaced.

"So have you talked to Kevin Marcus lately?" Holly asked cautiously.

Elle nodded. "He's in Baltimore for a couple weeks.

He called one night after having a little too much to drink. He probably regrets it now."

"Regrets the call or the break up?"

"Who cares? I don't need the angst."

Holly shrugged. "I still can't believe you don't want him. He's a rich, handsome attorney—"

"He is also a slacker. I swear if he makes partner, it will be a miracle. The guy has no drive. I don't want to end up like my mother, divorced and alone."

"So you'd rather always be alone?" Holly asked.

"No. I just refuse to jump into something."

"You dated Kevin for two years."

Elle looked into the mirror. She studied her thin, tired face. "And for two years I had to change my schedules, act like I was happy when I wasn't, and walk on egg-shells, like a wimpy female."

"But you are—" Holly began to say.

"I know, I'm female. You know what I mean," Elle said.

Holly walked to the door. "Do you want me to take care of your cat while you're gone?"

Elle shrugged. "Take him. I'm not sure he even knows I'm his owner. You have him more than I do."

Holly scoffed. "You can't just give away your pet."

"I don't think he'll mind or even notice. It's not like he gets much out of this relationship." Elle looked down at the black and white cat who licked its leg unconcerned about being the topic of conversation. "What do I have to offer? I don't think he's too worried about losing me."

Holly reached down to pick up the cat.

Elle put a hand out, stopping her. "I'll drop him off tomorrow, okay?"

Holly shrugged and left the two alone in the empty apartment.

As the door closed behind Holly, Elle took a seat on

the floor. She felt herself turning weak. It may have been two decades ago, but Elle remembered more about the Pennsylvania farm than she had ever told anyone. Much of it was a hazy fog and quick flashes of sights and people, but what she still saw clearly was a foreboding presence that lived on that farm. It was worse than any horror show monster, with bulging eyes, a sickly bluish face, and in her visions it was always swooping down on her.

She had never let that image fade. The guilt stabbed through her as though she were standing in a field and watching the monster take the life of the only sister she had. She remembered the crying and chaos that followed. Elle put her hands out in front of her and opened them. She traced the oddly shaped and palpable scars that covered her palms. She hated shaking hands. As she sat alone, she remembered the desperation she felt and the sadness that was still so strong in her. Sometimes, it hit her so hard she was unable to function.

She swallowed hard and wondered if she had done the right thing in agreeing to go to the farm. She turned and kneeled toward her cat. "Here, Kitty," she called in a sweet high-pitched tone. The cat looked up. "Here, Kitty," she tried again. "Please," she whispered.

As though feeling her pain, he cocked his head and stretched. He slowly climbed into her lap and cuddled up.

CHAPTER 2

The drive to Lancaster County took Elle through a part of the country she hadn't seen in years. The scatters of people and cement landscape of DC turned gradually into a wooded countryside of simple homes and endless rolling fields. Windmills turned slowly at each home, and several rustic wooden bridges linked the roads and broke up the monotony of the drive.

Elle watched the people in the fields and pastures. They were dressed in coveralls and work boots and were busy with brightly colored tractors and other large pieces of equipment. It's out in the middle of nowhere, she thought, contemplating what it would be like to live so far away from civilization. "An okay place to visit, but…" she mumbled.

The radio found little reception and nothing that kept Elle updated on the state of the conflict going on in the Persian Gulf. Economic sanctions had just been authorized, so Elle knew some type of action would happen soon.

She followed the directions she had been given by her new cousin, Cynthia. She was overly sweet on the phone, giving Elle a taste of what lay ahead.

The small country store was just as Cynthia had described. A sleek blue station wagon waited in the parking
lot. When Elle pulled up, a thin woman with oddly curled
brown hair hopped out from the passenger seat to greet
her.

"You must be Elle," she oozed, taking Elle's hand
with both of hers.

A small man with thinning hair opened the door of
the driver's side and struggled out. He adjusted his pants,
stood much too close, and extended a hand. "I'm John
Evans, Cynthia's husband. We're all real glad you decided to come up and talk some sense into that aunt of
yours."

Elle smiled awkwardly. "Well, actually, I just came
for a visit."

Cynthia laughed nervously and smiled through
spaced teeth. "What John means is that we appreciate any
help you can give us."

John piped up again, "Heaven knows no one else in
this family has the guts to face her."

"What does that mean?" asked Elle.

"She has the personality of a rock. No one in this
family dares to say anything, ever."

"Well, let's get you to Mary's house. I'm sure everyone is waiting." Cynthia took John by the arm and led
him away, trying to seem pleasant.

Elle followed them a short distance to a little home
that was set neatly back, into a nest of maple trees. Inside
Elle found a group of about twenty people, all short, and
either stocky or frail looking. She tried to smile and said a
weak, "Hello."

Several of the women smiled back and nodded. The
room was incredibly quiet, and Elle wondered if the rest
of the day would be as uncomfortable.

Cynthia took a stand in the center of the room. "Everyone, this is cousin Elle from Washington, DC." She turned back and smiled at Elle.

Elle grinned and lifted an eyebrow and wondered if she should say something or just stand there, smiling.

"I'll go around the room and introduce you to everyone." Cynthia began walking up to each of the muted relatives.

Elle nodded and said "Hello" as each one was introduced, wondering when Cynthia would introduce Kate. When Cynthia made it to the last chubby little woman, Elle stepped forward, expecting it to be her aunt.

"And this is cousin Deirdre," Cynthia said. "I'm sure you won't be able to remember them all, but at least you've been formally introduced."

Elle turned to Cynthia. "But where's Aunt Kate?"

John butted in, "She doesn't come to family things. She stays at her house—spends all her time with that guy."

Cynthia shot him a sneer and then turned back, her face flushed. "We'll be taking you to Kate's house after we eat."

Elle stood alone for a moment in the middle of the room. A round man with a flannel shirt and no ability to make eye contact approached her.

"They are ready to eat. Let's go to the dining room."

After the meal, Elle asked to be excused and made her way to the porch to be alone. She took deep breaths, relieved to be away from the gawks and glances of the strangers.

She felt a presence and turned, startled to see Cynthia was right behind her.

"Oh, I'm s—sorry," Cynthia stammered, as she interrupted Elle. "I didn't mean to bother you."

"You're not bothering me."

"I just wanted to let you know that we are about ready to go to Kate's house."

Elle nodded. "So, where is my mother's cousin, Dodie? Isn't that your mother?"

Cynthia gave her a sober look. "Mama's passed on. She's been dead about ten years now."

Elle looked at her with shocked humor. "Does my mother know this?"

Cynthia shrugged. "I figured someone had told Rose." Then she looked up and gave Elle a squeamish and oopsie-daisey grin.

Elle looked off, speechless. She remembered what Rose had said about Kate being shunned for not following the conservative ways like the others. She tried to imagine Rose, her gaudy clothes, painted red lips, and ratted hair, mixing with the plain likes of her distant relatives. She tugged at the hem of her shirt and straightened it around her hips. She knew her mother's expectations when it came to appearances, and she also knew regardless of how thin, how blonde or how flawless Elle appeared, there would always be something she could do more. It made Elle wonder if the stagnant and stifling air of her conservative relatives was what molded Rose into what she was and what she expected from Elle.

The drive to the farm was longer than Elle expected. The road followed a serpentine path, lined by willowy shafts of ripe oats. Sun filled the rows and made the breeze feel cool, as it whipped at Elle's long golden hair. She wondered what Kate was like and whether she knew of Rose's intent to get the money. Of course, if Kate was as naïve as the rest of the cousins, this could be an easy slam-dunk for Rose to score millions. All Rose wanted was for Elle to get rid of the guy.

The blue Taurus wagon turned onto a small dirt road dotted with large trees leading up the hill to a tiny brick house. A small garage sat off to the side and a white fence lined a yard filled with flowers and birdhouses. It was very pretty for a woman with the personality of a rock. Elle stopped her car, giving Cynthia room to make her escape.

Elle looked around and felt an odd sense of familiarity. She shook it off, thinking it was silly. It had been over two decades, how could she possibly remember anything about this place? And why would she want to?

Cynthia left John in the car and walked Elle up the stone path. When the door opened, a small thin woman peered out through round glasses.

"Hello, Kate. This is Elle…your niece," Cynthia cooed nervously.

"I know she's my niece," Kate snapped from behind the screen door. She stood silent, looking Elle over.

Elle stood in shock, quietly allowing the old woman to study her.

"Can she talk?" Kate asked.

Elle laughed to herself but forced a quick, "Yes, I can talk. Hello, Kate."

Cynthia disappeared, and Elle stood at the door alone, wondering if that's as far as she would get.

"I hear you had lunch," Kate said. She stood straight in a simple cotton dress, dotted with tiny blue flowers. A cream colored cardigan was draped over her shoulders and buttoned at her neck. Her thin hands were clasped in front of her.

"Yes, I did."

Kate opened the screen door. "Then I'll wait until later to make something."

Elle nodded and stepped inside. The home was clean, with tiny knick-knacks and paintings that covered every inch of the walls. "These are incredible," Elle said walking toward one landscape with fields of purple flowers.

Kate answered with a grunt.

"Who did these? How many do you own?" Elle asked.

"You haven't changed much from when you were young. You talked too much then, too." Kate stood squarely, her hands still clasped tightly in front of her. "Do you have an overnight bag?"

Elle felt the need to snap back, then she saw a ghost of a smile on the old woman.

"Yes."

She went out to the car, and as she sat in the driver's seat to pop the trunk, she felt an urge to quickly drive away. In the field that expanded around the house, a rustic sway-backed barn stood out from never-ending waves of crops. The sight tugged at Elle's mind, keeping her enthralled with the ragged wooden slats and high dormer windows that jutted out over the field. She squinted and saw that on the far side corner was a dark discoloration that covered the entire height of the structure. The sight of it made her gut tighten.

Elle tried to turn away, but the flames and smoke were everywhere. She heard her father call from outside and heard the words, "The barn's on fire." Elle ran up the stairs and out the door in a panic. "*Suzanne!*"

The word was clear in her mind, and she spoke the name softly again. Elle forced herself to turn away, and as soon as she did her mind cleared. She knew now why she hadn't been back to the farm.

Elle thought that after all these years, the pain would be gone, but instead it was like a nightmare that stayed with her even after she awoke. She wondered how she would be able to stay there and not obsess about what happened. She had to try. The air was cool and she took a deep breath of it, as she walked back into the house.

"Follow me," Kate said, as she led Elle down stairs

to an open room. The small windows let in little light, but Kate had obviously gone to lengths to make it suitable for her guest. A small bed was made with a beautiful hand tied quilt, and a bouquet of fresh fall flowers sat in a rose colored vase.

"This is very nice," Elle said, setting her suitcase down.

Kate turned toward the stairs. "We'll have dinner after our rest."

"Our rest?"

"Afternoon nap," Kate snapped back.

"Nap?"

Kate's tiny feet disappeared up the stairs. For several minutes Elle stood in awe. Then she paced. She needed a television, radio, anything where she could get news. She searched the room, finding nothing. She sat on the bed feeling trapped.

Boxes were stacked against every wall. She looked at the labels. Most were just dates. She wanted to open them but didn't feel she was quite up to that yet. After about fifteen minutes, she conceded and curled up on the small bed like she had as a child. The day seemed to rush through her mind like a flutter of strange places and odd characters. An afternoon nap! She lay wondering what could possibly happen next.

CHAPTER 3

Elle stirred and opened her eyes slowly. She couldn't believe she actually had fallen asleep. She blinked as she tried to focus on her watch.

A gruff voice came from behind her. "Are you going to sleep all day?"

Elle turned quickly to her side. There stood Kate. She held another beautiful quilt in her arms.

"You'll probably need this tonight. It gets cool down here."

"I can't believe I really fell asleep. I'm not used to taking naps. What time is it?"

"It's almost five, and you should get used to it. You need to drink more water, too. Your skin is dry and water will flush the impurities out."

Elle sat up wondering what else to expect.

Kate motioned toward the stairs. "I made scrapple and greens. It's ready when you are."

Elle stood up and straightened her sweater. She wondered if she would ever be truly ready for Kate.

The greens were green, so Elle assumed the perfectly squared piece of speckled cornmeal was the scrapple. A bottle of maple syrup sat on the table. Elle sat poised, waiting for a cue from Kate as to what to do. Kate sat and stared back. She had white hair that looked like brushed cotton and skin like cracked ivory. Her dress looked handmade but well-tailored, and the tiny blue flowers matched the blue lace that lined the collar and cuffs of her sweater.

"Aren't you hungry?" she asked Elle.

"Oh, uh…yes. I've just never had scrapple before. I'm not sure how to eat it."

"You use a fork," Kate answered back.

Elle smiled and looked down at her plate. The gruffness was funny but starting to wear on her. "You're probably wondering why I came to visit you."

"No. You came because your mother wants the land."

Elle looked squarely at Kate. "She was worried about you and asked me to come for a visit." She imagined Rose looking at millions slipping away.

Kate smiled broadly for the first time since Elle had arrived. "Your mother hasn't worried herself with me or anything else out here for over twenty years."

"I know. It's just she heard that you were changing your will, and, well, I guess the family is worried that someone is taking advantage of you." Elle heard the words come out but cringed at the sound of them.

Kate stood up. "The family? They aren't my family. I've run this farm without any help from them for decades. The only interest they've ever shown in this land was to degrade it. They want to bulldoze it to build a tacky restaurant. You can go back to your mother and tell her no one is going to ruin this land. It will stay with people who care about it."

Elle sat stunned and quiet.

Kate went to the fridge and brought out a bottle of milk. "I have orange juice, too, if you don't want milk."

"Milk is fine," Elle mumbled.

They sat silent, picking at the greens and scrapple.

"I'm beginning to see it was a m—mistake for me to come out h—here," Elle stammered. "Maybe I should leave."

Kate stared at her plate, as Elle pushed herself away from the table.

Elle hesitated at the stairs and then went to retrieve her things. It was useless to try and reason with Kate. Rose would get an attorney, and then let a judge decide who family was. As she straightened the covers on the bed, she heard the stairs creek behind her. Kate stood silently, but Elle heard a familiar noise coming from her hands. She looked back at Kate and noticed her clicking her nails, just as Elle did when she was agitated or nervous.

"Do you get along with your mother?" Kate's monotone voice asked from the stairs.

Elle shrugged, "Yes, when I'm not around her."

Kate nodded. "Let's go for a walk, and I'll show you why I don't get along with her either."

The sun was still up and warmed the air, but conversation still hung like a cool cloud around them. Elle tried to make small talk about the weather, but Kate just mumbled answers and walked quietly beside her. For an old woman, her pace was quick and sure. The breeze did seem to be turning cooler and Elle wished she had brought a jacket. When they reached the top of the hill, Kate stopped and looked over the fields. They seemed to spread out endlessly.

"All of this is our land," Kate said. "We've farmed it for two hundred years. It has taken care of a lot of people."

"There's so much of it. Why does John need all this for his diner?"

"I wouldn't give him one square inch for his tacky old restaurant. This land won't be violated by that."

Elle admired her aunt's passion for the land, and, as she surveyed the expanse, she understood why her mother saw dollar signs. She shaded her eyes from the sun and noticed a small house in the distance and a stable and pasture nearby. "What's that?" she asked.

"That was the original farm house. It's where your mother and I were raised. She hated it here, always walked around complaining about the work and how she was going to leave the day she turned eighteen. Rory is staying there now."

"Who's Rory?"

Kate looked at her, surprised. She smiled with her eyes. "It has been a long time, hasn't it?"

Elle was oblivious.

Kate scoffed. "I'm surprised they haven't given you all the gory little details."

Ah hah! thought Elle. So this younger man has a name and has already staked his claim on the land and living in the family home!

They turned to the east and Elle stopped and stared again at the large red barn. It was worn and swayed and looked like it hadn't been used in years. The same odd, haunting sensation rushed through her. It was so powerful, she lost herself in thought for a moment, trying to push the memories away.

"It's just an old barn, Elle."

Elle continued to stare. "It's where she died isn't it?"

"Yes."

"I don't remember much about this place, but when I saw that barn, I remembered what happened...or at least some of it. I remember I always was afraid to go in there, even before she died."

"You ran all over this place when you were a little

girl. You used to love it here. It is sad how things turn
out."

Elle turned away from it, but still felt pulled to know
more. Her instincts as a journalist picked at her constantly. She wanted to open the pages of her past but knew
that only pain would come from learning the truth. After
all these years, she knew there was a reason she held
back. Elle felt the nauseating wave of memories rush over
her, and she shook her mind free of its grasp. Even
though the curious pull was strong, she would continue to
keep what secrets were in that barn pushed far away from
reach.

A dust cloud appeared in the distance, and Elle saw a
white truck making its way up the path on the other side
of the hill. Soon she saw a cheery, smiling face behind
the wheel as the truck slowed down to greet them. She
looked over to Kate who smiled broadly and Elle figured
this must be Rory. Kate approached the truck, as the smiling man rolled down the window. "How are you, Kate?
It's so nice to see you out."

Kate beamed at the man. He was older than Elle expected and was rugged and unkempt. He hardly seemed
like the young swindler everyone had painted him to be.

"I want you to meet my niece. This is Elle McCord.
She's up visiting for a couple days. Elle, this is Ervin
Coughlin.

Elle nodded.

He smiled even brighter. "A niece. That's wonderful.
Nice to meet you. What did you say your name was?"

"It's Elle," she said.

"Elle. Like the letter?" he asked.

"Like the letter."

Kate laughed. It was hearty and Elle knew it was directed at her, but it was different from the gruffness she
had been enduring.

"Ervin here has worked on the farm for about ten years now," said Kate.

Elle realized he wasn't the young love in Kate's life.

"I've checked the back sections and things look really good. We should be harvesting by next week," he announced.

Kate patted him on the arm, as he drove off in another cloud of dust.

"So you still run this entire farm?" asked Elle.

"No. Ervin does most of the work, but Rory oversees it now that he's here. I help with some of the books when I can, but I don't hold up like I used to." She began to walk back to the house.

"So this Rory person works for you?" asked Elle, feeling the courage to pry.

"I'd prefer to say he works for *us*. And my idea of work is different than yours."

"Really?" asked Elle, humored. "How's that?"

"Do you like your work?"

"I love my work. My work is my life," Elle announced proudly.

"Your life is unhappy. Your work is making you sick," Kate said, still staring out as they walked.

Elle looked over at her, surprised. "I know the stress of my job is not good for me. But my job is my life."

"You'll have no stress at all when you're dead." Kate clasped her hands behind her and walked toward the house. "Time for bed."

Bed? It couldn't have been past seven. Elle stood on the porch as the sun faded into the distance. It gave her a chance to really look at the land and remember her short time living there. She tried to imagine what it was like for her mother to grow up with the open spaces and quiet serenity. Rose had often talked about the fields and animals, but the picture she painted was dismal and dirty. Elle had never had the desire to visit, based on her mother's description.

She surveyed the property, feeling an odd sense of security and solace. It was as though she could hear the voices of people who lived there before, talking in the wind. Elle heard Kate in the house, putting dishes away in the kitchen. She thought about what Kate had said about Elle's life being unhappy. What did Kate know about her life, thought Elle, and just what exactly is happiness? She had a great job and she was thin and young. What more was there?

CHAPTER 4

Elle awoke feeling more awake and refreshed than she had in months. The quilt was heavy and warm, and she hoped Kate wasn't waiting for her. She pulled on her robe and tiptoed upstairs. The door to Kate's room was closed, so Elle took a quick shower and dressed in the bathroom. She carefully combed her long hair into its usual sleek, straight pony tail. It was the only way she could keep it from succumbing to its natural curl and looking frivolous and unprofessional. She penciled in the dark, sharp curve of her eyebrows and gave her lips a quick swipe of ruby glisten lip gloss. She heard Holly's voice chiding her about trying to impress the hayseeds, but Elle refused let herself go for even one day.

When she opened the door, Kate stood with an armful of towels. "I'd like to take you to Cynthia and John's chicken place today," she said and then turned toward the kitchen.

"Okay," said Elle, wondering why, and calculating in her mind how much time that would take, as she was looking forward to getting back home. It had been almost two days without news and she was beginning to worry about what she had missed. She ate a quiet but tasty breakfast of grits and eggs and then walked with Kate outside.

"Would you like me to drive?" Elle asked.

Kate shrugged. "We can take my car." She paused and looked back at the garage.

Elle stopped. "Really? You drive?"

"You act as though you're surprised I can even feed myself." Kate walked over to the garage and tried to lift the door.

Elle saw her struggling and helped her raise it. Inside was a perfectly undisturbed 1965 white Thunderbird. Elle gasped. "It's beautiful."

"It was a gift," Kate said smiling. "It was brand new when I got it, and I've kept it all these years." Kate's voice had softened and she spoke as though there was no one else around. She turned to Elle. "I don't take it out much anymore."

"Would you like to?" Elle asked.

Kate nodded slowly as she stood and stared at the car. It was obvious from her gaze it was the source of many memories. "Here, you drive it." She searched her purse and pulled out a set of two keys. "I'll sit and enjoy the ride."

Elle smiled and almost skipped to the driver's side of the car. As she opened the door, she paused, noticing a horse and a figure in the fields. She walked around to the side of the garage and shaded her eyes from the sun. It was a man. He stood watching her, as his auburn hair blew with the same rhythm as the oats. Even from a distance, Elle could see he had dark, handsome eyes.

His shirt hung closely over sculpted shoulders and Elle found herself tracing his lines with her eyes. She put her hands to her side as if trying to still the tremors in her legs. She caught his stare, and he gave a small smile.

Stunned from her dreamy gaze, she scowled back. He started to wave, but instead turned back to the horse. She watched him as he mounted and reined the animal up the hill toward the corrals.

Again, Elle found herself mesmerized—the shape of his back, the way he sat, strong and at ease in the saddle. He looked back, and seeing Elle still watching him, spurred the horse into a gallop, leaving a billow of dust. It was obviously Rory and he must have suspected that Elle was there to do more than just visit. She walked back to the garage, as Kate sat in the passenger seat, her white tufted head barely showing above the dash.

"Would you like the top down?" Elle asked with a grin.

"Why not. It's warm today."

Elle smiled, surprised, and pulled the flawless beauty onto the road. She looked out over the fields. The man had ridden his horse up the hill to watch them drive away. He leaned on the saddle horn, his large arms brown from working in the sun. Elle strained to get a better view of his face. Even from a distance she could see his dark eyes studying her the way she found herself inspecting him. He tipped his head to the side and smiled with teeth so perfect and white against his tanned face, she almost missed a bend in the road.

Elle tucked a stray lock of her long blonde hair behind her ear and ignored him like one of the cows grazing along the road. It would take a lot more than good looks to shake her from her mission. Being a robust hunk may work on some, but he had no idea with whom he was dealing.

How *dare* he try to scam her aunt? Maybe her country cousins could stand idly by, but she wouldn't. A couple of phone calls to attorneys, and he'd have little more than the horse he rode in on. Elle turned to Kate, who leaned back and enjoyed the wind rushing around her. An old woman, a Thunderbird, and a trip to the diner through oat fields. This will surely have them talking at the station.

The guttural hum of the engine was intoxicating. Elle and Kate both relished the combination of speed and wind. Elle didn't look forward to seeing Cynthia and her husband. She leaned back and thought about her life in DC, how she appreciated all that she had waiting for her when she got home.

"People actually wonder why I've kept this car all these years," Kate said, staring out at the road. "I hide it in the garage, because everyone's always trying to swindle it away from me. It's worth quite a bit."

"I'm sure it is. It rides great and you say you don't drive it much?"

"Never."

"Really? So why do you keep it, if you don't drive?" Elle asked.

Kate smiled. "You don't have to drive to enjoy the ride."

The smell of old leather and clean rural air was an interesting mix. Elle settled back into the soft molded seat and dropped her hand out the side window. The car hummed along hypnotically as the two of them watched the fields go by.

Elle wanted to ask Kate more questions, especially about Rory, but when she tried, Kate gave quick one-word answers and kept her eyes on the road, so Elle stopped asking. It wasn't like Elle to back off from questioning, but she began to realize the story wasn't complete until she interrogated the offender in all this. Elle knew that with her schedule, that would probably never happen.

Country hills slowly turned into a town. After several

streets of stores and neighborhoods, Kate directed Elle to turn into the parking lot of a small restaurant. The sign was large and poorly done with the words, Finger Lickin' Chickin'. The glorious scents of the day had turned to the rancid odor of old corn oil.

"This is Cynthia and John's diner?" Elle asked.

Kate nodded with a snide smile.

Inside, the place was busy. At the counter were two young men in goofy red-striped suits taking orders. John Evans peered from the back and yelled out a shocked, "Kate is here!" He ran around to greet the two, invading their personal space, as Cynthia appeared from a back office. She looked frazzled as she straightened her dress and hair.

"What a surprise," Cynthia said. "You should have called. We must look like a mess."

"Elle wanted to see your place. Pretty impressive, isn't it?" Kate said with a twinkle in her eye.

Elle titled her eyes. "It's a restaurant, all right."

John tucked in his shirt and strutted along the counter. "We started this place from nothing. Now Finger Lickin' Chickin' is one of the largest chicken places in all of Lancaster County."

Elle looked at Kate who sat with an indulgent grin. The image of that tacky diner on her pristine land was a dreadful sight, and Kate knew the only way of getting that across was by showing Elle.

John ordered Cynthia to bring out some samples for Elle. It looked like regular fried chicken and she picked through it, giving them gracious grins as she tasted it.

Kate sat at the bench quietly as John took Elle on a tour of the operation. When they returned, Kate looked pale and weak.

Cynthia sat close by and looked up to Elle as she approached.

"She just started mumbling. She doesn't look well," Cynthia said, distressed

Elle grabbed Kate's hand and lifted her chin. "Kate, are you all right?"

Kate tried to nod. "Just get me out of this chicken place. The smell is getting to me."

Elle turned to Cynthia. "Call an ambulance and get her some water." She turned back to Kate. "We're getting help. The ambulance is on its way."

Kate looked up to Elle with fragile eyes. It was strange to see her like this. The usually brash old woman was weak and frail. When Rose had said Kate wasn't doing well, Elle had no idea that she was really sick. She just thought she was old. Kate took a sip of the water and muttered softly to Elle, "Call the farm. They need to know."

Cynthia lifted an eyebrow at John who walked back to the office and screamed, "Did someone call nine-one-one? We've got an old woman dying out here!"

Elle wanted to slap him, but instead squeezed Kate's hand. "Don't worry, I'll call."

Elle got the number to the house from Cynthia and called from the hospital. A low, gentle voice came over the answering machine and Elle rattled off what had happened.

Elle sat in the waiting room perusing outdated magazines. Time crawled by as she contemplated how much had happened in less than two days. Elle considered calling Rose, but hoped to get more information about Kate's condition before making the call.

One of the small plump cousins from the day before came into the waiting room. Elle tried to muster a smile but it was useless.

"How is she?" the woman asked.

"I don't know yet," Elle said. She couldn't remember

the woman's name, but remembered her from the lunch and was actually glad that someone other than Cynthia and John had made the trip to the hospital.

As if knowing Elle didn't remember, the cousin leaned over and whispered, "I'm Mary, and we're all so glad you're here. We feel like we should be doing something, but no one has ever been very close to Kate."

Mary was cut from the same cloth as the others, and yet she had a genuine sincerity that Elle could sense. She trusted her for some odd reason and was comforted she was there.

A thin, older doctor walked into the room, "Are you Ms. Taylor's niece?" he asked Elle.

Elle looked at her recently acquired cousin, who nodded for her. "Yes, I'm her niece. Is Kate all right?"

"She'll be fine. The chemotherapy drugs make her weak, especially at her age. She needs her rest, but you can see her now," he said, directing Elle toward the hallway.

"Chemo drugs. Does she have cancer?" she asked the doctor, as he led her to the door.

"Yes," he answered, surprised at her question. "She has pancreatic cancer. That's why she's lost so much weight."

Elle thanked the doctor before quietly opening the door to Kate's room. She crept in to find the young man from the field sitting with her, his back to the door, unaware that Elle had entered. He was dressed in clean work clothes and his hair was still damp from a rushed shower. Kate slept as he held her hand and stroked her arm.

Elle watched as he looked at Kate tenderly and straightened the blankets around her.

He seemed Herculean next to Kate's frail, tiny form. Elle found herself lost in the slope of his back and the spread of his shoulders as he hovered over Kate.

Having seen enough, Elle knocked on the door.

He turned back and stood up from the bed. His dark eyes looked at her, questioning.

"I take it you're Rory?" Elle asked.

He nodded, keeping steady eye contact with her. He was rugged and uncombed, but had gentle pristine features that Elle couldn't help but notice.

"I'm Kate's niece," she announced.

"Yes, I know. It's nice to see you, Ellie," he said with a smile. "She said you were coming." His voice was low and deliberate. Silence. He looked down and licked his lips as if searching for words. Then he took a sweeping glance and gave Elle a smile that made her blush.

"My name isn't Ellie, its Elle."

His smiled faded.

They stood awkwardly in the room, as Kate slept peacefully. Elle looked over to her and studied her calm weathered face. She looked even more unfamiliar without her glasses.

"I had no idea she had cancer," said Elle.

Rory nodded. "She's had it over a year now. The doctors didn't think she'd last more than a couple months."

Elle scoffed. "That's very convenient for you."

Rory stared at her, stunned. "What did you say?"

"Listen, maybe you can snow an old woman, but I know what you're doing. Cut the concern, because I know what you're really after."

Rory stepped toward Elle, his eyes burning with anger. "I see. They've got to you already. Brought up the past with lies and rumors, I suppose," he said, in a hoarse whisper.

Elle smirked. "Did you expect to get away with it and have nobody say anything? All I've heard is that you're stringing my aunt along, acting like you care about her, so you can take her money."

Rory took another step, making Elle back up. "Acting?" he asked angrily. "I care more about Kate than any one of her judgmental relatives. Your family is the one who ran out on her. I love her more than anything. How dare you come out here and try to act like you know what's right!"

Kate stirred in her bed. She opened her eyes slowly and looked around the room. "Rory?" she called.

Rory went to her side and took her hand. "I'm right here, Kate."

Kate looked at Elle. "Elle, take me home. Rory needs to get back to work."

"Don't you be worrying about that," Rory tried to comfort her.

Elle sighed. "I'm going to go talk to the doctor. I'll be back in a minute." She walked to the waiting room where Mary was sitting. "Have you seen the doctor?" she asked.

"No," answered Mary. She looked up at her with questioning eyes. "How is she?"

"I think she'll be fine, but she'll need rest."

Mary sighed. "We're just so glad you'll be here for her."

Elle looked at her with concern. "I can't stay. I just came up for the weekend. I have to go back to work."

Mary's face turned sad.

Elle shook her head. "What about the family? Can't someone come and help her?"

"We all have the harvest. Even our children are out of school for it."

"What about Cynthia?" she asked, looking around but not seeing her or John in the hallway.

Mary grimaced. "Kate wouldn't allow it. She's shunned them ever since…"

Elle watched her try to pick her words. "What?" she asked.

Mary leaned in close. "I shouldn't talk about it."

"Oh," said Elle. "The situation with Rory?"

Mary gave Elle an unsure nod. "Well, kind of," she answered, obviously not wanting to explain any more.

Kind of? thought Elle, as she walked away, hoping to find the doctor and figure out what she should do about Kate. She couldn't possibly stay any longer. Tensions were rising in the Persian Gulf. The newsroom was sure to be hectic for months. It wasn't as though she had any obligations to Kate—they had just met the day before. If anyone should be there helping out, it was Rose, but Elle knew that would never happen.

She went back to Kate's room and was relieved to find that Rory had left. She looked down at Kate's weary face as she slept. The hospital gown drowned her tiny body, making her seem helpless; Elle wondered if she would survive the week. A nurse came into the room.

"Do you have a home health agency here in town?" Elle asked.

"Yes. There are some pamphlets at the nurse's station."

Elle made arrangements for a nurse to stay with Kate full-time for a week. She even paid for it. She turned back to the waiting room, feeling much better now that she had attended to her aunt.

"I've taken care of everything," she announced to Mary.

Mary's face lit up with delight. "Then you'll be able to stay and take care of her."

Elle's heart dropped, knowing she would be disappointed. She sat down next to Mary and pulled out her daily planner. "You don't understand. See, here is my life." She opened the book, exposing the many appointments and notes. "I can't just leave all this. I have people counting on me. I produce a national news program. It's not as though the news can take a day off. I hired a nurse to take care of Kate. She'll be there every day."

Mary swallowed hard. "I can try to come by and I'll talk to the rest of her family. I know how Kate is, and I don't think she will let any of them help her. She wanted you here."

"Really? I only came out to check on her. I didn't even know her until yesterday. If anyone should be out here to watch her, it should be my mother. S*he's* the one who's set on wanting the money."

Mary nodded sadly. She took Elle's hand. "Your mother is like most of the old family. She had a hard time with what happened. We were counting on you. The rest of her family has burned their bridges with Kate."

Elle made her way out the door.

She was left with myriad questions as she sat alone in the waiting room. She wondered where to go and what to do. Her things were back at Kate's house, but she didn't have a key. She thought she should probably wait and get Kate settled back at home, instead of abandoning her at the hospital. She walked back to the nurse's station to find out when Kate could leave. In the hallway stood Rory. His face was weary, but he stood tall. Elle felt exposed in his gaze.

"I thought you had left," he said.

"No—sorry," Elle snapped back.

Rory shifted. "It's just that I saw Mary leaving and I thought—"

"I'm Kate's niece."

He looked her in the eye. "I know who you are, Ellie...or Elle. But I don't know why you've come back after all these years. I don't know what you want."

"Why do you keep calling me Ellie?"

"That was your name."

"Is that what Kate told you?"

Rory began to answer and then stopped and looked at her perplexed.

Elle shook her head. "I'm going to get Kate settled at home and then I'm going back to DC. I've hired a nurse to help her. I'll call and check up on her daily."

"She won't have it," he warned.

"Won't have what?"

"She won't put up with a stranger in the house. I'll stay with her."

Elle tilted her eyes. "Don't play saint with me. Besides, what about the harvest?"

Rory nodded. "We'll lose some on it. I'll have to hire other men to take my place, but we'll still clear enough."

Elle didn't expect his answer. She threw her hands up. "Whatever! If you don't want the help, fine. But don't say I didn't try."

"To whom?" Rory asked walking to her.

"What do you mean?" she asked, backing up.

"To whom would I say you didn't try?"

"What are you talking about? I don't know," Elle answered.

"If you left today and never spoke to Kate again, no one would ever say a thing. Your so-called family shunned her years ago. They don't care what happens to her."

"Well, it isn't as though she's real accommodating, and how do you think they feel with you around? That's got to make them a little uncomfortable," she said, trying to keep her voice down.

Rory shook his head. "How would you know? Your parents took off just like everyone else. You're not the only one who lost someone during that whole mess. I lost my father because of it. You've been around less than a day." He turned and walked into Kate's room.

Elle felt her head spinning. Evening had set in and she was exhausted. She followed him, barking out questions. "What are you talking about? What's all this have to do with your father?"

Rory turned to her. "I have had to deal with what happened my entire life. I don't need to discuss it with you. If you came here to dig up the past, then leave us alone. Go gossip with the others."

"I don't want any part of this place!" Elle yelled back at him. "I lost my only sister here. Do you think I enjoy being back? I just want to get out." The rage she felt was not only directed at him but at her mother for not explaining everything to her. She turned and started toward the door, but then paused. "I need the key to the house to get my things."

"The back door doesn't lock," Rory answered. "It's always open."

҂ѹ҂

The drive back to the house was cold. In the frustration of the moment, Elle had left the top down. Before she realized how chilly the night had become, she was halfway back to Kate's house. She pulled the car into the garage and walked to the back door. Sure enough, it was unlocked. Inside, Elle hesitated at the paintings and the dirty breakfast dishes in the sink. She washed them, then quickly went downstairs, gathered her suitcase and headed for her car.

Without looking back, she drove off, wanting to get as far away as she could before she let the country air escape her lungs. As she continued to drive, she mulled over the events of the last two days, and wondered how such a short period of time could impact her life so strongly.

Again, she became angry with Rose. Elle hated being in the dark and feeling as though she didn't have the whole story. She was convinced that Rose knew the whole truth and there was a reason she had kept it a secret all these years. There was obviously more to Kate than an ornery personality and a younger man.

That brought her thoughts back to Rory. What was it that made her feel like she had one foot off a cliff? She had dated handsome men. She worked in network news. Elle spent her days with some of the most attractive men in the country.

And these men weren't just good looking, they were successful and driven. She loved the polished look of a man in a designer suit and with hands that looked like they handled money, not manure. Why was this unkempt cowboy making her lose her head?

He truly was an enigma and now that Elle had left, he had gotten his way. This infuriated her. It was wrong that she, the closest relative to Kate, be forced out. She pulled off the highway and tried to gather her thoughts. Two days ago, she had never given Kate a second thought, now she considered using her precious vacation time to take care of her.

If Rose knew that Elle took time off to spend it with a little known relative and yet fought tooth and nail to stay away from her own mother, it would kill her. Elle smiled at the grief it would cause. Besides, she actually enjoyed Kate. Her brash and blunt comments humored Elle.

She looked down at her hands as she clicked her nails feverishly and thought about going back. I'll take Monday off, just to make sure she's settled, she thought.

Then I'll evaluate the situation and decide what to do after that.

As she pulled back into the driveway, she noticed a dark green truck in front of the house. She knew it had to be Rory, and she sat in the car dreading the encounter. It made her mad that he flustered her so. His eyes watched her in a way that made her feel exposed. When he smiled, it made her face heat up and the back of her neck sweat. It drove her nuts that his simple actions brought about such a rise in her. After all, he was the outsider, not her. She was family, what was he?

She walked to the back door and opened it confidently. It flew open, hitting the house and shattering the stillness of the dark night.

"Did you forget something?" Rory called from inside the kitchen. He had a Levi jacket on, and stood at the counter with his keys, as if he had just arrived or was just leaving. His eyes danced in the dimly lit room and Elle was struck by the length and number of lashes that framed them. I'd die for those, she thought.

Elle caught a warm smile begin to form at the corner of his mouth, as she stood agape. She tossed her head and walked to the sink. "No, I just went down to the store to pick up some things I'll need."

"It's Sunday night. Nothing's open except in Hershey." He leaned up against the counter, waiting to hear what she'd say to that.

"I realized that. It's why I don't have anything with me," she said, holding out her arms.

He shook the keys as he walked toward the door. "What do you need? I thought you were leaving tonight?"

"No," she snapped back. "I'll be staying…till tomorrow. I want to make sure Kate is settled before I leave."

Rory shook his head, "And then what?"

"What do you mean?"

"Will you go another twenty years without giving her a second thought?"

Elle's eyes flashed and she threw her purse on the table. "How dare you come here and criticize me? I'm not the one being all flirty with an old woman in the hopes I'll get a bunch of farm land."

"What?" Rory said. "You think I'm...that Kate and I are...Good grief!" He took Elle by the shoulders. "I ought to knock your head off for saying that."

Elle struggled against him, "You lay one hand on me, and I'll have you thrown in jail."

"Is that what they're saying now?" he said, keeping his grip firm. He released her and Elle backed into the corner away from him. "I don't care what they say about me," he continued. "But it'll kill Kate to hear that, and I won't allow it. I want you to go home."

Elle's heart thundered in her chest and her breathing was heavy. "If it's a lie," she gasped, "then why are you here? It's obvious you don't just *work* for her."

"I don't work for her. I help her. Kate raised me. Don't you remember anything that happened? There are times I wonder why I came back," he answered, still heated.

He ran his fingers through his long hair and paced the floor. Part of Rory's shirt was untucked and Elle watched as it brushed his upper thighs. His legs were sturdy but lean and his jeans followed his striking form, ending over well-worn boots. Why was she noticing that?

"I probably should have never come back here," Rory said, "but I knew she needed my help."

"Come back?" Elle asked.

He looked at her, annoyed.

"What?" she asked confused. "I have no idea what you're talking about. Come back from where?"

Rory took a deep sigh as if explaining anything to

her taxed him of his last bit of energy. He pulled out a chair and sank into it. "I have had to live with all the rumors my entire life. I left and went to college in Pittsburgh. I should have stayed there. No one knew anything about what happened back here."

Elle was hesitant to appear anymore deluded, but wanted to know more. "This place has so many skeletons. What did happen? Kate didn't say a word to me about you, only that you worked here." Her hesitation to delve into the past began to dissolve, but like the sting of frostbite beginning to thaw, Elle knew she would regret her desire to know more.

"She probably thought you remembered. I thought…well, that's all you need to know. I have to go back to the hospital. You can leave now. I'll take care of Kate."

Elle shrugged. "I'm not leaving," she said, defiant.

Rory turned back to her. "Why? To prove a point to me? Don't bother."

"I don't care the least about what you think. I only care about her," she answered.

"Yes, enough to stay a whole extra day. Good for you. Maybe we'll see you again in twenty years."

Elle pushed past him to the stairs. "I'm staying for two weeks. Then after that I'll come up on weekends. You'll see so much of me, you'll think I live next door," she spouted back. "If you think you're going to get rid of me, you're wrong. I'll call work tomorrow and take my two weeks' vacation now, and I don't want to see your sorry butt anywhere near here."

She bounded down the stairs to her room. *Oh God what did I do?* Elle thought, as she sat on the bed and listened for his footsteps on the wooden floor above. She couldn't back down now, but what excuse could she possibly give her boss, allowing her to stay an entire two weeks?

ℰ✺ℰ✺

Rory stood at the table, keys in hand, rubbing his chin. She was brash and yet something about her kept gnawing at him. The sight of her green eyes glaring while unruly strands of blonde hair whipped as she talked made him realize he hadn't been around a younger woman for months. Now she was here for two weeks and already he found himself dreading the fact that he would be working the field from morning until night. He pushed the thoughts from his mind. She was already poisoned by the others. Having her be civil to him was about all he could wish for now.

CHAPTER 5

Getting Kate back home was easier than she had thought, but it was caring for her that was difficult. It was a long night and Elle got little sleep, as she hovered over Kate, worried she might die while under her watch. The next morning someone knocking on the door awakened her.

"You have a key," Elle yelled, knowing it was Rory. "You even told me the back door never locks." She straightened her hair and threw open the door. There stood a thin young woman holding a large leather bag, a stethoscope around her neck. Elle looked at her with surprise. "Can I help you?"

The woman tried to smile. "I was looking for Kate Taylor. I'm Mindy the home health nurse."

Suddenly it came back to Elle. "Oh, I forgot…" She heard the back door close and she turned to find Rory standing in the kitchen. She pulled the robe tighter around her. He walked to the door, but didn't say anything.

"I was going to cancel the service, because I've decided to stay and help her myself," Elle said, trying to ignore Rory.

"Oh," the nurse said, ignoring Elle and studying Rory.

Rory stepped forward. "You did say you needed to get some things for your stay," he said to Elle. "Maybe she could stay today while you get what you need."

The nurse smiled up at him and Elle looked back at Rory with dismay. He shrugged and walked back to the bedroom to see Kate. Elle invited the nurse in.

"Is Ms. Taylor your mother or your husband's?" she asked.

"He's not my husband. Ms. Taylor is my aunt. He's her...uh...friend."

"Oh," the nurse said coyly, looking back toward the bedroom as if appeased.

Elle arranged with the nurse to care for Kate after Elle's two weeks were over. The nurse seemed thrilled with the arrangement and left Elle her card.

Elle watched the perky girl leave and then placed the card in the letter slot by the phone. She wondered if she should go into Kate's room or if she should go back down stairs. She decided against both and headed to the shower. When she was finished, she peered out of the bathroom, cautiously wondering if Rory was still around. Seeing the path was clear, she wrapped a towel around her and darted back downstairs. She then realized she had only two changes of clothes and wished she hadn't let her stubbornness keep her from utilizing the nurse for the day.

It was going to be a challenge keeping her cool around Rory. There was something about him that made her snap. His calmness made Elle want to slap his flawless face. She stood staring at nothing, but mulling over the shape of his mouth in her mind. The line of his jaw was strong but his lips were so...

She blinked and realized several minutes had passed and she was standing in the middle of the room, wrapped

in a towel, with her mouth open. She shook her mind
clear and chuckled at her idiocy. She towel dried her hair
and it fell messily around her face. She stopped and studied the thin scar on her forehead, and then pulled her
bangs over it. She searched for the rubber band to pull her
hair back into her usual pony tail, but even after scouring
through her bag and even crawling around on the floor,
she found nothing. Elle rolled her eyes wondering what
else could go wrong. Looking in the mirror, she rolled her
eyes again at the curls and waves already forming in defiant pleasure.

She walked quietly up the stairs and noticed the door
to Kate's room was open. Rory must be gone. She went
to the kitchen and noticed him through the back window.
He approached a horse that was tied to one of the fence
posts. Elle stood and watched, admiring his broad shoulders and strong legs. He could actually be handsome
dressed in a nice suit. He mounted the horse and turned
back to the house. Elle ducked down, not wanting him to
see her staring. She peeked up and watched as he rode off
toward the larger home.

She leaned against the counter and wondered what
she had gotten herself into. Why did she think she could
care for a dying woman? She pulled open the refrigerator
and looked into it wondering what to fix to eat. Her stomach growled as she looked over the fresh fruits and vege-
tables. Even the butter and milk were in containers that
Elle knew weren't from any store.

The cupboards were full, but not with anything Elle
recognized. Nothing pre-packaged like she was used to.
Instead, baking ingredients. She found a box of corn
flakes. They tasted good, but she knew she couldn't live
like that for two weeks. And besides, what would she
feed Kate? She pulled out the coffee maker and started a
pot, then rinsed out her bowl. She walked back to Kate's

room and tried to peek in without making a noise.

"Do you plan on staring at me the whole time?" Kate asked from her bed.

Elle pushed open the door. "I didn't want to wake you."

"Wake me? It's almost nine o'clock," she snapped. "Where's Rory? Did he leave already?"

"Yes."

Kate turned to her side and tried to push herself up to sitting.

Elle walked to the side of the bed. "What are you doing?"

"I'm getting up."

"You can't get up," Elle said sternly.

"If I don't, you'll be cleaning these sheets," Kate snapped back at her.

Elle didn't like the sound of that, so she took Kate's arm and gently pulled her out of bed and walked her to the bathroom. As she waited for Kate to finish, she looked around Kate's room. Large, beautifully framed oil paintings covered the walls; most were of a pretty young woman with curly red hair. One in particular caught Elle's eye. It hung above Kate's bed and the colors were soft and warm. The same young woman sat in an ornate chair, holding a child as it nursed. Sunlight radiated from the woman's face as she peered lovingly at the child. Elle walked closer to it and tried to make out the inscription at the bottom of the painting. She wondered how such a bitter old woman owned anything so beautiful.

Elle asked Kate what she wanted for breakfast. She was relieved when Kate said corn flakes, and yet even that presented her with problems.

The milk bottle splashed onto the bowl and all over Elle. It was her only clean outfit, since the only other clothes she had were dirty from the day before. Now she stood with milk stains on her shirt and jeans.

"Could I use your washer? I only brought one change of clothes," Elle asked, as she sat the TV tray in front of Kate.

Kate nodded and actually thanked Elle for the breakfast.

Elle went down stairs and took her other clothes from her suitcase. "I might as well wash these, too," she mumbled. She started the water in the outdated washer and threw all her clothes in. She felt something was missing. She realized there was no dryer. Elle walked back upstairs and asked Kate how she dried her clothes.

"There's a line just out the back door. The clothes pins are in a basket under the sink."

Elle stood stunned, then quietly asked as she motioned at the robe she was wearing. "I have no other clothes. How long will it take them to dry?"

"It depends. Jeans will take all day, at least. That's why I wear cotton. If you need a change of clothes, there are some things you can look through in the closet down by your bed. They should fit you fine."

Elle nodded and went back down stairs to the closet. Inside she found a dozen flowered cotton dresses. Grudgingly she tried one on. Oddly enough, it was extremely comfortable and fit nicely, made for a tall woman, like herself. If only Holly could see her now.

Elle went back to the kitchen and took the empty breakfast dishes away. Kate was back in bed. Elle paused for a moment and then dialed Holly's number.

"Make-up," Holly answered.

"Hey, it's Elle."

"Oh my god! Elle, what happened? They said you were staying in Pennsylvania for two weeks."

"I need to take care of my aunt. She's really sick."

A long pause came from the other end of the phone,

and Elle held out the receiver wondering if the line had gone dead.

"*You're* taking care of her?" Holly asked cautiously.

"Yes, I am." Elle answered back, indignant. "I need your help with something, but I'm not going to put up with your sarcasm."

"Fine. What do you need?"

"I don't know how to cook."

Holly giggled.

"I mean it. I'm supposed to be feeding her, and all I know how to do is put stuff in a microwave."

"She doesn't have a microwave?"

"No. She doesn't even have a clothes dryer."

Holly sighed but then pondered how she would teach Elle to cook over the phone. "What did you want to make?"

"Lunch," answered Elle.

She twisted the phone cord and clicked her nails. She found an old envelope and fumbled for a pen while Holly rambled off the directions to grilled cheese sandwiches.

Elle quickly hung up before Holly could ask any more questions. She went to the cupboards and the refrigerator and found ingredients necessary to make sandwiches.

What should she do now? It was at least four hours until lunch and she couldn't leave Kate alone. She looked around again at the paintings and wondered about the bitter old woman in the other room.

Elle thought about Rose. She had left a quick voice mail message, since Rose was on a cruise to Catalina. She was back now and the message would surely come as a surprise. Elle debated whether or not to call or wait to hear from her.

Since she had nothing else to do, she picked up the phone and dialed Rose.

"Are you really staying at her house?" Rose asked in shock.

"Yes."

"What has she said? Is she really leaving all the money to that kid? Did you see him?"

Elle wanted to scream at Rose, but knew she would only wake Kate. "Yes, I've seen him. I don't know anything about the money except that the chicken guy is a creep. I think you should fight for the land yourself and keep the chicken people out of the picture."

"How?" asked Rose.

"You'd have to do it in court," Elle said lowering her voice. "Even if Kate wills her half to this guy, you can get some of it because you're family."

Rose gasped. "Is she really dying?"

Elle paused. "I think so. Sometimes she seems so sick and then all of a sudden she will lash out with all the energy of a badger."

"So, now you know Kate," Rose said with a laugh.

"I don't know her at all. I have no idea what I'm even doing out here."

"I am not sure either, but I'm glad you are."

Elle shrugged as she hung up the phone. She wondered what to do with her time. Why was she out there? Was it her stubbornness that had made her stay or was it the money? Briefly, she thought about the change millions of dollars could make in both their lives. She thought about new cars, clothes, and trips, but ended up with an awkward empty feeling that tasted bitter and stale.

As the day rolled along, the wind picked up and skies threatened a storm. The house became chilly and Elle again went to the closet. She found a soft cardigan sweater mixed in with the cotton dresses. As she began to go back upstairs, she found herself staring at the neatly stacked boxes in the closet and wondering what was inside. Elle fought her curiosity. All good journalists had it. She knew they probably contained nothing more than old tax returns, but there was always the possibility there was more.

She carefully sat on the bed and shimmied off one lid. Her eyes widened as she looked down upon hundreds of pictures, sketches, and small paintings. She sifted through them looking for anything she recognized. Most were of a red haired young woman, and Elle wondered if it was Kate. Maybe underneath that gruff exterior was the soft and happy woman in the pictures. Then again, thought Elle, it couldn't have been. The woman in the pictures was tall and thin. Even though Kate's body was wasting away, she was at least five inches shorter than the woman in the photos and sketches.

As she sorted through the box, Elle came upon a sketch that caught her eye. It was hastily done on the back of a postcard. It was of the same woman, but this time she was scantily dressed and lying back on a rolling hill. Elle was surprised that Kate, who seemed so conservative, had something that provocative.

The floorboards creaked on the staircase behind her and she turned to find Rory. His dark brows furrowed and his eyes danced with intrigue. Even without the height of the steps he loomed large above her. His vigorous build filled the stairwell, making Elle feel vulnerable. A strand of sun streaked auburn hair fell on his forehead as he looked at her and then down to the open box.

Elle stood up, startled. "What are you doing?" she demanded.

"What are *you* doing?"

"Do you make it a habit to sneak up on people?"

He looked at her as his eyebrows furrowed. "Do you make it habit to rummage through other people's things?"

Elle looked down at the box. "I'm not rummaging. I'm just looking."

"For what?" he asked.

"Nothing. Is there something wrong with looking at family pictures?"

Rory smiled. "Oh, is that what they are?"

Elle felt awkward as she stood there in the borrowed dress and her bare feet. She tried to walk past him. "I need to go check on Kate."

"I already did. She's sleeping."

"Then I need to go make her lunch."

Rory didn't budge, but watched as she tried to slide past him. His jeans were dusty and his cheeks had lines of sweat, but his scent made Elle close her eyes and take a deeper breath.

"Don't you have a harvest or something you're supposed to be doing?" she asked.

He smiled. "I'll be leaving in a minute. I just wanted to see if you needed anything."

"No."

"You sure?"

"Yes!" she barked back.

❧❧❧

Rory chuckled as she stomped up the stairs. He watched as the sunlight glistened down the staircase giving him a full view of her sleek figure. He smiled and started to look away but then followed her upstairs with the urge to talk some more. Anyone who rivaled Kate's stubbornness was worth knowing better. There was something that fascinated him about her. Her coarse disdain made for quite a challenge, or was it that he had been alone for a very long time? Either way, he was drawn to her. It saddened him that she was never able to look at

him with anything but disdain for what happened long
ago.

℘℘℘

Rory walked to the kitchen and found Elle scurrying
between the refrigerator and the counter. He leaned
against the doorjamb and watched as she put the butter
next to the cheese and bread. She stood stupefied, looking
up and down the counter.

"Is this what you're looking for?" Rory asked, as he
held the envelope with Holly's recipe for grilled cheese
sandwiches.

Elle glared at him and held out her hand. "Give me
that!" She was horrified that he had discovered her weak-
ness, even if it was about cooking.

Rory smiled and ignored her. He began to read the
recipe.

Elle walked to him and tried to snatch it from him.

He lifted the envelope in the air and chuckled.

Elle, without thinking, jumped for it, landing very
close to him. For a moment she found herself inches
away and looking into his eyes. They were dark green
and made her shudder. He was unshaven today, and his
beard was slightly lighter than his hair.

"Fine, you make lunch!" she said, brushing past him
and down the stairs.

Elle felt his gaze and turned back to him. It had been
years since Elle had someone look at her in that way, and
it made her uneasy. His shirt hung over his large shoulders and his dark, weathered hands still held the envelope.

Without saying a word, she continued down the
stairs and to the washer, her heart beating so hard she put
her hand to her chest. There she paused, wondering what

had just happened. She took a deep breath and tried to recover as she lifted the lid of the washer. The clothes were spun and ready to hang. She piled the wet cold load into a basket and laid the clothespins on top.

She dreaded going back upstairs and facing Rory and that bothered her even more. Maybe she could wait until he left, she thought, as she put the basket down and sat on the bed. She smelled butter frying. Rory was making the sandwiches.

"This is ridiculous," she mumbled. She waited until no more sounds came from the kitchen. She picked up the basket and walked confidently up the stairs. She set the basket on the table and looked down the hallway. Kate's door was closed. She peeked out the front window and saw Rory talking to Ervin Coughlin, who was sitting in his truck. It was her chance to slip out the back and hang up her clothes to dry.

She grabbed the basket and carefully opened the back door. She dropped the basket near the clothesline. She felt her tensions ease for a moment and then felt the twinge of curiosity pull her around to the side of the house. Without looking around the corner, she strained to listen to what the men had to say. Most of the conversation centered on the harvest and consisted of measurements and yields, which Elle found interesting.

"So, is her niece still around?" asked Ervin.

Elle's ears strained to hear Rory's response.

"She is."

"Why haven't we seen her before?" Ervin said over the hum of the truck.

"Kate's sister moved to California years ago and that is where Elle was raised. They haven't been back since…well, you know," Rory explained.

Ervin looked at the ground. "So, why is she back now?"

Elle stood as close to the corner of the house as possible, straining to see.

"I'm not sure. Probably to see what she'll inherit," Rory answered.

"Do you think she'll cause problems with the plans?"

Rory shrugged. "If she does, it won't be the first setback. If I have to keep commuting, then that's what I'll do."

"Is she married?" asked Ervin.

Rory laughed. "I don't know."

"She's very pretty."

Elle leaned in as close as she could for Rory's response.

"She is, but she's got a personality like sandpaper," Rory said with a chuckle. He glanced down as he dusted off his jeans. He studied the house with lowered eyebrows. The flutter of cotton fabric caught his eye. "Excuse me a minute," he said to Ervin, as he walked slowly towards Elle. He rounded the corner and found Elle crouched down. Startled, she stood up. She gasped and glared at him, then ran to the back of the house, his triumphant chuckle following on her heels.

That night Elle lay in her cool basement bed and wondered why it bugged her that Rory thought of her as rough, and why it gave her hope that he thought she was pretty. As she continued to think, it irritated her that she cared at all. He was obviously doing something that he wanted to keep a secret, and yet his leading man good looks and personality seemed to only prick her interest more. It was embarrassing. Here she was supposed to bring him to his knees, and she found her own knees weak when he was near.

CHAPTER 6

After only three days, Elle learned the situation at work had already intensified. She found herself sick with envy upon learning that Secretary of State, Dick Cheney, had flown to Saudi Arabia. The 82nd Airborne and several fighter squadrons had been dispatched. Elle felt trapped in another world, as she went through news withdrawal, and watched her dream event happen for someone else.

The next morning she found Kate fully dressed and as chipper as if she were never sick.

"You're up?" asked Elle.

Kate nodded. "I don't believe in sleeping in."

"But you seemed so sick yesterday."

"That was yesterday. We need to bring in the horses at the main house. Rory is out in the fields trying to stop the flood from taking the back corner."

"Flood?" Elle looked toward the window. As she approached, lightning streaked across the sky and she wondered how she could have slept through blowing wind and thunder. "My clothes! I forgot all about them." Elle cried out, running to the back door. She opened it to find the clothesline empty. "Where did they go?"

"They're on the kitchen table. The storm came quick. They're still a bit wet," Kate said, pointing to the dripping basket.

"Did you haul all of this in?" Elle asked knowing Kate was still weak.

"God, no! I didn't even know they were out there. Rory brought them in."

"Oh," mumbled Elle with pangs of uneasiness, as she thought about Rory handling her underwear.

"We'll have to use the truck and the field roads. The mud has blocked the main road up to the house," said Kate, pulling on her sweater.

"You can't go out in this. You should be back in bed."

"If we don't get the horses into the stable next to the main house, they could be struck by lightning. There is no shelter in that pasture."

"I'll go," Elle said, knowing she'd regret it.

"You?" Kate chuckled. "How are you going to catch a horse and lead it into the stable?"

"No worse than you," Elle snapped back.

Kate smiled and cocked her head to the side. "Fine, but I think I should at least go with you in the truck."

"No. Where are the keys?" Elle demanded.

Kate handed them to her. "Follow the same path that we walked the first night you were here. It will curve to the left. Just stay on it."

Elle pulled the sweater around her. "Do you have a rain coat or boots I can use?"

"I believe there may be some in the closet downstairs."

Elle found the boots and slicker. She opened the kitchen door and braced herself for the storm. In just the run from the door to the truck, every part of her that wasn't covered was sopping wet. She started the engine and pulled on the lever that shifted it into four-wheel drive. It lurched forward and carried her easily up the road and past the large red barn.

Elle closed one eye hard, trying to keep horrible recollections from assaulting her mind. As she peered out through thick wet film on the windshield, she saw the blue face and bulging eyes looking back at her. She blinked and forced it out. She knew the reason she saw smoke and flames, but the dreaded monster that went along with it was something she couldn't explain. What she did know was that the tragedy surrounding the old barn was something she wanted to be far away from.

Elle felt the tires slipping and spinning as she tried to guide the truck along. Soon the tall white gables of her mother's childhood home emerged through the storm. Elle pulled up to the house and looked out to the fenced area surrounding the stable. There the two horses thrashed and bucked in the rain.

"What was I thinking?" she mumbled, "I can't go out there. They'll kill me."

She slowly opened the truck door and squinted against the downpour. Braced against the wind, she slogged toward the fence. The horses seemed to grow larger and stronger with every footstep. She held her hands out, hoping to calm them. Instead they snorted and heaved as she got closer. When she reached the fence, they ran off toward the far side of the small pasture.

Elle could see the stable gate and prayed that by opening it they would go inside on their own. She quickly ducked under the fence. A gust of wind blew back the hood of her raincoat, dousing her hair and leaving her wiping her eyes just to see. She looked up to find the horses approaching her. Elle stood up quickly, as her breath was sucked from her body.

"Stop!" she yelled at them. The larger of the two horses' ears fell flat and he reared up in front of her, making her fall backward into the mud. She screamed and covered her head, expecting the horse to come down upon her. Instead she felt her body being lifted from the mud and carried away. She pushed her dripping hair from her face to find Rory. His face was white as he looked down at her with concern. She felt the strength of his arms supporting her, and wondered where he had come from.

"Put me down," she urged.

He placed her safely on the other side of the fence. "Go to the house," he ordered. He walked off toward the horses, as rain came down in harsh flashes.

He had picked her up as though she were a feather, a child, and she hated feeling weak and foolish. She sloshed back to the house and pulled off her mud filled boots, placing them along with the dirty raincoat on a chair next to the door. Even with the slicker her dress was wet and clung coldly to her. She walked slowly down the hallway, noticing the walls filled with paintings. The hardwood floor was smooth beneath her bare feet and the warmth of the house was even more comforting.

Then it hit her and she gasped. *This is the house. No wonder I didn't recognize anything at Kate's home. This is the house where we lived.* The door opened and Rory stood staring at her with concern.

"Are you crazy? You could have been killed," he yelled.

"What do you care?" Elle snapped back.

Rory ran his fingers through his wet hair in frustration. "What were you trying to do?"

"Kate said the horses had to be put in the stable. She would have done it if I hadn't."

Rory scoffed. "I swear I never thought I'd ever meet

anyone stubborn as Kate, but I was wrong. It must run in the family."

"Oh, go away—for good."

"I probably will after I strangle the both of you," he said, walking to the pantry. "I'll make some coffee. You go take a shower. There are towels in the cupboard under the sink. Put your clothes outside the door and I'll get them dried."

He walked off to the kitchen before Elle could object. Inside the bathroom, she peeled off the sopping clothes and opened a crack in the door to drop them out. The heat of the shower was heavenly. Not since she was a child did she remember having to take a shower to wash away actual dirt.

Rory knocked on the bathroom door. "I have a robe for you," he called to her.

Startled, Elle looked over the top of the shower door. "Set it next to the door," she yelled back. She turned off the shower and dried, wondering how she would ever digest everything that had happened in the last week and a half. A flash flood, chicken dinners, an old T-bird, Kate, and of course Rory. She couldn't get the feeling of being in his arms out of her mind.

What was it about him that irritated her so much? Maybe it was her attraction to him.

What was it about him that she even found appealing? Yes, he was strong and young and handsome, but he had none of the qualities Elle usually went for in men. And she had never been attracted to auburn hair. He was obviously poor and under-educated. He didn't dress well or have a prestigious job, and Elle saw no benefit from the relationship whatsoever.

She had never dated anyone with less than a master's degree and certainly no one who made less money than she did. They were usually older and enjoyed coddling her. They always started out seeing her pert attitude as cute, but that didn't last.

She had never dated a man just for the pure enjoyment of it, and maybe that's what perplexed her so much now. She was almost thirty and the thought that this could be anything more than a silly crush made her skin tingle. She looked in the mirror and wondered if Rory felt the same about her. She closed her eyes and thought about loving him. It made her sigh.

Elle combed through her wet hair with her hands. She wrapped the long thick terry cloth robe about her and stepped into the hallway. She heard the shutting of cupboards in the other room and walked toward the noise. The house was dimly lit and dark skies gave the rooms an orange glow.

"Your clothes should be ready soon," Rory said, hearing her footsteps.

"Thank you," said Elle.

He looked at her with surprise and then turned to the coffee maker. "Would you like a cup?"

Elle nodded.

He poured it and handed it to her. "I've got sugar and milk."

"No, thank you. I take it black."

Rory shrugged and smiled.

"What's that supposed to mean?" asked Elle, annoyed.

"Nothing," Rory said with a sigh.

Elle took a sip. "You are so smug."

Rory laughed out loud. "Me?"

Elle sat the cup down and sat back in her chair. "Yes, you. I don't know what it is, but you really think you're something."

Rory clasped his hands tightly behind his neck and leaned back. "Who came rolling into town on her high horse just three days ago, thinking she knew it all? You still act high and mighty, even after I had to pull you out of the mud."

"Give me a break. Just because I'm not used to farm animals doesn't mean I need your help. Not every woman is weak and helpless. I've been in gang crossfire before, so save the manly man stuff for someone who falls for the type." Elle stood up and pushed the chair back. She tightened the sash of the robe and began to walk off.

Rory took her arm and nudged her back. "You love putting me down. Stay here. I'm not finished."

"Too bad! Let go!" she demanded.

Rory gently eased her toward him. He looked her in the eyes, perhaps wanting to see something other than ire?

Elle tried to push against him. Her heart raced and she wondered just how mad he was as he looked down at her.

A clap of thunder crashed overhead.

Elle felt her insides shudder. Rory took her face gently in his hands and bent down as if he were going to kiss her. She stood in shock wondering if he would.

Elle worried that her hair was drying weird or that her face looked ruddy without her crème foundation. He was so handsome and flawless. Rory hovered above her still holding her face gently and she felt no need to struggle against him.

The room was hauntingly silent as another flash of lightning silhouetted them like the headlights of a Mack truck. He pulled her close.

With exquisite sweetness, he lightly kissed each of her eyelids, then her cheek.

Elle knew what was happening but couldn't believe it. He was strong and sure and she enjoyed being held. She relented into his chest. He smelled wonderful, and through the thick cotton shirt, she felt his strength. Then he stopped. He released her from his grip and stood upright, looking out toward the fields.

"What is it?" she asked.

"Listen," he whispered.

Elle shook her head, "I don't..." Then she heard it, the faint sound of sirens. "What does it mean?"

"It's the flash flood sirens. Kate's alone in the house. It's at the base of the hill, so I've got to get to her." He looked away. "Stay inside. I'll be back," he said as he pulled on his coat and walked to the door.

"I'm coming with you," she demanded, following after him.

"No, you're not," he said, bluntly.

"Why?" Elle asked.

He looked back at her and paused. "Because I don't need to worry about you, too."

"Oh, here we go again. Mister Save-the-Day. Trust me, I don't need you to worry about me."

Rory shook his head. "Did you ever think that maybe I was trying to be nice to you? For someone so pretty, you are such a..."

A clap of thunder deleted his last word, but Elle was quite sure she knew what it was. She stopped and watched him open the door. She didn't know if she should be insulted or touched.

Rory began to leave but then paused with the door open. The wind bellowed into the house. His mind was obviously full and he tried to speak. "I'm sorry," he said softly, and then he closed the door behind him.

For the first time in years, Elle wanted to cry. She watched him walk out, into the rain. What did he mean? Was he sorry that he had to leave or sorry about the kisses. What upset her more was the fact that she cared. Her heart dropped as she watched his truck pull onto the muddy path toward the big barn. Was she really that de-prived of affection or was she actually feeling something for him?

CHAPTER 7

For hours Elle paced the floor of the old farmhouse. She touched the walls and reminisced in her mind about the years she had spent there and tried to make sense with her past. Her desire to know more was strong but even more persistent was the tortured chaos that kept her curiosity in check. She was an investigative journalist and yet the most intriguing story of her life was one she was unwilling to uncover.

In her perusing, she had found a small black and white television. After several failed attempts to find reception, she got a faint and snowy picture. It wasn't much, but it gave her enough news to learn that the war was coming quickly. The United Nations had placed economic sanctions on Iraq, and President Bush announced the deployment of more troops. Elle felt her dreams quickly slipping through her fingers.

She pulled her clothes from the dryer. They were dry, except for the sweater. She found a wooden hanger and draped the sweater over it to dry naturally. The warm cotton of her dress felt good against her, but nothing like the feel of Rory's strong and solid arms. She found herself lost in thoughts of what had happened, wondering why he had affected her so.

Thunder pounded above her. Elle cringed as the noise shook the old house. It would have been nice to hold him, be near his warmth during the storm. She walked up the polished wooden steps, looking into each room and wondering where it was that he slept. As she opened the door to what looked like the main bedroom, she was surprised by the decor. It was covered with pictures, but the furniture was old and intricately carved with lace doilies and crocheted throws. Hardly a room she expected Rory to have. She went to the closet and opened the crystal knob. Inside was nothing but a long row of the cotton dresses. They were smaller sized than the one she wore. A chill went through her.

She went to each room, searching through the closets for any signs of Rory. In one of the smaller bedrooms Elle found a duffel bag full of his clothes and some toiletries. His musky scent again filled her head, but she shook it clear, as her curiosity became more intense.

Something was awry. Elle knew when she was being duped. The clothes in the closet were women's. There wasn't anything that could have been Rory's, so Elle knew this wasn't where he lived. But why did Kate lie about that? It made no sense.

While she continued to search the house for clues, she heard the brakes of the truck pulling up out front. What should she do? Part of her wanted to meet him at the door and throw herself into his arms again. Part of her wanted to interrogate him, find out who he really was.

She stood in the kitchen, wishing she had the long sweater Kate had lent her. She heard the door of the truck slam and the sound of his heavy boots on the wood floor. Elle pulled out a chair to alert him as to where she was. Soon he appeared in the kitchen. He looked to a chair where the robe was placed and then to Elle in her freshly washed dress.

"The roads are open now," he mumbled.

"How's Kate?" Elle asked.

"She's fine. She was more worried about you."

Elle cocked her head. "Really?" she asked, surprised.

Rory nodded. "I can take you back now." He said it with hesitation.

Elle's mind was torn between wanting to grill him with questions and being pulled into his arms. She quietly gathered her things, left the drying sweater, and followed him out to the truck. They sat quietly as the truck rambled home in the dark.

As they pulled into the drive, Rory turned to her and Elle hoped for at least a kiss.

"I should have never done what I did," he said, holding her hand.

Elle felt her heart fall and her insides churn. He regretted it. The humiliation was overwhelming, and now he held the upper hand.

"You're right," she snapped back, pulling her hand away from him.

"I'm sorry," Rory called to her, as she pushed open the truck door.

Elle slammed it behind her and ran to the house, trying to dodge the puddles that crowded the path. Inside she fell back against the door and waited as she heard the sound of his truck pulling out and rolling down the road. She sank to the floor, wishing to blink her eyes and transport herself home. What had this place done to her? Elle took a deep breath. Then her thoughts turned to Kate.

Elle pulled herself up and walked down the hallway to Kate's room. She gently pushed open the door and found her sleeping. She started to close the door again, but then slowly walked inside toward one of the closets.

She turned back to Kate to make sure she was sound asleep, and then quietly opened one of the doors. She felt herself gasp as she looked over the rows of men's shirts, jeans, and boots. These were Rory's clothes. She felt their worn smoothness. Then, her journalistic instinct kicked in and Elle looked back to where Kate lay sleeping. What is going on here?

The storm kept her awake for most of the night. It was the sound of footsteps on the floorboards above her head that jolted her out of bed and to the stairs. She tried to creep quietly up them but the old boards creaked and moaned. A faint light came from the kitchen and Elle walked in to find Kate sitting at the table with a glass of milk.

"Kate?" Elle asked softly, as not to startle her.

Kate turned to her slowly. "I didn't mean to wake you," she said without a whisper. "I just needed a sleeping pill."

Elle motioned to the cupboard. "Let me get one for you."

Kate put her hand on Elle's arm. "Sit down. I've already taken two."

Elle did as she asked. Kate's face looked worn and tired and her hands shook as she tried to lift the glass.

Kate looked up to Elle. "I hate feeling weak. I've always been able to take care of myself and now I am helpless. I think I'm ready to die."

Elle stared at her in shock. "No."

"Don't worry. I'll wait until you leave," Kate said, taking another sip.

Elle sat back and shook her head. Even with the sleeping pills taking their effect, Kate's bite came through. "Why didn't we stay in touch?" Elle asked. "Did you and my mother really hate each other that much?"

Kate lifted an eyebrow. "I don't know if we cared

enough to hate. Your mother couldn't handle being a part of the ridicule. The family turned their back on me, but that's okay. They showed their true colors. I still have friends. Many have passed on. And even if I lost every friend and family member I had, it didn't matter."

"What did you do that was so bad?" Elle asked, wondering what could possibly be worth losing everything.

Kate took a long and labored breath. "I fell in love."

Elle sat up straight. The words seemed foreign coming from Kate.

"It was hard for people to accept."

"What was so awful?" Elle asked, leaning forward.

"It was just the circumstances. There were a lot of raised eyebrows."

Elle scoffed. "And my mother turned her back on you for that? She has a lot of nerve to talk. She's had more husbands than I can count."

Kate chuckled. "It was more than that, and remember it was over twenty years ago. Things were different then. So often we do what everyone else thinks is right, and we throw away happiness trying to please people we don't even care about."

"So why is everyone talking as though Rory is to blame in all this? He said something about losing a father."

Kate nodded sadly. "It's been hard on him. He was just a young boy when it all happened."

Elle felt a sickening chill go through her. "You mean his father was the one?"

Kate shook her head. "I don't want to talk about it anymore. Help me back to bed." She tried to push herself away from the table, but her arms shook under the strain.

Elle was still full of questions, but relented and took her arm, helping her up.

Kate demurred as she tried to stand on her own. "If someone as skinny and sickly as you is helping me around, I really must be close to death."

Elle sighed, as she guided Kate toward her room. "For such a sick old woman, you can sure spit nails. Do you talk to everyone like this?" She tucked Kate in as if she were a child and then turned toward the door.

"The only person I say much to is Rory, and he doesn't seem to mind."

Just the mere mention of his name shot chills through Elle's spine. She wondered what Kate would think if she knew that just hours before she was in his arms. "Why doesn't he? Mind, that is?"

Kate shrugged her little shoulders. "He's the only child I've cared for. He's been with me for so long, I guess he's used to it." Her words became slurred as she tried to hold back a yawn.

Elle sat back down on the foot of the bed. "Did you raise him?"

"We sort of raised each other. I got to deal with the hormones and teenage attitude. However, he had to live with an ornery old woman, so I guess it was a draw. Any more questions?"

"Just one," Elle answered, knowing Kate was fading fast. "Why are Rory's clothes in this closet?" She pointed to the large doors.

"It's his closet," Kate answered.

"But I thought this was your room."

"It is for the time being. When I got sick, this was more convenient, closer to the main road."

"You mean you gave Rory this house?"

"I didn't give it to him. This was originally his parents' home."

"Did you adopt him?" Elle asked.

"No, and now it could cost him everything. He is as

close to a son as anyone could be, and with everything he's had to endure because of me, he deserves everything I have. You're the only one who can keep them from changing that." And she began to slip off.

"Is that why you let me stay here?" Elle asked.

"I hoped that you might see what's right in all this. Your mother always talked about how independent and strong willed you are. I see those things as strengths. I hope you'll leave here on Sunday at least knowing what's right."

Elle nodded. She understood what Kate said, but still wasn't convinced that her sentimental sickbed talk was worth giving up millions.

However, she was intrigued with the story Kate started to reveal and wanted to know more. She actually liked being around Kate and felt some pride in the fact that she was related. She had spent more time with her ailing aunt in four days, than she had spent with her mother in two years.

cↄeↄ

It was late morning and Elle sat at the kitchen table alone, finishing off the last crumbs of a casserole some-one had left on the front porch the day before. It was warm and tasted heavenly compared to what was becoming a routine of burnt cheese and cold cereal. When she had served it to Kate, she took a bite and looked up at her surprised.

"This isn't bad. What's in it?" Kate asked.

Elle stood awkwardly by the bed. "Just a little of this and that," she mumbled unwilling to let on that she wasn't the creator.

Kate lifted an eyebrow and grunted. "I was beginning to think you were trying to kill me with an overdose of cheese," she huffed as she picked at her meal.

Elle smiled to herself as she sat that next morning enjoying the leftovers. She peered out the side window and watched birds fluttering in puddles and hopping about. She heard Kate come into the kitchen and turned to her.

Kate looked out the window and looked back at Elle. "The rain has stopped."

"Yes. The birds are out." Elle pointed off into the distance. "There is a crow picking at something on the road. It doesn't look like food, but something shiny."

Kate strained to see. "That's a raven."

"What's the difference?"

"A lot, if you're a raven." Kate pointed at it. "It's twice the size of a crow and they are more aggressive. They are here year round."

"They don't fly south?"

"Nope. They stick it out and find what they can to live. I've seen them kill baby ducks and raid the songbirds' nests. They work as teams."

"That's awful," said Elle, with disdain.

"That's survival."

Elle nodded, but looked at the large bird with skepticism.

∽∾∽

The breeze through the small kitchen window was soothing and the cotton dress billowed as Elle sat and stretched her legs in front of her. Her jeans and sweater were clean and folded in her suitcase, but Elle decided to stay with the dresses. A knock came at the front door. She looked out the window. It was Cynthia Evans. Elle opened the door, and Cynthia cocked her head sideways, giving Elle a big-eyed grin.

"Just wanted to bring you by a little something from John and me. You've been working so hard, we wanted to lighten the load." She extended a bag that was greasy on the bottom and filled with fried chicken.

Elle tried to smile back, but found it impossible. She opened the door and motioned for Cynthia to come in.

"It's such a nice day, why don't we talk outside?" Cynthia asked, looking past Elle, trying to see if Kate was in sight.

"She's asleep," Elle said.

"Oh. Well, maybe for just a little while," Cynthia said, slipping into the house, as if she were preparing to burglarize it. She took a seat on the sofa, looked around at the varied paintings, and tsk-tsked as if they disgusted her. She tried in vain to be pleasant, talking quietly as she asked polite questions about Kate's health and how Elle's week had gone.

Elle answered and found that having another human being to speak to was actually inviting, even if it was Cynthia.

It didn't take long for Cynthia to cut to the quick and begin talking about her plans for the diner. It was John this and John said that. It made Elle's stomach turn to think of the creepy little man enjoying any part of the hillside that Elle considered hers.

"I'm not so sure a restaurant is the right thing to put here," Elle said, cutting in. "Maybe Kate doesn't like the idea of her land being desecrated by a chicken diner."

Cynthia sat upright and stared at Elle as if she had spit on her. She gave an insulted little huff. "Kate has already cheapened and defiled this land far beyond what any of us could do. Allowing respectable folks to be here will only improve this hill."

Elle sat stunned as her sticky sweet distant cousin turned irate. She leaned forward, amused by the rage she had evoked and continued to extract what she could.

"Respectable folks? Just what has Kate done to get you so worked up? What is this big dark sin she's committed?"

Cynthia swallowed hard and looked toward the door as if gauging how quickly she could sprint from the room. "Don't you remember what happened with your sister? It all comes back to the same thing. It isn't something I'm going to discuss. The quicker we can all get past it the better."

"What do you mean by that?" Elle asked.

"What she means is the quicker I kick the bucket the better," Kate said, as she stood squarely in the hallway.

Before Elle could look back to Cynthia, she was at the door. She looked flustered, as she searched for something to say. "That isn't what I meant. I'm a Christian. I wouldn't wish that upon anyone."

"You're a hypocrite," Kate said calmly. "And you're married to a fool."

Cynthia swung open the door and disappeared.

Elle looked for Kate, but she was already shuffling back to her room. Elle stood up to follow her, but wasn't sure what to say, so she sat back on the sofa and let the awkward silence surround her. What was it? What was this secret that had everyone so uptight and hushed? It left Elle in the dark and yet most everyone acted as though she knew everything. If she hadn't thought it might jeopardize her situation with Kate, she would surely have been more forceful with her questions, but for some reason she held back, not wanting to distance Kate by prying or seeming too interested. It went against all her instincts, but still she hesitated. Deep down the dread of knowing kept picking away.

CHAPTER 8

There was no television back at the small house and Elle felt lost. She found CNN on the radio and kept it on constantly, yet every time she called her station, the station manager, Richard Prescott, scolded her for not using her time for a true vacation and shooed her off. This was her war and if it started without her, she'd never forgive herself.

Elle sat at the table drinking a tall glass of whole milk. It was thick and tasted like cream, but she soon had gotten used to it and smiled at the fact that she could make a thick mustache with it. She was sure the fat content was incredible, but it was all that was left in the fridge. She needed to go to the store, and she was well aware that Kate was getting tired of cereal and grilled cheese sandwiches. There was no microwave, and Elle never used a regular oven, but she figured she could find something.

She paced the floors, deep in thought about Rory. For two days he avoided the house. Elle thought she heard his truck late one night, but by the time she threw on her robe and got upstairs the noise was gone. She continued to lis-

ten in the nights after, but soon she gave up on his returning.

⌀⌀⌀

Elle stirred one night as she remembered lying
awake as a child and hearing the same sound as her father
left after a fight with Rose. The shouts and sounds of
things breaking always preceded the start of his engine
and the loud revving before driving away. One night he
drove off and never came back. That was the last time
Elle saw her father.

The questions and secrets continued to pick at her.
During one of Kate's chemo treatments, Elle found time
to make her way downtown to the local newspaper in
hopes of delving into their archives to learn more about
the fire that killed her sister and possibly why her nightmares wouldn't end. She knew there was more to what
happened. No one was being forthcoming with anything
that could explain why her past was still such a blur.

The glass door of the small office was heavy and a
cowbell was tied to the handle with a piece of twine to
announce her entrance. A very young man with terrible
skin and a few hairs that danced wildly above the well
minded others looked up from his desk, confused. He
pushed thick glasses back on his nose.

Elle raised her eyebrows in an attempt to receive
some sort of greeting. Instead he sat stunned, so she
cleared her throat and pressed on. "Hello. Can I speak to
someone in your research department?"

The young man stood up slowly. "Research department?"

"Yes. Who does your archival work? I need to find
any articles your paper may have printed about a fire that
happened years ago."

He exhaled loudly. "Oh, well, I can help you with that."

"Good," said Elle, wanting to pat his head like a puppy. "Do you have the archives on microfilm? Or computer?"

The young man smiled uneasily then pointed to a room without saying a word.

The cowbell clanged again and Elle jumped.

"Hello, Ed," an older man called from behind her. He gave Elle a big smile.

Ed nodded. "Hey, Jake." He paused a moment and put up a hand to Elle. "What can I do for you?"

The man was rumpled, but kind looking. He glanced at Elle and then to Ed. "I didn't mean to butt in. I can wait. I was hoping to get a copy of that story you did on my boy last week."

Ed stood a bit taller. "I can do that. How about I bring it over to you on my way home? I have to cover the planning and zoning meeting, but I should be done at around seven."

Jake shook his head. "Is this the meeting to vote on the vet clinic?"

Ed nodded.

"What a mess. Why are people standing in the way of Dr. Beau?"

Ed shrugged. "They should be making a decision soon."

"It drives me nuts when these big city folks come in here trying to take over. You've done a good job keeping on top of it," said Jake with a nod of emphasis. He turned to leave. "I'll see you tonight."

Ed beamed and then brought his attention back to Elle. "We keep the past papers in that room," he said, leading the way.

"Great!" Elle exclaimed. She walked with him. "I'm Elle McCord. I work for World Network News So, you are a reporter here?"

The young man piped up. "Yes. I'm Ed Stuart. I also edit the agriculture section and do the layout."

"Wow," said Elle, wanting to stroke his ego, in hopes he'd be more help. "How many reporters are there?"

"There are three of us—the publisher, the managing editor, and Diane. She works from home and also does the classifieds."

Elle smiled at the unpretentiousness of it, but also realized how close to his readers Ed must be. He reported on things that not only were local stories, but also about people he could, and most likely would, bump into in the store or at church. The accountability he had as to what he wrote struck Elle hard. She tried to remember when she personally ever had any tie or purpose in the stories she covered over the years. Her pride in the size and stature of her position diminished as she realized she had no idea what impact any of her stories had ever made on anyone.

Elle followed him through the door and found stacks of old newspapers neatly sorted on floor-to-ceiling shelves. Her heart sunk, but she smiled and asked, "Are they labeled by month and year?"

He nodded.

"Okay. Can you show me where I can find the year 1971?"

His brows furrowed. "That would be part of the flood damage."

Elle shook her head. "What does that mean?"

Ed walked over to the wall and pointed out a discolored line about three feet up from the floor. "Everything below this line was soaked when the building flooded in 1984. Most of it was from 1952 through 1980." He walked over and pulled a paper from one of the stacks. "We did save most of 1964 though." He handed it to Elle as though this would appease her.

"Soaked meaning destroyed?"

"Gone," Ed said, matter-of-factly.

"Are there other newspapers in the area that may have covered it?" Elle asked frantically.

Ed gave an impish smile, shrugged and shook his head.

Elle left feeling even more clueless and frustrated about her entire situation. A visit to the local library yielded nothing. Years ago, Elle had discovered that the story was never listed in the *New York Times Index*. With the story being destroyed here, it wouldn't have made a difference if it were. She was met with shrugs and silence when she tried the local library, looking for someone who remembered the events of 1971.

Next, she tried the volunteer fire department, hoping to meet with an old-timer who might remember the fire. The same shrugs and silence were her answers. Elle was convinced there was a big ugly secret that was shared by everyone in town.

❧❧❧

Sunday morning came upon Elle quite suddenly. The night before, Kate awoke and cried out, and when Elle went to her, Kate took her hand and held onto it for hours. It gave Elle time to study her aunt as she lay sleeping in the dimly lit room.

The strange secret she was hiding made Elle wonder about Kate's long life. She had so many questions and yet now she was leaving. She found herself worrying that the nurses wouldn't be able to take care of Kate. At one point she even contemplated coming back and checking on her.

When she returned to Washington, she would call and make sure things were in order. She knew that Rory would be around, but Elle wasn't sure if that was a comfort or an annoyance. There came a knock at the door. It was Mindy, the pixy cute nurse who had come two weeks before. There was no need for Elle now, and she was free to go.

Leaving became even more painful as Elle tried to squeeze back into the jeans she had worn the day she arrived. The whole milk and cheese had taken their toll and now Elle looked round and soft. She gave a grunt as she looked in the mirror, trying to stretch the jeans. She placed the dress in the hamper, but not before she gave it one last stroke and smiled at its simple softness. Elle gave the nurse instructions and then went to Kate's room.

"I don't want her touching my things," Kate said, as she sat up in bed, "and I don't like her voice. It's high pitched and hurts my ears."

Elle smiled. "She's not here to rob you or talk to you. She's here to take care of you."

"I don't need her. Where's Rory?"

Good question, Elle thought. "She'll only be here until Rory finishes whatever it is he's working on. Let her do her job or I'll have to come back," Elle said, raising a threatening eyebrow.

"Heaven forbid," Kate chuckled.

Elle started to back out of the room. "I'll call," she said. "Collect."

Kate smiled, and Elle stood, surprised but glad to see Kate had appreciated her sarcasm. Elle beamed back at her, and as she walked through the house, she felt an unusual sensation of loss. She truly cared for Kate and the thought of never seeing her again really hurt. She held back tears as she drove over the hill, away from her mother's childhood home.

As she drove, Elle popped in her old heavy metal tape and cranked the volume. She sat back and let the music fill the car and her mind. She needed to push the last two weeks as far into oblivion as possible. She didn't need anything clouding her thoughts when she stepped back into the studio and turned her focus to the war.

In a couple of weeks Elle would fulfill her dream of a lifetime and produce a bomb-dropping, missile-shooting, list-of-casualties war. She took a deep breath and sorted through the options of sidebar stories and special reports.

℮ↄ℮ↄ

The first week Elle was back in Washington, she found herself digging out from a stack of things to do. It was good she was busy, because her thoughts were definitely not focused on her job. Rory's handsome face often filled her mind as she sorted through papers. She found herself off somewhere and came back to reality by having someone ask her a question.

"You look different," said Holly.

"I know, I know. I've ballooned about ten pounds. I look horrible," Elle huffed, as she continued to toss papers in the trash.

"I think you look wonderful. Your skin is clear and smooth, and your eyes are shiny and alert. You look healthy and rested."

"What's being said about me?" Elle asked, still keeping to her task of sorting.

"What do you mean?" asked Holly.

"I haven't been here for two weeks. Aren't they wondering where I've been and who I've been with?"

"Not really," answered Holly without thinking.

"Well, they don't need to know."

"You look so different." Holly cringed, right after she said it, knowing that what she meant and what Elle heard were completely different.

"Gee, thanks. There was nothing but pure fat everywhere I turned. No gyms anywhere, so yes, I gained a little."

"So how is your aunt?" Holly asked, trying anything to change the tone.

"Fine."

⁊ϭ⁊

It was now eleven and Rory would be checking on Kate. The nurse should have already started lunch and hopefully Kate hadn't already run her off. Elle felt the band of her skirt cut into her stomach and she longed for the light flowing feel of the farm dress.

"Welcome back."

The voice startled Elle from her daze and she turned to find Hal Norland, the bureau chief and her boss. "Thank you, I'm so glad to be here." Elle leaned back in her chair and smiled. "So much to get caught up on."

"Maybe more than you think." Hal paused for affect and it worked.

Elle leaned forward, "Really? Why do you say that?"

"I have a very interesting proposal for you. Can you have lunch with me today?"

"Sure!"

"I'll bring my car around for you at one." He paused again and looked at Elle. Then he smiled. "Vacation was good for you. You look different. It's good."

"Thank you, sir."

Hal nodded. "I'll see you at one."

As he walked away, Elle wondered about the proposal. Hal was one was of Elle's favorite people, maybe

her most favorite. She was an intern when she first met
him and he scared her to death. He was tough and bois-
terous and had no problem calling people out when things
weren't the way he felt they should be.

Elle had worked herself up the ranks, but never remembered not reporting to Hal. He was who she looked
up to and there was no secret that he adored her, too. He
was the reason she always enjoyed her work. Seeing him
beam and give a loud wide-eyed holler when she snagged
an exclusive, is what Elle lived for.

This lunch meeting was different. Although the two
spent hours together each day, the tie rarely followed
them outside the station. In fact, the last time she had
lunch with Hal it was with a group of people from the
newsroom--producers, assignment managers, and senior
reporters. It was to announce that Matt Porter, the special
projects producer, was leaving to take a similar job at the
main station in New York and that his job in DC was up
for grabs. It was the job that Elle held now. It made her
wonder if someone else was leaving and what it could
mean for her.

Then her thoughts turned to Rory. It still bothered
her that he kept coming into her mind. Why hadn't he
come around when she left? Elle shook her shoulders as
if brushing the thought from her mind. She didn't care
about him, or at least she wouldn't. He wasn't what she
needed and he certainly wasn't someone who could make
her happy. Rory was simple and conventional. Certainly
not someone Elle would really be interested in. She sat
and let the events of her time in Harrisburg play in her
mind.

She smiled at the biting comments of Kate and the
quiet of the farmhouse. She knew she needed to help in
some way to keep her from being taken by those para-
sites, John and Cynthia. When Kate died, the land would

be Elle's and then she could tell them all *no way.*

She didn't have to sell it to them. But what would Rory do? Then she realized she had been sitting there for almost an hour. She still had too much to do and her lunch with Hal was just a couple of hours away.

Her phone rang and Elle jumped. It was Holly.

"What are you doing?" she asked.

Elle looked across the large newsroom and saw Holly on the phone. "What do you mean?" she answered.

"Don't you see who just walked in to the newsroom? Look behind you." Holly whispered loudly and flipped her head, directing Elle.

Elle turned around.

Holly grunted. "Don't look now. Geez, he'll see you looking."

"You told me to look. Who is it?"

"It's Matt Porter. He's back from New York. Gosh, he's gorgeous. Why is he back here?" Holly asked, excited.

Elle felt her heart jump. Matt would never leave New York. It was his dream job, unless he was being put on-air. Matt was a perfect candidate for being on-air. He was striking and infallible. There had to be a link. Maybe she was being considered for New York. She was certainly qualified to do anything that he was doing there. She looked over at him again. Being in the same city with him could be trouble. Elle casually swung her chair around and acted like she was searching for something in a desk drawer. She glanced up and found Matt smiling at her. She tried to look surprised and then smiled widely at him. She waved him over.

"Oh, my God!" Holly whispered loudly on the phone. "You are good."

"Gotta go," said Elle, with a lilt.

She hung up the phone and stood up to greet Matt.

She put out her hand in a friendly but professional greeting.

Matt took her hand, pulled her to him, and gave her a not so professional embrace.

Elle felt her knees tingle as the trace of expensive cologne and a well-honed body pressed against her. Holly's eye bulged and she sank down into her chair with her hand to her mouth.

"Wow, you look great," said Matt, as he released her. He cocked his head and studied her. "Something's different. Did you cut your hair?"

Elle was still in awe and just shook her head and took a deep breath to avoid speaking.

"So have you heard?" Matt said softly.

"Heard what?"

"Has Hal talked to you?"

"We are having lunch today."

Matt smiled and nodded. "I won't blow it then. Let's just say, I hope you're game." He winked at her and walked off toward one of the editors whom he greeted with a hearty pat on the back.

Elle watched him a minute then turned back to her desk. Her phone rang and she looked across the room where Holly was standing, phone to her ear, wide-eyed. Elle answered, "Yes?"

"If you don't go for him, you're nuts."

Elle closed her eyes tight and sighed. "The only thing I'm going for is his job."

CHAPTER 9

It always felt good to step out of a limo even if it was a couple of miles drive. Elle pulled her suit jacket down hoping it covered her expanded hips. Even with the number of comments she received about her healthy and glowing good looks, she felt out of sorts with her new size and uncomfortable in her clothes. It would take a while for her to get back to her fighting weight, and without the farm food, she felt it was only a matter of time. Right now she needed to focus on furthering her career, not on her thighs.

She stood straight and walked with purpose into the Gray Whale restaurant. Hal lifted a glass filled with iced tea and greeted her with a smile. Hal was past retirement age, but had no desire to leave his post as Washington bureau chief. He was of average height, with a full head of dark gray hair. His face looked like marble with flecks of age spots and freckles, and his smile looked like it was ready to fall onto the table at any moment. He was respected at the station, but also feared.

Elle loved Hal because he was like her in many ways. News was his life and he never let anything else come between him and a story. He made a difference and he was her idol.

"Elle, come sit," Hal said, pointing to the chair next to him.

Elle did as she was told and cocked her head. "So what is my new position?" she asked, bluntly.

Hal blurted out a half laugh, half gasp. "You always were to the point." He smiled and took a swig. "That is why you are where you are. I am proud of you, Elle. You are someone I saw a lot in from the very beginning. You're tough and don't let anyone or anything get in the way of news. You remind me of me."

Elle lifted an eyebrow, flattered. "So, am I going to New York?"

Hal scoffed. "New York? Who wants New York right now? The big news is in the Middle East. I am sending you where the action is."

"Iraq?"

Hal shook his head. "Not just Iraq, but right in the middle of the war."

"War?"

"I'm sending you and Matt to do something that has never been done before. You'll be doing hour-long specials on the Middle East."

Elle listened, but only heard the part about Matt. The news smoldered in her gut. She was the producer. There was no need for two on the assignment. Plus, she had never forgiven herself for letting Matt break it off first. She obviously must have found something attractive about him back then. They dated for almost a year, but it wasn't long before she saw through him.

Matt was ambitious, like her, but different. Elle was aggressive and good at her job, Matt used other tactics. And that is how he treated Elle when it came to their relationship. If she had something to offer, then everything was good, but as soon as something better came along, he was gone. She was ready to lower the boom on him, when he up and practically announced his engagement to another woman. He married an editor at *The Washington Post.* Elle was so glad when he was sent to New York. It gave her a reprieve from having to watch him use his sleazy charm to land interviews and set up stories.

"You look stunned," Hal said, signaling the waitress to refresh his tea. "This is huge, Elle. You'll be right in line for the bureau chief's job in London if you pull this off. The network is already planning a four week run during the February sweeps."

"London? Wow, I'm honored, Hal, really. But why do they feel the need to send two producers?"

"It's a big assignment. Don't look at it as a competition. You'll all be working as a team."

"Does this have something to do with the layoffs?"

Hal's smiled faded. "No, just scaling back. We need to be more efficient."

Elle took a long gulp of the iced tea that Hal had ordered for her. "Can I pick my crew?"

Hal laughed. "Of course you'll pick the crew. Matt said he prefers Dan Otto as the chief photographer on this, but you can decide."

Elle shrugged. "Dan's good. Who will be our interpreter? Will they be traveling with us?"

"Whoa! Not now. I want a nice lunch. You can drive me crazy with the details later."

Elle nodded, and then quietly asked, "How long will I be gone?"

Hal leaned back and studied her. "Does it matter?"

Elle shrugged.

Hal tipped his glass and swallowed the last of his tea. "You'll have to fly out with military troops. They have very set schedules, so once you're out there, you are there until another transport can be arranged. I expect your first tour will be about a month."

Elle nodded, thinking.

"So, tell me about this aunt of yours. I heard she died. Sorry to hear it."

Elle sat up straight. "Who told you that? She's not dead yet…I mean she is very sick, but she's doing better."

"Oh, I guess I wasn't listening as well as I should. I heard you were visiting a dying aunt. Is she leaving you her fortune?" He laughed and began to choke. He cleared his throat. "Sorry, dear. I shouldn't joke like that. I didn't think you had any family except the crazy mother in California. This aunt must be pretty important for you to spend that kind of time."

Elle nodded, uncomfortable. "Yes, I suppose." A knot rolled in her stomach and she turned her attentions to the menu, hoping to brush the thoughts of Kate, Rory, and the estate from her mind.

She enjoyed her image of toughness. She was a survivor. Elle had committed herself to that attitude at a young age.

She learned early on that she was just a side dish on the menu of men her mother ordered up. When she learned not to care, life became easier.

It worked for her. She believed that caring for Kate and being attracted to Rory would eventually leave her hurt.

It could leave her mother without the land and without the money. Rose would torment her with it forever.

"So when do we leave?" she asked.

Hal smiled, happy to see his young protégé hadn't lost her edge. "November first."

Elle mentally counted out the days she had to prepare. "What will I wear?"

"Ha!" Hal blurted.

Elle recovered. "I mean, do I have to wear those saris or burqas or can I wear normal clothes?"

Hal smiled. "We have a Middle Eastern translator hired and she should be able to give you wardrobe tips. All I know is that it's hotter 'n blazes."

Maybe I should bring my farm dresses, thought Elle, day dreaming about how cool they were in the late summer afternoons. She smiled to herself and caught Hal watching her as she drifted back to reality. Then the strange twinge of longing hit her and she suddenly felt sad.

"You okay?" Hal asked.

Elle nodded and tried to force a smile. "Couldn't be better."

When she arrived back at the station, her head was full of story ideas and Peabody Awards. She kept catching herself with a Cheshire cat grin. This Middle Eastern trip wasn't just another assignment. It was a task for Elle to prove herself. She had always been Hal's golden child, and this was his way of giving her the upper hand and allowing her to prove it. It was a choice assignment that would give her all the ammunition she needed to keep her job solid.

Elle walked to the rack that held dozens of newspapers from around the world. She pulled off several copies and stuck her nose in the world section of *The New York Times*. She studied the sorrowful faces in a photograph taken at the sight of a mass killing. It was the eyes of the women, barely showing under black scarves wrapped tightly around their heads and faces that called to Elle.

The visual story she was about to tell would probably be the most important work she would ever do. She could change lives. It was something she never talked about, but thought of often. Her job was her life, her identity, and the main reason she chose that profession was its

ability to change the world. Every time she turned in a
story, she sat back and waited for the letters and phone
calls that it generated, the more controversial the better.

This was a gift she was given by Hal. She would be
able to expose horrendous acts, and human injustices,
making every person who watched want to stand up and
do something. Every sound bite from an orphaned child,
every tear the camera caught would be sent home to the
station in a compelling and unforgettable package.

She felt the newspaper fly from her hands. Matt was
in her face and lifting her off the floor. Flustered, she
tried to set herself back down, but it only made her skirt
slide awkwardly to the side, putting her in an even more
uncomfortable state.

"Can you believe it, Elle?" Matt asked, close enough
to kiss her and smiling broadly.

Elle squirmed and opened her eyes wide, trying to
give him a sign that the holding and lifting weren't the
best show of professionalism.

He put her on her feet and then bent one leg slightly,
clenched a fist and thrust his arm down. "Yes! This is going to be so great."

Elle smiled. "It is exciting."

"It's more than exciting," he continued. "It's our
dream." He leaned in closer to her and away from the
other ears. "We talked about this all the time. You and
me, doing what we love and making a difference."

Great. There it was, flapping in the breeze. Now she
remembered why he exhausted her so. He was non-stop
energy.

She smiled at him. "Yes, it is quite the opportunity."

Elle motioned for him to follow her, and he danced
behind her like a child who had just been told that he was
getting a new bike. She walked quickly from the newsroom and down the hallway toward the water fountains.

When they were out of sight, she turned and looked him in the eye. "What do you mean about this 'you and me' stuff?"

He threw his shoulders down. "Elle, don't you remember? We used to talk all the time about how cool it would be to work on a special project together. We planned on covering major events as a team. Now we can."

"So you're talking strictly about the job, right?"

He squinted at her, and then realized what she was alluding to. He started to talk then turned and walked a couple of steps away with his hand to his chin. He turned around and studied her.

Elle shifted. "What?"

"Do you still think about us?" He lifted a mocking eyebrow.

She shook her head wildly and almost yelled her answer. "No."

He smiled, obviously not believing her, and began to speak.

She held her hand out to silence him. "It's just this talk of 'you and me.' I wanted to make sure *you* weren't thinking anything."

He walked to her and looked at her differently than before. His eyes seemed to stare deep into her and she swallowed so hard it made her eyes water.

"Well, at least I hadn't been thinking anything…up to this point," he said, as he walked past her and back to the newsroom.

She stood alone in the hall and wondered why her world was always turned crooked when he was around. It had been a very productive and sane three years. She had a feeling that her world was about to change.

CHAPTER 10

Elle was jolted out of bed by the telephone's scream. She looked at the clock, seven a.m. Who was bothering her at that hour on a Saturday? She felt like she was weighted down and then she remembered the big dinner she had with her crew the night before. She grabbed the phone and fell back against the pillow.

"Yeah?" she asked, hoping the caller knew she was disturbed.

"Elle?" the voice asked.

Elle sat up straight. "Kevin?" she asked back. What the heck? she thought, two ex-boyfriends within twenty-four hours.

"Are you okay?" he asked.

"Yes. I just had a late night. What do you need?"

"I don't need anything. It's just, well, I got a phone call this morning from Rose and—"

"My mother? Good grief. What is she doing now?" Elle threw herself back on the bed. "She really needs to get over the fact that you and I are done."

There was a pause on the other end.

"I'm sorry. She just drives me nuts."

"Elle, this isn't about us. She called for legal advice. She wants me to help her get the money and land she deserves from her father's estate. I was flattered. I never really felt she thought much of me as an attorney."

She doesn't, Elle said to herself. She's looking for cheap legal advice. "You don't need to bother. We can find an attorney."

"It's not a bother, Elle. This is an easy case and I have time. Unless you don't feel comfortable working that close with me."

Elle rolled her eyes. "I'm fine working with you. What do you want me to do?"

"Actually Rose gave me all the legal descriptions and the phone numbers I need for the county surveyors. The reason I called was just to make sure this was all okay with you. I'm fine with us working closely together, but I just wasn't sure how you'd be."

"I'm great actually. I know you'll do a good job, and I'll feel good knowing it's you doing the work." Elle couldn't wait to end her call with Kevin so she could call her mother and berate her over the phone.

"It sounds like a slam dunk here, Elle. The entire piece of property should go to the family, which is legally Rose and you. And when you sell it like Rose was saying, you will end up with quite a nice little chunk of change."

"I don't know what my mother has planned. I do have to wonder why her father gave all the land to Kate and left Rose high and dry. In Rose's case, I can only imagine." Elle was exhausted after the emotional day before, and quite frankly she was to a point where she didn't care who got the land.

"Can we meet and start the paperwork?" Kevin asked.

Elle sniffed. So this is the plan? "Get everything put

together first and then give it to me."

"Well, okay. Do you know what attorney is working for your aunt?"

"No. I don't even know if she has an attorney. I didn't talk to her about that at all."

"Yes, Rose told me you had gone out there. She also said something about a guy who was trying to steal the land somehow. Did you get a feel for that situation?"

Elle paused.

"Elle?"

"Yes, I'm here. Um, there is no problem with this guy. It's just some hired hand that Kate is close to. He's…nothing."

"Okay then. I'll have the papers drawn up and get with you when they are ready for a signature."

"Great."

"So, when?"

"I don't know. I'm going to Iraq. I should be there about a month. I'll meet with you when I get back."

"A month?"

"Yes. I'll be setting up stories and getting some file footage. The stories are set to start airing in November and so I expect to be back then. It won't be a problem. Kate isn't dying any time soon."

Kevin cleared his throat. "It's not that. It's just…"

"What?"

"That's quite a long time to be gone."

"Not really. I am always on the road."

"Yes, but you usually come back after about a week or so before you go again."

"Yeah, so?"

Kevin paused.

"Is there something wrong?"

"No. Don't worry about it. I'll see you when you get back."

Elle hung up the phone and lay back in bed, pondering the reasons why Kevin seemed even more strange and clingy than usual. She knew she hadn't made a clean break, but she was tired and impatient at the time, and so she simply started avoiding him. That was over a year ago and he still called and came around.

Kevin knew she considered them over, but he clung on as though eventually she'd see her mistake. Then he'd be there to catch her and bring her home. Kevin Marcus was handsome in a college professor sort of way. He was tall and fit, with thinning hair, but with deep-set eyes that Elle found lovely, at least when they first started dating. He was stable and safe. But her feelings faded quickly and she found herself irritable and annoyed with him, especially when he was trying his best to woo her.

Her mother had schemed her way into free legal advice, and Elle knew that despite his feeble manner, he was an effective and respected attorney. At first, Elle was attracted to his appearance, but then it started to annoy her, because he spent more time on his hair than she did. He was a strong debater in the courtroom, but in the love department, Elle found him whiney and selfish.

Elle rolled to her side and looked at the clock. It was twenty minutes away from the alarm, so she pushed herself to sitting and stretched her arms up high. She needed to get things organized and plan for her trip to the Middle East. She only had a couple of hours before Holly came by to interrupt her solitude. Elle went to the cupboard and pulled a coffee tin from the shelf. As it brewed, she sorted through her suitcase and began putting things away.

In the pile of rumbled clothes, she found the bulky cardigan sweater she wore when Rory rescued her from the mud and horses. She pulled it close and took a whiff of the sweet smell of the Pennsylvania farmhouse. She wondered how the sweater had made it into her suitcase.

She hadn't seen it since just after her fall in the corral and wondered where it ended up.

She straightened it and hung it carefully in the back of her closet.

❧❧❧

"So what happened that you had to stay two weeks?" Holly asked, as she set the small kennel on the floor. The cat eagerly stared out and then leaped into Elle's lap.

"I almost wish you didn't bring him back. Now I'm leaving again."

Holly smiled. "Are you really going? So, what's the deal with Matt now? He seemed awfully chummy."

Elle shrugged.

Holly giggled. "You didn't answer me about the Pennsylvania trip. So, were your cousins as weird as you thought?"

Elle looked at her and thought for a minute. "Just two of them...a married couple." She went back to unpacking. Elle tried to ignore the questions and wished Holly would stop making her think about Kate...and Rory.

"Tell me! Come on. I know you have some great stories after all that time. What was this aunt like and what did her little boy toy look like?"

"It wasn't at all what I thought. I did what I needed to do. It just took a little longer."

"So, you're getting the money?" asked Holly with a lilt.

Elle really wished for Holly to stop talking and leave. "Yes. I'm getting the money. I really must get some things done. I've got a lot to get caught up on. Thanks for taking the cat."

Holly stood up to leave. "Okay, I'll see you at work tomorrow."

Elle sighed. She felt something for the young woman who always tried too hard. "How about lunch tomorrow? I'll buy for taking care of the feline."

Holly turned back and gave Elle a genuine grin. "Really? Okay."

Holly closed the door behind her and Elle took a seat at the small kitchen table. She heard a rustling and looked over to see the cat batting at an empty plastic bag. It paused, realizing it was being watched.

Kevin had given the cat to her when they were together. He named the cat Kevin Junior or K.J. He used the cat as an excuse to see Elle. At that moment as she sat there face to face with it, she found herself somewhat amazed that it even survived under her care, but loved it when, at certain times in the morning, it brushed against her leg in a show of affection.

The phone rang and she looked at the clock, wondering who was calling so late. The caller ID read "R. Davenport." That was her mother's third husband's name. Even though Rose had been married five times, she liked the way that one sounded best, and since she was currently available, she decided to use it. Elle stared at the ringing phone and prepared her attack before answering it.

"Hello?" Elle answered with a huff.

"Elle darling, I got your message, but I couldn't call until now because I was at the auxiliary meeting."

"Mother, why did you call Kevin? You know I'm not seeing him anymore. It's so irritating and awkward."

"Elle, who else should I have called? I don't know any attorneys and we need one. You are so busy that I wanted to help."

"Then stay out of it. You asked me to go up there, so you obviously didn't think I was too busy to spend two weeks of my life doing your dirty work."

"Elle, I am not doing anything wrong here. That is

my home up there and I...we deserve it. It should stay with the family, not go to a stranger."

Elle grit her teeth. "You're planning on selling it anyway. It isn't staying with the family."

"Why are you arguing with me?" Rose asked. "Do you want all that land and money to go to that punk?"

Elle paused and thought about Rory. "Tell me what you know about this so called punk. It seems everyone has her nose in a twist about him, but I can't get a straight answer from anyone about what's really going on. Before I went up there, you had me thinking he and Kate were living in sin."

"Elle, why do you have to be so crude?"

Elle laughed. "Mother, don't try to make yourself out as a wholesome prude. After five marriages, it isn't going to happen."

"Well, at least I've been married."

"What is that supposed to mean? Do you really think a bunch of failed marriages is something to be proud of?" The conversation was beginning to sound like the dinner table rapport of every Christmas holiday she had spent with Rose.

The topic Elle was hoping to discuss always got lost in an explosion of pent up anger and lightning quick tempers.

"Well, at least I've tried," Rose, continued. "I haven't given up on love and marriage. I've tried to be happy, Elle. You don't even try. You act like you want to be lonely and single."

Elle wanted to fire back, but was too exhausted.

"Elle, are you there?" Rose asked after several seconds.

Still pondering whether she should answer, Elle took a deep breath.

"I can hear you breathing," Rose sang in an off key lilt.

"Only because I haven't completely tightened the noose," Elle shot back.

"Elle, please just let Kevin put the papers together," Rose whined, ignoring Elle's sarcasm. "At least we can trust him and he won't charge us the way another attorney would. He says it will be easy and all you will have to do is sign some things. He says because we are the only blood relatives, you probably won't have to do much more than appear one day in court. Is that too much to ask?"

Elle sighed hard. "No. But I still don't understand why this is all on me. It was your parents who owned the place. Why has this come down to me?"

"It's all just a lot of stuff in the past. I was angry and didn't think things through. I should have never given up my claim to the land."

"Wait a minute," Elle asked, surprised. "You never told me that. If you gave up your right to the land, then this is a lost cause. If you don't have a claim, I certainly don't. Is that why you sent me out there? To try and convince them that I should?"

"No. You see…" Then Rose started to stumble. She paused and started several times, until Elle got frustrated and knew that something evil had been plotted long before her trip to see Kate.

"What is going on, Mother?"

"The land is yours because Daddy wrote you in."

"What? When?"

"It was years ago. You were still young. But there are some provisions."

"Provisions. Like what?" Elle asked.

"I don't know. That's why I sent you out there. I

didn't know that Daddy had changed the will until last month."

"So, I am the only one on the will?" asked Elle.

Long pause.

"Wait a minute. You don't have anything." Elle then laughed hysterically. "It's all becoming so clear now."

"Knock it off, Elle. You're being terrible."

"I'm being terrible? You just sent me on a wild goose chase and all because you wanted me to be the pawn in your greedy little plan."

"The land is ours, Elle...all of it. I'm not being greedy. I just don't think that your granddaddy's farm should be in the hands of anyone that isn't family."

"So, if I sign the papers and get the whole thing, what then? When we do get the land, what will we do with it then?"

"Sell it."

"If we sell it, then it won't be in the hands of family any longer."

"Yes, it will. I already told you. Cynthia and John will pay two million."

"Whoa. Wait." Elle sat up straight.

"What?" Rose asked.

"No. No way. Those two are sleazy little vermin."

"What are you talking about, Elle? That's our cousin. It's two million."

"No. You don't understand. They make my skin crawl. I don't want them anywhere on that land."

"Elle, we need to sell it to get the money."

"That's fine, but not to them."

"Then to who?"

"I don't care. Anyone but them. Family or not."

"Why? That could take years. What difference does it make? If they have the money, why not?" asked Rose.

Elle tried to answer, but couldn't find the words that explained her adamancy against them.

"Elle, we're selling it to John and Cynthia. That's always been the plan."

"You're forgetting one very important thing, Mother. *You* are not selling it to anyone. If a sale is going to take place, then *I'm* the one that will be doing it. Remember? The land is in my name, not yours."

"Elle, why do you have to be so evil to me? You find great joy in punishing me and for what?"

Elle just shook her head and stared off. She then noticed the silence on the other end of the phone.

"Mother?"

"What?" Rose shouted. "Are you going to ignore the question?"

Elle sighed. "What question?"

Rose scoffed. "You never listen to me. I want to know what your plans are for the holidays. Is this work trip going to mess things up?"

The holidays. How Elle dreaded the words and the question. But this year she may have an actual excuse. "Yes, I will probably be in the Middle East." For the first time Elle actually had the perfect excuse. She'd be thousands of miles away from the maddening and painful experience of holidays with Mother.

"Oh," said Rose with a bit of surprise. "I guess that's good. I thought you'd have other plans, so I planned a trip to Cancun with my bridge group this year. I made the flight plans last week because I thought you'd be spending it with Kate."

Elle slowly sat back in the chair. This stunned her. She never had realized until then that, whenever Rose asked her to come to California, Elle at least felt she had someone who cared, someone who wanted her there. She wasn't just another one of the thousands of single, driven worker bees, who put career first and ignored just about anything else.

"I didn't want her to be alone on the holidays, especially since this might be her last," said Rose. Her voice trailed off as if pondering the sadness of Kate being gone.

"Give me a break, Mother. You know as well as I do that this is all just a big guilt trip to get me out there and do your dirty work. Besides, Rory will be there."

"That is exactly what I don't want. He'll have his hooks into her even more now. He's a criminal that destroyed everything and now you are going to give it to him."

"I find that hard to believe. What did he do? Besides, I am the one on the will, not him."

Rose gave a loud sniff. "Sounds to me like he's got his hooks into you, too."

"What does that mean?" Elle raged.

"You're going to give away millions of dollars because of this guy. If you don't show that you want the land, then it will be put back into the estate and then it will be divided amongst everyone. We'll get a fraction of it. Kate will give him her part and then he'll have a stake in it. You and Kate are both blind to it. So, go ahead, let him have the land and the money."

"I'm not letting him have anything. I can't pick up and go out there on a whim."

"This isn't a whim. It's the holidays. You being out there could change Kate's mind about who is her family."

"Do you really think that me being around for a couple months is going to make a difference?"

"It already has."

"What? How?"

"When I talked with Cynthia last week she said the building project had been stopped."

"What building project? If you mean that stupid chicken diner, good!"

"No. That is what should be going in. That leech of a kid is building a business there."

Elle sat down, confused. All that talk about keeping the land for farming and for raising animals. Was she being snowed? "Are you sure?"

"Yes. Cynthia said that because we filed the papers, the construction was put on hold. So, it is working."

"No one ever told me anything about him building a business."

"I'm not surprised. I think there is a lot that is being hidden from the family. That is why you need to be there. Otherwise, we'll lose it all. Don't be taken in by this guy. Kate already has and now we risk losing everything."

Elle sat wondering if what her mother was saying could be true.

"Elle, sweetheart, please go out to Kate's for the holidays."

"I can't. I'll be working. We'll just have to hope that the attorneys can work out whatever deal it is we get."

"Hmm," Rose whined. "That's sad. Really sad."

"Yes. Yes, it is."

CHAPTER 11

The month and a half Elle had to prepare went quickly, but time also seemed to drag on because of her anxiousness to secure her promotion. She couldn't wait to step off that plane and get to work proving her worth.

Holly took the cat and Elle had just put the last of what she could fit into her zippered mobile home. She often thought about getting a new suitcase, but this one had been with her for so many years, had seen so many of the things she covered, it was as though she'd be giving up a friend.

The trip to Iraq was hopefully to be one of her last. Then the suitcase could retire to the back of her closet, unpacked and empty. This assignment was to clinch her position at the network and that meant promotion to bureau chief. It was her dream job.

Elle took one last look around the apartment, wondering why she felt she missed something. She looked at the phone and felt the need to make a call. She hadn't talked to Kate since she left. Now she wanted to check on her and let her know that she would be gone for a while.

Elle wasn't sure why she felt the need to contact Kate, and she didn't know exactly what to say, so she just stood there staring at the phone. Suddenly it rang loudly and she jumped back startled.

"Good grief," she blurted out. She grabbed the receiver and answered it.

"Elle?" the voice asked. It sounded familiar but not one she immediately placed.

"Yes?"

"It's Rory Beau."

Rory. "Is Kate okay?" Elle asked, as her heart sank.

"Yes. She's okay."

"What's wrong?"

"Nothing. I just wanted to see if you can come up for the holidays."

Elle almost dropped the phone.

"If you're going to be free, that is," Rory said, in a direct and formal tone.

"Uh…" Elle stammered, unsure what to say. She felt strange having Rory on the phone, and surprised at the invitation. "It's just that I'm not sure where I'll be. You see I was just getting ready to call you…"

"You were going to call me?" Rory playfully interrupted.

Elle snorted. "I meant Kate."

Rory chuckled and Elle felt her face turn red. "I wanted to see how she was doing and let her know that I'll be gone for a while to the Middle East."

"Really. Why would you want to go there? Isn't a war about to break out?"

"That is exactly why I'm going. Can I talk to her?" Elle asked.

Rory paused. "Actually, Elle, Kate is pretty weak. She doesn't want to worry you, and she certainly wouldn't want me calling and inviting you for Thanksgiving. She never admits she wants to celebrate the holidays, but I'll be busy and I really don't want her alone. They've put her on chemo again, and she isn't handling it as well as we'd like. She's fine, but just not her normal sweet self."

Elle smiled, thinking about Kate's caustic demeanor. "What about the nurse? Isn't she helping?"

"She is. But I don't want Kate spending the holidays with paid help. I want her to have family here."

Family, thought Elle, I guess technically I am, but I'm certainly not that close to be spending the holidays there. *Seal the deal.* She thought it was curious that her mother had wanted her to go see Kate and now she was being invited to go by the very person standing in Rose's way to millions.

"I don't know when I'll be returning. It really depends on what happens over there. If we do go to war, I have no idea when I will come back."

Rory's end of the line was silent. He cleared his throat. "I understand. So, should I get in touch with you if…if something happens?"

A sickening grumble went through Elle's stomach. Something happening meant that Kate had died. She didn't know how to respond. It angered her to think he may be using it as a way to make her feel guilty.

"Why would you say something like that? Are you trying to guilt me into coming back?"

"Is that the only reason you would?"

"You idiot. Why are you even involved? If I want to see my aunt, I will and it won't be from an invitation from you."

"Elle, I'm not trying to start a fight. I'm just being realistic. She isn't well and I thought you might want to be in the loop." Rory continued, "How do I contact you over there?"

Elle couldn't keep thinking about Kate being gone. She numbly gave Rory the main number at the news desk in Washington as a contact.

Rory returned to his formalness. "Well, since I won't be seeing you, have a happy holiday."

Elle just sighed, annoyed and irritable.

"And Elle…" He paused.

"Yes?" she asked sharply.

"You be careful over there."

Elle huffed.

He gave a small laugh, which irritated her even more. "Maybe I'll see you when you get home."

She hung up the phone and took a seat on the sofa. Home, she thought looking around the apartment. Why did it all of a sudden seem so cold and impersonal? She sat up straight and shook herself back to reality. What is it with me lately?

Elle took the handle of the suitcase and reminded herself of the awesome assignment she'd been given and the daunting task of saving her job. She was about to take an adventure. Even though she had been alone for years, it was the first time the loneliness of being alone hit her.

Home. The word rang out in her head. She walked out the door and closed it behind her. She put the key in the door to lock up the apartment, and as she turned the bolt, she thought about how little was in there that she'd actually miss if it were stolen.

CHAPTER 12

Early November, 1990:

The flight was long. Matt slept most of the way, as Elle sat scheming story ideas and ways to outdo him. Dan Otto, their photographer, picked at the nuts and pretzels they were offered from the cheery flight attendant.

"How many times have you been overseas on assignment?" Elle asked him, noticing his boredom.

He looked up at the ceiling as if counting. "I can't even remember. I used to think it was an honor, but then I figured out the real reason I keep getting chosen. It's more a matter of being disposable."

"Disposable. What does that mean? You're one of the best in the business."

Dan laughed. "Maybe, but do you really think the three of us are being sent out here because we're indispensable?" He shook his head. "We are all disposable employees. They aren't going to send someone out in the middle of a war zone that isn't. None of us have families. We're all a bunch of single workaholics who no one would really miss. The last thing the network needs is a funeral with a grieving spouse and a passel of little ones to ruin their image."

Elle started to disagree, but realized she really had no defense. She turned to the window.

Dan reached over and jokingly patted her on the shoulder. "It's not all bad. It's actually job security. And besides, I'm so close to being done with all this, I can taste it."

Elle smiled and realized that Matt was awake and groggily looking over to her. He winked. Sly boy, she thought, as she gave him a sappy grin back. She turned quickly to the window. She unbuckled her seatbelt when the pilot sat the plane down and stretched her arms above her head, anxious to get out of the flying tube and get to work.

They landed in Jordan, and along with the rest of the journalists and their precious visas, Elle, Dan and Matt found themselves wandering the airport in the hopes of securing the transportation they had arranged for back in the states. No one awaited them.

Elle knew that once she was at the Al-Rashid hotel, she had an ace in the pocket, a guide arranged through Hal and a former production assistant who was from Iraq and still had ties. The heat of the Jordanian desert was thick, and along with the frustration of not having everything arranged easily to get into Baghdad, it felt even more smothering.

Dan found a transport bus to share with several of the crews from the other networks and Elle loaded her suitcase into the back of the large, antiquated van. The sun shimmered and waved above the black of the pavement as they drove. The sight mesmerized her.

It was a long drive from Jordan into Iraq and eventually into the capital city where they would be based. As they drove, the land seemed to stretch out forever. Small towns appeared out of the sand and the van slowed along dusty, single lane roads where lines of people walked and carried large bundles and baskets.

People stared at the faces peering from the windows of the strange bus. Both men and women were draped in robes, and the women wore veils that covered everything but their eyes. Elle found herself smoothing down her hair and feeling like her lipstick was far too red.

In between bouts of restless sleep, Elle groggily peered out the van window and thought about the parched desert and how it differed from the wandering hills of oats and fall leaves of the farm. The remaining hours of jostling and boredom gave Elle more time to plot her stories and her ploy for securing her job.

At the hotel, a woman that looked to be Elle's age greeted their van. She appeared slim, even being covered almost completely by the dark robes of the burqa. She had large brown eyes and in the bright sun, her skin glowed like satin. Elle quickly guided her to the side, away from the others. The woman gave her a brilliant and confident smile.

"Are you Elle?"

Elle nodded.

"Hello, I am Faiza. I will be your guide here. Welcome."

"Thank you. I am..." Elle started to speak, but was interrupted by Matt, who put his hand out quickly. He was obviously already engrossed with the Middle Eastern beauty and wasted no time flirting with her. Elle squinted and watched as he gushed about the honor of covering her people's plight, and a bunch of nonsense.

Faiza was polite, but not flattered. When Matt began asking questions about her job and life, she quickly changed the subject and moved closer to Elle. Her English was impeccable and Elle watched Matt fall all over himself. Faiza seemed to float as she walked with them into the hotel.

The Al-Rashid hotel was ornate and elegant. Intricate and colorful tiles covered the floor and walls, and gold plated sconces gave a soft spill of light around the large foyer. Faiza continued to talk, as Elle studied the hotel. Faiza explained where they would be able to go and how they could contact her when needed. Dan stayed behind, as he examined the video gear he had carefully loaded onto the van's storage rack.

Elle and Matt checked in at the front desk. The clerk was friendly and welcomed them genuinely, as if his smile could change the tensions building everywhere. Elle and Matt took their keys and followed Faiza to their respective hotel rooms. They reached Matt's first. He gave her the gunpoint and wink, as he opened the door and stepped inside.

"Catch'ya later," he said with a grin.

Faiza smiled, uncomfortable. When Matt was safely inside and out of earshot, Faiza walked with Elle down the hall. "If you want me to help you in your attire, I can do that," said Faiza.

Elle looked down at her jeans and t-shirt. "Is there something wrong with what I'm wearing?"

"No. But—"

Elle interrupted her. "You were hired to guide us, and if I need it, I will ask you for fashion advice." She looked back at the young woman who swallowed hard as desperation spread across her flawless face.

"Yes, of course," Faiza whispered. "I will be in the lobby until you need me."

Elle closed the door and threw the key on the table. She zipped open her old suitcase and began unloading and sorting a couple of things into drawers and onto hangers. She was a master at packing. Elle had taken so many trips for her job that the layouts of hotel rooms were homier to her than the apartment she had lived in for the last five years. When she finished, she picked up the phone and called Dan's room.

"Meet me in the lobby in ten minutes so we can plan." She heard laughing in the background. "Who is that?"

"It's Matt. He just showed up. Hey, Matt, Elle wants to meet in the lobby in ten," he yelled. "Matt says to bring Faiza, too." She heard Matt cat calling in the background.

"We're supposed to be working here, not acting like we're at a frat party," Elle said sternly.

She slammed the phone down and went to into the bathroom. She washed her face in the sink and blotted it dry with one of the clean but rough hand towels. She looked in the mirror and studied her skin. She was Faiza's age, but she looked much older. The lines around her mouth from years of tension and lack of sleep made her lips looked pursed. It was a long flight and even longer drive, she thought, rationalizing her haggard appearance.

She brushed her hair back in to an elastic and changed her shirt. She kept stewing about what Faiza had said and wondered how her appearance could possibly hinder her ability to get the stories she needed. It had never played a role before.

Again, she gazed in the mirror and turned to view her figure from the side. It had been weeks since she returned from Pennsylvania and she was slowly getting her figure back. It had taken a lot of missed meals, but it was worth it. No more whole milk and rich cheese and meat for her. She was almost at her fighting weight and she felt like she would soon be fighting for her life.

She put the room key in her pocket and pulled the

door shut. In the lobby sat Matt, Dan and Faiza.

"Elle, I already have an interview tomorrow with one of the staff at the US embassy. There is talk they will be closing it soon," Matt said.

"Really. How'd you get that so fast?" Elle looked over to Faiza and then back to Matt.

"I met the guy at a statehouse presser a couple years ago. It pays to schmooze."

Elle had never schmoozed anyone. She knew Matt well enough to know he was needling her. She had talked long and hard about getting stories through respect, not brown nosing. They had completely different styles and she was quick to point that out. Matt enjoyed showing her that her way wasn't always the most effective.

Elle took a chair next to Faiza. "Since we have to share you, we need to plan what days you'll be going with Matt and what days you'll be going with me."

"Since I already have an interview for tomorrow, it looks like she'll be with me," said Matt, talking to Elle, but smiling at Faiza.

"That's fine. I need tomorrow to research and set things up anyway," said Elle. "But I do need to know how to get a taxi so I can get around and see this place."

Faiza shook her head. "You can't venture out on your own. It's too dangerous."

Elle frowned. "I don't want to sit around the hotel."

Faiza looked anxious. "I will find a guide for Matt. I will go with you and show you the people who will talk."

"Whoa there," Matt blurted out. "Why not find a guide for her instead?"

Faiza looked desperate for a good answer. "It will be easier for me to show her the town since I live here. Any driver can take you to the embassy."

"Hmm," Matt pondered. "You sure you're not just trying to avoid me?" He winked.

Faiza started to shake her head, but Dan spoke up. "It is a good point. And we don't need an interpreter to get to the embassy. We should be fine."

"Then guys against girls it is," said Matt, as he gave Dan the man's thumbs up. He stood up. "Isn't there a bar or something around this place? I'm going to walk around the block and see what we've been sentenced to for the next month."

Elle just watched as Matt walked toward the door. "You coming with me?" he asked Dan.

Dan grunted and continued cleaning the already spotless camera lens.

Faiza sat back in the chair. "So, tell me how you want me to help you with your stories."

Elle pondered the question. Then she looked back toward the door to make sure Matt was really gone. "I've read some unofficial reports about mass executions, Holocaust type killings. I want to show what these people have been living through. I want to talk to witnesses."

Faiza looked pained. "That's going to be very hard because the people are scared of what might happen. They want things to change, but if they speak out, they too can be killed."

"But if we don't tell that story, the only information that is going to get out is propaganda that the Iraqi government is letting out."

"I don't know," said Faiza. "Many people don't trust the Americans any more than they trust the Iraqi army."

"What do you know?"

Faiza looked down at her hands. "Enough to know they will be afraid to talk."

Elle sighed. "Well, I'm not going to just sit around here and talk to a bunch of officials who won't admit what is happening. I want to talk to real people. They are the ones who are hurt by all this."

Faiza nodded. "I can try. Maybe you can help them."

"Help them. What do you mean?"

"Show things and encourage change."

Elle held up her hands. "I can't take sides about any of this. I can't get involved or become a part of any of this or I am not doing my job."

Faiza was lost in thought, and didn't respond.

"It's almost dark. I must get some sleep so we can head out early," Elle said. "Tomorrow I want to start in the downtown area near the statue of Saddam Hussein."

Faiza stood up. "I will meet you here in the lobby in the morning. I will have a car for us."

"Good," Elle answered. She stood and awkwardly sent Faiza on her way. When she had left the hotel, she turned to Dan. "We have to separate ourselves from the others. They will see and hear things and we can't be sending back the same press conferences and staged file video as the rest."

Dan scowled. "Well, no kidding. So, what do you have planned? It's not like we know this place. We'll get nothing if we don't at least cover the official statements and meetings."

"Matt can worry about that. I'm finding something else. I'll use our lovely guide. She knows stuff, and even though she claims she is just a guide, she's got to know more. You can't live in this place and not have some idea of what is really going on."

The next morning, Faiza waited as she said, in the lobby. Elle looked around to see who else was there, but only saw a photographer she didn't know wandering the foyer like a tourist. When Faiza saw her, she smiled broadly. "I have a taxi waiting outside."

"Where are we going?"

"I will show you around the city and give you some

idea of how things are laid out. We can see the palace and some of the official buildings."

Elle nodded, but hoped that it didn't turn out to be a day of sightseeing. However, at the moment she didn't have a better plan and did need to get an idea of the area she would be covering. They walked outside and crawled into the dusty, beat up cab. Faiza gave him directions in Arabic.

"I thought it would be much hotter here," said Elle, wishing she had dressed more warmly.

"It is fall. Most foreigners' think it is always hot and dry here, but in winter we have rain, snow and freezing wind. From now until April, I would at least bring along a jacket."

Elle looked out as they drove through the narrow, poorly paved streets. People were dressed in loose clothes, many robes and drapes, and some of the men looked no different than those back home wearing pants, collared shirts and athletic shoes. Their skin was mahogany and most had dark, deep-set eyes.

"Do they all speak Arabic?" Elle asked.

"Most do. Many speak Kurdish. Some Armenian. Some speak English."

"What do they know about Americans?"

"Not much, but they worry about what is going to happen. They know something has gone on in the south, but all they hear is that Saddam is trying to protect them. Now they wonder why the United States is getting involved."

"What do you think?"

Faiza gave her a weary smile. "What history has shown doesn't make me feel that any good can come out of what I am hearing. I worry that things will get worse for my people, not better." She looked out the front window and then pointed. "That is the mosque."

Elle looked out at a large building with a colorful dome, decorated in gold and dark blue tiles. The sun reflected off it, giving the round globe a shimmer. "It's very pretty," said Elle, not really seeing it, but instead contemplating what Faiza had said. "What is so bad here?" Elle asked, trying to egg on something more than a scripted response. "I've heard about Saddam killing those who are disloyal, but I figured that was all military and government stuff. If you're just a citizen, is life really that bad?" Elle motioned to the people on the street. "They don't seem unhappy. Does this all affect them?"

"Yes." Faiza stopped, catching herself. "There is much more than what you see on the streets."

"That's what I want."

Faiza sighed.

"Faiza, you asked yesterday how you can help me and that is how. I want to talk to real people who have suffered under Saddam. I want to find out how this affects them."

Faiza demurred. "I am just an interpreter. I don't know if I can put my people at risk. This is just a job for you. For them it is their life and the lives of their families. I don't think anyone is willing to risk that."

When the sun began to set, and they had covered most of the landmarks in the large city, Faiza directed the cab back to the hotel. Elle didn't offer much in the way of parting words, but Faiza told her she would be back the following morning and Elle acquiesced. The lobby was full of fresh cut flowers, and the fountain cascaded happily in the middle. It was a stark contrast to the dry and lifeless feel of the street just outside the door.

At the counter of the lobby sat Mat and Dan. They had found reception on a small television and were snacking on rice crackers. Matt turned with a grin. "So how was the sightseeing?"

"I was researching," Elle snapped back.

Matt made a face and sat back against the bar. "We just finished feeding our interview. We got that along with some great video of tanks rolling out of the Iraqi Army headquarters."

Dan looked at Elle as if apologizing for being in the right place at the right time.

Matt continued, knowing he had Elle on the ropes. "And we bought a car."

"Why?" asked Elle.

"We figured we could get around a lot easier. It was only two hundred dollars. And we can drive." He smirked and sat back.

"What does that mean?" Elle asked.

Matt started to speak up, but Dan silenced him. "It isn't common for women to drive here. It's better we don't draw attention. But it's no big deal. We thought it might be easier to get our own car, especially since we're all competing trying to get rides."

Matt tried to act nonchalant, but Elle saw his victorious grin. She knew she was defeated for the day, but she was hardly ready to give up the entire trip. The story she wanted to tell was far more powerful than what Matt could dig up. Her challenge would be convincing people to talk, and Elle knew that her abilities were lacking when it came to giving off the appearance of caring concern that was needed for them to trust her. She'd been behind the scenes too long and needed to brush up on her interviewing skills.

She tried to act unaffected and quickly escaped to her room.

Elle washed her face and stood in the bathroom looking in the mirror and thinking about the day. She acted out in the mirror, her facial expressions, as if listening and reacting to their stories of struggle. She furrowed her eyebrows and nodded her head as if responding.

Elle pushed aside her attempts and began to plot on how to get people to talk without the use of sappy sentimentality. She had less than a week to turn in something or be too far past the deadline to recover. Regardless of her standing with Hal, if she failed here, her job was at stake.

CHAPTER 13

That night Elle awoke to the sounds of a scuffle. It wasn't close but the voices were loud and a high-pitched wail pierced the night and kept her from sleeping. After several minutes of loud engine noises and distant yelling, she turned on the nightstand lamp and sat up. She tried to form productive thoughts, but usually found herself drifting back to her brief time on the Pennsylvania farm. She longed for the peaceful openness and the simplicity of her time with Kate. She longed for Rory.

Elle looked at her suitcase lying open near the fan on the desk. She had spent so much time living out of it, that she often wondered why she even had an apartment. Lately, she spent more time at the station because Hal Norland was nearing retirement, and he asked her to fill in a bit more than usual. Elle was flattered and hopeful that it was a sign that she was the heir apparent. She knew that with Hal on her side, she really didn't need to fear the layoffs, but her fight or flight instinct kept her from being lax. There were plenty of sharks in that newsroom.

Elle reached over and turned off the light then scooted down into the blankets. The disturbance continued most of the night, and each time she drifted off, a new round of clamor shattered the silence.

That morning she wandered down to the lobby, where Faiza waited. She was dressed in a long flowing robe and her dark hair was covered with a black scarf.

Elle put a hand on her jeans and wondered if her bright pink blouse was too much.

"Where are the others?" Elle asked.

"They are already gone. I have a car and driver that can take us around. It is waiting outside."

Elle nodded. "Good." She looked around the lobby. "Is there coffee somewhere?"

Faiza smiled. "I have taken the liberty of arranging a meal for you at my family's home. It is not far from here. There will be coffee there."

Elle looked at her, surprised. "With your family?"

Faiza looked apologetic. "It won't take long."

Elle smiled. "No, that's great. I'm looking to talk to real people. This is a good start."

They walked out of the hotel and onto the street. It was an anthill of activity. Elle was overwhelmed at the number of people just going about their business after what sounded like a war zone the night before. The men wore long beards and the women were all in black drapes and veils.

As the women walked together, it reminded Elle of the flocks of ravens that floated above the fields back at the farm. Their shiny ebony bodies mesmerized her as they glided in formation, each a carbon copy of the other. Elle wondered if she shouldn't have taken Faiza's offering of attire. The stares and double stares were a bit disconcerting. But she stubbornly refuted the thought and stood tall.

Once in the cab, Elle was relieved. Faiza spoke to the

driver in Arabic and he pulled away from the curb and through the sea of people. As they headed out of the hub of the city, the crowds thinned and open, barren land was visible again.

"Where are we going?" Elle asked.

"We will go to the city of Dujail. That is where much of the activity has happened."

"So where is your family?" asked Elle.

"They live in Saba al- Bor; it's a small village on the way."

As they drove, Elle caught the cab driver giving her unfriendly looks in the rear view mirror. He mumbled something to Faiza in Arabic and she answered him sternly.

"What was that about?" asked Elle.

"He is not used to having an American in his cab. He is worried that the Sunnis will single us out," she answered.

"I'm a journalist. I'm here to tell the stories about what is happening."

Faiza looked pained.

"They will do more harm than good, by hurting me."

"I don't think they care. It seems everyone is trying to make a point. It's best to stay under the radar. That is why I suggested…"

Elle put a hand up. "Please don't tell me that we might be in danger because of the way I look."

Faiza stayed silent.

Suddenly both Faiza and the driver stared out at the road and then anxiously looked back at Elle.

"Get down," ordered Faiza.

Elle started to balk, but Faiza put her hand on Elle's head and thrust her toward the floor of the cab.

"What's going on?" she yelled from the floor. Then a loud, low rumble shook the floorboards. It got louder as they drove. She stayed down, wondering what the noise was. It soon subsided and Faiza slowly directed her back to the seat.

"What was that all about?" she demanded.

Faiza kept staring straight ahead. "Militia."

Elle looked out the back window, as a procession of large open bed trucks and dozens of armed men drove into the distance. She turned back around and sat silent the rest of the ride.

At a small stucco home in the middle of a cookie cutter maze of others, Faiza signaled the driver to stop. Elle waited by the door of the house, as Faiza talked with the driver. When she turned to Elle, the cab sped off and Faiza rubbed her eyes and groaned.

"What?" asked Elle.

"I asked him to return for us."

"So, what's the problem?" Elle asked.

"He doesn't want problems."

"Then we'll find another."

"It will be difficult to find another and there aren't many in my town."

A young boy appeared around the corner and walked with confidence up to Elle and Faiza.

"Why aren't you inside, Muki?" asked Faiza. "Does your mother know you're running about?"

Muki was thin and dark and wore a black circular cap, blue shorts and a striped t-shirt. He had large expressive eyes that smiled, even when he wasn't. He ignored Faiza and studied Elle.

"Who is he?" Elle asked.

"He lives in the flat next to ours."

Elle studied him back. She noticed a leather strap and a stone in his hand. "What is that?" she asked him.

Muki stayed quiet.

"Muki, don't be rude. Answer, Elle."

He smiled. "It's a sling shot. I can hit a target at fifty meters."

Elle raised her eyebrows. "I'll make sure I stay on your good side."

He smiled and ran off.

Faiza looked tired as she went to the door of the small home. She knocked twice, waited, and then knocked twice again. She then used a key, opened the door and stepped inside.

"Mother?" she called out.

The room was small with colorful rugs and tiny gold and ceramic trinkets on wooden tables and shelves. Two older women in similar dark robes came around the corner from the back of the home and greeted Faiza with smiles. When Elle stepped inside, the older of the two looked at her and then back to Faiza with concern.

"This is Elle," Faiza said. "She is the journalist I told you I was working with."

The older woman nodded then mumbled something in Arabic and left the room.

"Elle, that was my grandmother Houda, and this is my mother Gali," said Faiza.

"Nice to meet you," said Elle, extending a hand.

The woman smiled politely and then looked back to Faiza. "How long do you have?"

Elle smiled. "You speak really good English."

Faiza laughed. "Many of the people here understand and speak English. Some don't or just don't want to use it." She undid the scarf around her chin and unveiled a cascade of glorious black hair.

Elle was in awe. "Why do you hide your hair?"

Faiza giggled. "I don't hide my hair. I cover. It is part of being Muslim."

"What are you required to cover?"

"I cover everything but my hands and face when I

am out in public. It is something I do any time I am around any male who is not a relative. It is part of what we believe."

Elle thought for minute. "Why did you want me to wear one? I'm not Muslim."

"No. But even many who aren't, wear it here because it is custom and it shows respect. Sometimes it is a good thing to blend in."

Elle nodded. "It's really different from what I'm used to." She wanted to say more but knew that her comments would offend. She bit her tongue and continued to study what she was seeing.

Elle continued to look around the home and was surprised at how similar it was to any other home she had been to. There were pictures and knick-knacks and other signs of family.

They sat at a small table and Gali brought out a tray of baked goods and a coffee pot. She placed a tiny porcelain cup and saucer in front of both Elle and Faiza and poured the thick black liquid from the pot into each cup.

Elle watched and wondered if Gali had noticed that there was a thick layer of grounds on each of the cups. She looked up at Faiza to see her response. Faiza smiled and put the coffee to her lips. She took a small sip and then to Elle's horror, she began to chew the grounds. Elle looked back at her own cup and then over to Gali, who had taken a seat across the table. She, too, took a sip and began to chew.

"This is Turkish coffee," explained Faiza. "It may be a bit stronger than what you are used to."

Elle picked up the cup and pointed at the grounds-covered liquid. "So, is it supposed to have this stuff on the top?"

Faiza laughed. "Yes, and if you don't like it we can strain it."

Gali began to stand up and Elle signaled her to stay put. She took the cup and raised it slowly to her mouth. She sipped what she could without drinking the grounds on top. She licked her lips and smiled at Gali. "It's good."

Faiza laughed again. "It reminds me of the first time I tried to eat pizza. The grease was awful, but now I'm hooked."

Elle looked at her surprised. "Really? Me too. But I can't touch it. I'd weigh a ton."

The women sat around the table and talked about Faiza's childhood. Elle learned that she had lived in the town of Dujail most of her life. When it was time for college, her father wanted her to have a better education and sent her to Georgetown University.

"That's amazing. You probably know the city, as well as I do," said Elle. "Have you been back?"

"No."

"Why, not?"

Faiza tried to answer then shrugged.

Elle looked around the room and noticed Houda sitting in an adjoining room doing some type of sewing in her lap. "Does anyone else live here with you?"

"No," Gali quickly answered.

Elle looked to Faiza, surprised.

Faiza smiled sadly. "It is just the three of us."

Tenseness filled the room and Elle sensed it, but she continued. "What about your father? Is he still alive?"

Faiza's brow furrowed and she looked down at her hands. "No. Like I said, it is just us."

Elle knew when to stop so she simply nodded and tried to drink the coffee again. After she finished it, she became anxious and was ready to get out and see the area. The rest of the day was spent driving. Faiza, with her covers back on, called for another car and driver. Elle thanked Gali and said good-bye to Houda, who made no effort to return the gesture.

Even in the walk from the house to the waiting car, Elle was met with disapproving stares. She hated to admit it, but she knew that Faiza's suggestion for alternative clothing was not only in line with the culture, but was crucial to getting the story.

"I heard what sounded like a big brawl last night. There were people screaming and it sounded like trucks full of people. Do you know what happened?" asked Elle, as the car pulled onto the main road.

Faiza shook her head. "It happens so often, I hardly notice."

"So, how do you feel about the United States Military getting involved over here? Are you glad they're standing up to Saddam Hussein? Do you think it's going to help the people?"

Faiza put up a hand to silence Elle.

Elle noticed the cab driver looking back at her cautiously. She stopped the questioning and looked out the window. They continued driving and Elle studied the people along the roads, standing by small stucco houses and always carrying what seemed to be their lives on their heads or backs. After about an hour of driving on the small dusty roads, they arrived in the town of Dujail. It was desolate. The driver seemed uneasy.

"What is this place?" Elle asked, looking at the lifeless fields and sterile block shaped buildings.

Faiza signaled the driver in Arabic and he nodded. She turned to Elle. "This is Dujail. I wanted you to see it. This used to be my home."

Elle nodded and stared out the window. It looked like a ghost town, but there was evidence of life. Trucks and cars were parked about and yet it seemed like a work camp rather than a town. "Why did you move?"

"Let's get out and walk for a while."

Elle nodded and followed Faiza out onto the sandy street.

"This used to be a beautiful town with fields of grapes and orchards of date palms. We had a good life here."

"So, what happened?"

"Saddam came to give a speech. People cheered as they were ordered to do, but when his motorcade was leaving the city along this street," she said, pointing down the road, "some men who were hiding in the date palms fired on him. Because of that he ordered those men be found and killed. The problem is they hid and so the military just killed and killed. Dozens of men were lined up and shot. The families of those men were taken away and made to live in a prison camp. One day they came and said Saddam had forgiven everyone and they were allowed to come home."

Elle looked around. "So, if this is your home, why don't you live here?"

Faiza shrugged. "Look around. It's no longer our home. When we returned, we found nothing. Our house was burned and torn down. The orchards were also nothing but charred dead trees. They even told us the land had been given away. We had nowhere to live, so we moved into the place we are now. My brother's father-in-law owns the building, and he let us move in next door."

The driver circled back and Faiza and Elle got in. The car headed back toward the road they traveled. Faiza sat quietly in thought and Elle decided to ask questions later. The horizon was filled with dark rain clouds, and yet at closer look, Elle realized that the clouds weren't filled with rain but red dust. People along the roads pulled their scarves and clothes around to hide their faces from the chafing storm.

"Sharqi," said Faiza.

Elle gave her a questioning look of concern.

"Dust storm," Faiza continued. "They are more common in the summer, but we get them in the fall, too."

As the sand cloud reached them, the sound of biting little particles beat against the metal of the car. Elle flinched, knowing how hard it must sting against bare skin or even clothes. In just a few short minutes, the wind stopped and the sand settled. The sun appeared and life went on as it had before.

Faiza signaled for the cab to stop and the women got out on a side street that led to a large open-air market. The air felt gritty and Elle could see grime literally settle on her skin. As the two walked, the intense heat in the middle of October stunned Elle. The streets were badly paved, wide and littered with debris. The market was a buzz of people of all ages. Vendors called out to shoppers, and there was a plethora of items from jewelry to rugs to fruit to live birds.

Elle was mesmerized by the color and activity. It was a far cry from the sterile stores and perfectly attired and coifed crowds she was used to at the mall at Pentagon Station. The older people had crooked lines carved deeply into their dark and weathered faces, and even the children had looks of helpless fatigue.

Again, Elle was met with disapproving glares and huffs. "I thought being judgmental was a problem in my country, but this is ridiculous. They treat me like I'm a harlot just because I'm not Muslim."

Faiza shook her head. "No, it isn't because you are not Muslim; it is because you are not covered. It is simply custom, not just a matter of religion."

Elle was unconvinced. "Doesn't it bother you at all to live in a place that treats women like that? You lived in the US. Why would you want to come back here and be a second-class citizen? You'll never find a man here who will treat you like an equal."

Faiza chuckled.

"What?" asked Elle.

"It is different from what you are used to. We have definite roles here for men and women. But I like that."

Elle sighed, unconvinced, but brushed it off quickly. "Speaking of men. What about your father? Where is he?"

"There are things I can't talk about, especially..." Faiza looked around cautiously. "I have to watch what I say, or I could cause trouble for my family."

"I just asked where he was."

"Please. I want to help you while you're here, but there are some things I can't talk about."

Elle wanted to press her for more but relented. They continued to walk and Elle bought a few small items to use as a reminder of her time in Iraq. She finally got fed up with the stares and bought a head scarf which she wrapped attractively around her blond waves. Then she turned to Faiza. "Let's go back to the hotel."

On the ride back, Elle felt defeated. She had spent the entire day and returned with nothing. She knew that when Matt returned, he would have an incredible interview and be strutting around like a morning rooster.

When the cab pulled up to the hotel, a small white car was out front and a Middle Eastern man stood next to it talking with Matt. When Elle stepped out of the cab, Matt smiled and walked toward her. Seeing the trinkets she held, and the pretty scarf, his smile grew. "Nice day of shopping, ladies?"

"Shut up," Elle grumbled.

Matt motioned to the man. "This is Zev. He has offered to help us with our stories on the Sunnis and Shias. He has some great contacts."

Elle acknowledged him. He was short and thin, with perfectly combed black hair and a kidney shaped birthmark above his right eye. He wore tan cotton pants and a navy polo shirt.

He gave her a nod with no smile. Elle then realized Faiza was still sitting in the cab. She bent down, knowing that Faiza was feeling her job was threatened. "Same time, tomorrow? I want to bring Dan and start some interviews with the people in the market. I'll need your help taking us around."

Faiza nodded. Elle closed the cab door and ignored Matt as she walked into the hotel. Dan was inside, putting tapes neatly on the table next to perfectly bundled cables.

"How did it go today?" Elle asked.

Dan raised his shoulders. "Okay, I guess. We're not winning any awards with this stuff. It's all talking heads."

"Who is this Zev guy?"

Dan looked up at her. "He approached us at the embassy. I thought he worked there at first, but he's just some Joe. He claims to know his way around. He's got Matt's shorts in a twist."

"What about Faiza?"

"What about her?" Dan asked. "Doesn't seem like she's done much but take you around sightseeing. She can't even drive you herself."

The comment annoyed Elle, and she became defensive. "If I wanted to interview officials, I would. I'm not out here to do stories that we can be covering back in DC. I want stories about the people here. When they send the talent in, do you really think they are going to want to spend their time interviewing people they could have snagged back in Washington?"

Dan raised his hands in defense. "I'm not criticizing you, Elle. It's just we've been here a week now and Matt has already fed back four stories. You have yet to feed back anything. The crew back home, well…they're notic-ing."

"What do you mean? What are they saying?"

"I'm keeping my mouth shut. I'm here to shut up and shoot."

Elle stomped off toward her room. Then she turned back to him. "I will need you tomorrow."

"What do you got?" Dan asked.

"Hal wants stories about the people. I want to show the market. I want to start talking to the people and get their feelings about what is going on."

Dan nodded, unimpressed, but answered, "Sure thing."

CHAPTER 14

The next morning, Faiza was waiting. She smiled when she saw that Elle was wearing the pretty scarf around her head. The three loaded into the car Dan had purchased and headed back to the open-air market from the day before. The vendors had bright colored canopies to shade the glare of the Middle Eastern sun. The fabric billowed softly.

There were few stares this morning, and Elle enjoyed the breeze as she tried to gauge what angle to take, since she really didn't have an idea for a story when she asked Dan to come along.

Dan stepped out of the car and pulled his large camera from the trunk. He swung it up to his shoulder and looked over to Elle. "What's the plan?"

She looked around. "Follow me."

Faiza scurried behind and the three went headlong into the crowd. The people saw them coming and many fled from the streets. Some stood and stared, and others glowered.

Elle approached one of the merchants. "Do you speak English?" she asked.

The merchant looked directly at the camera and put his hand up. "No!" He shooed them away.

Elle tried again, stopping a woman walking by. The woman shook her off and kept walking. After several more tries, Elle looked at Faiza, feeling crushed and beaten.

Dan walked past them and began shooting activity on the street. After a while the normal pace resumed. Elle walked to the shaded side of the street and leaned up against the corner of one of the shops. Faiza followed.

"I give up," Elle said to herself, aloud. "Matt's won and I might as well go back to running the teleprompter in the studio."

Faiza went to say something but stopped.

"What?" asked Elle.

Faiza shook her head.

Elle threw up her hands. "You can't say anything. Why do I expect you to? I know you're just a guide, but why not give me something to work with? Matt's got Zev handing him interviews on a silver tray, and I can't even get a peasant on the street to talk to me."

Faiza snapped around and faced her. Her eyes were filled with furry, and she shook her head as the rest of her body stood rigid. "I told you the first day you were here that I would help you with your dress and you brushed me aside."

"Clothes? Do you really think that clothes are going to make a difference?"

"They will make all the difference. The head scarf is a help, but it's not enough. These people don't trust you, and why should they? You don't respect them."

Elle stood straight and looked for Dan. "I'm getting out of here."

"Why not? You can go back to your pristine life and never think about any of this again."

Elle turned back to her. "You act like you want to be a martyr. Do you enjoy living like this? Is that why you don't leave?"

Faiza stopped and tears filled her eyes. "Why do you want to know? You don't really care. This is a *job* for you. What you want me to do for you will risk my family. I can't do that. I will find someone else to guide you." She turned and headed toward the car.

Elle watched her walk away, as she leaned back against the smooth stucco wall of the storefront. She started to call for her, but then a low rumbling of engines silenced the chirps and bustle of the market. It was so loud Elle felt the vibrations in her chest. She looked around anxiously. The market turned into a beehive of frantic confusion.

Elle turned back to see Faiza trying to make her way through the crowd. She caught Elle's eye. Terror filled Faiza's face. She shook her head in desperation and disappeared into the mass of bodies and dust.

The clamor of trucks filled the entire street. The stark faces of the shoppers turned to pleading, in hopes they would be spared. Elle stepped behind the building and hid as she watched men pile out of four large open bed trucks. They walked through the market studying the wares and taking what they wanted.

Elle searched the street for Dan. She saw him behind a storefront, camera poised and rolling. She watched silently as the men strutted amongst the shopkeepers, lone stragglers who weren't able to get away without notice.

After making their point, they relaxed for a moment against their trucks, eating the fruit they had looted, and spitting the pits onto the street. Elle again looked back to where Faiza had gone, wondering where she was and what was happening.

Elle wanted to go to her, but stayed still behind her

shield, knowing if she was spotted, it could mean trouble.

She walked backward to a small alley and hid. She scooted down the small path that ran parallel to the market. About a block down, she crept up to Dan and stood silently while he continued to shoot. After a few seconds, she saw him glancing down at her hands. She was clicking her nails. He gave her a quick, annoyed growl and went back to his work.

A scuffle began at one of the tented vendors. Elle peered around and saw a short man in a white robe and small round red and white cap talking loudly to one of the armed men. With little provocation, the Iraqi security officer, in a swift blow, knocked the man to the ground. This action stirred the crowd to frenzy, and they stampeded away in chaos. The other officers became annoyed at the clamor. They began to swing at them indiscriminately as they passed, knocking them to the ground.

Then the people on the streets became even more frantic and that stirred the rampage even more. A gun was raised high in the air. The sharp crack of gunfire rang out. Elle flinched back, surprised at how loud it was. For a moment the crowd was silenced. Then the panic became even greater. Within seconds, the officers were menacing both men and women, leaving them cringing in clumps and taking swings at others as they tried to escape. Dozens of shoppers hovered on the ground, looking up and wondering what had just happened and why.

"We're going in. Stay right behind me," Dan ordered.

"They'll see us," Elle said, pulling at his shirt.

Dan pressed on without answering.

Elle felt dizzy and numb but followed him.

The market had turned into a mass of injured bodies and wails. Elle tried to take it all in, wanting to bury her face and hide. Dan was all work. He flowed from one nightmarish scene to the next. Not a second went by that his camera's red light was not on recording. Some of the injured reached out to him in pain. Without expression, he shot their pleading faces and simply moved on. Elle stayed with him. She felt her knees buckle and her head was spinning. She was being dragged and then propped up against a wall.

"You okay?" Dan asked, camera still on his shoulder.

Elle blinked, trying to clear the blur from her eyes. "What happened?"

"You landed on me. I think you passed out."

"No."

Dan sighed heavily. "The officers have left and now I have clear access. I'm going back in. I'll get you when I'm done."

Elle looked around and saw that she was out of the way. She didn't feel as though she was ready to stand up yet. "Dan, please don't tell anyone."

"You mean don't tell Matt."

Elle started to object.

"Don't worry. Everyone will still think you're a tough gal."

He turned and jogged back to the action. From her out-of-the-way post, Elle watched heartbreak and ruin unfold like a tragic play. She began to compose the story in her head.

There were mounds of injured people. Others were either trying to help, or just simply rocked and wept at what had happened. Every so often, a new person entered the scene and discovered a loved one, terrified and in pain. Cries split the muggy, noise filled air. Each time, Elle flinched. Their sorrow hurt her ears and pierced her heart.

She thought about Faiza. Where had she gone? She scanned the area, wondering if she was still around or if she had gone back on her own. She realized that, for Faiza, this was her reality.

Elle searched the crowd for Dan. She wanted to run away from it before it claimed her strength once again. Heavy footsteps behind her made her come to. There was Dan, smiling down at her.

"Amazing," he said, quietly. "I have never been this close to it happening. It was right there. I even got the initial scuffle that started it all."

Elle just stared numbly.

"You still don't look so good."

"I'm fine. Can we head back?"

Dan nodded. "If we leave now, we can feed it back for tonight's show."

Elle pushed to standing. She steadied herself. "I don't know where Faiza went. We must find her." Elle looked around again, as she followed Dan back to where the car was parked. Standing nearby were two older men. Both were throwing hands in the air and shaking their heads as they talked. When Dan and Elle approached, they scowled and walked away.

"We need to go back to the hotel," Dan said.

"We can't leave Faiza. How will she get back?"

"Elle, she's supposed to be helping us find our way, not the opposite. She's obviously gone."

As they pulled away, Elle turned and looked out the back window. Dust still rose into the midday sky and tortured faces were everywhere, but the cries were silenced. She watched as the scene grew smaller and soon was just a haze in the distance. Then she turned around.

"I need to stop at Faiza's," she said.

"What? No. We'll miss our satellite window," Dan said. "You can see her tomorrow."

"Drop me off then. I'll find my way back and you can feed the tape."

Dan shook his head. "What is with you, Elle? She's just a guide."

"I know, but I need her help. How else am I going to get around?"

"Zev can help us. He's got good connections."

"Please just drop me off, I want to make sure she got home okay."

Dan nodded. "Tell me where to go. I'll wait for you, but make it quick."

When they arrived at the small home, Elle quickly went up to the door and knocked. Muki appeared in the door at the home next door.

"Muki, did Faiza come home?"

Muki nodded and then slowly closed the door.

Elle knocked again. No one answered. She looked back at Dan in the car and shrugged. He started to wave her back, but then Elle remembered the special knock that Faiza had used. She turned back around knocked twice, paused and then knocked twice again. After several seconds, the door cracked open and Gali peeked out.

"Gali, is Faiza here?"

Gali looked anxious as she peered past Elle and at the waiting car. "No."

Elle started to leave then heard Faiza call from inside. The door opened wider and there Faiza stood. "Come in," she said.

Elle looked back to Dan and signaled him that it would be just a minute. She closed the door behind her. "How did you get home?"

Faiza didn't answer. "Why are you here? And why did you bring him with you?"

"I wanted to make sure you got home. Dan is fine, you can trust him."

"I don't trust anyone."

"I don't blame you."

Houda entered from a back room and the four wom-
en stood in silence.

Faiza walked to the door. "You should leave now.
Please don't bring anyone else to this house."

"I won't," said Elle. She stopped before opening the
door to leave. "I'm sorry for my attitude today. What was
that today at the market? Why did those men start beating
on people?"

Faiza was annoyed at Elle's naiveté. "Fear. They ter-
rorize us like animals so we don't forget they have control."

"You're living a life that I can't even imagine."

Faiza's eyes were defiant and intense. "I don't want
pity."

"What can I do?"

Faiza pondered the question. "Listen to what I tell
you. It is for your safety as well as my family and me. I
have no choice, but you do."

"I want you to continue working with me."

Faiza nodded.

Elle left the house. Back in the car, she sat silent,
even when Dan asked her what had happened. He weaved
the car through the small streets and back to the main
road to the hotel.

"Do you think she'll continue to work for us?" Dan
asked, after a while.

"She has no choice."

"What does that mean?"

"Look around. Can't you see it? It's in all their faces.
They are trapped like mice and a big hungry housecat
stalks them every second of the day."

Dan reeled back. "Isn't that a little dramatic?"

"I don't think so. These people aren't just looking for
jobs or trying to raise kids; they are trying to stay alive.
Every day they watch their backs, wondering if they'll be

targeted next. They are little old ladies buying fruit and store owners trying to sell fish. They are watched and, if they step out of line, they get cracked in the head. These people are chattel."

Dan shrugged. "It's a story."

"God."

"What's with you? It's like you're a different person, Elle. You used to be a barracuda with this stuff and now you seem…"

"What?" Elle asked, defensive.

Dan just raised his eyebrows.

"What do you care how I am?"

"I care because I want the story. We've came back with stuff today that was mind blowing. But, Elle, that was total luck. We stumbled onto it, just the way Matt and I stumbled into seeing all that military fanfare near the embassy. I'm talking stories. You're good at digging up stuff. I'm tired and this is my chance to hit it big and get out. You need this too."

"What's that supposed to mean?"

Dan looked at her dolefully. "Matt hasn't slowed down since we arrived here. It won't be long until he breaks something big. He knows this is do or die for him."

"I don't care what he does."

Dan scoffed. "You should. It's do or die for you, too."

CHAPTER 15

Morning came quickly and Elle felt stress rise up through her back and settle in her neck. She had stayed up most of the night, wondering if she should fight for her job or curl up in a ball and surrender. She contemplated calling Hal to find out just how on the bubble she was. He'd tell her straight and besides, even if she didn't get the job in London, it wasn't like she'd be out of a job completely.

They wouldn't do that to her after all these years. Or would they? She felt like the winded runner who sensed the field gaining, as her legs cramped and gave out. She used to be a young pup, now she felt like an old dog. She slowly dressed and tried to ignore the noise in the street below.

She wondered if she would be working with Faiza today or looking for another guide. She pulled on her jeans and again brushed her long hair back into a sleek ponytail at the nape of her neck. She dabbed cream on her face and felt her dry skin suck it in. Then she donned the scarf.

When she entered the foyer of the hotel, she was relieved to see she wouldn't be spending her day without her guide.

Faiza looked agitated as she waited in the lobby. She stood near the door and peeked out the small window toward the street.

"What is it?" Elle asked as she approached her.

Faiza looked back concerned. "There is a gathering. I think they are arresting someone."

"For what?"

"For whatever they choose."

Elle looked through the window at the crowd. Two men dressed in street clothes, with red and white scarves covering their heads, walked quickly from a small house. They were dragging a man without shoes, who was mumbling to the sky. An older woman in black robes and two young children followed, wailing. An unusually tall man with a black scarf shoved them back and then divided the crowd. They paraded the man through and into the car. The tall man looked around and seemed to catch the stare of Elle in the window. She ducked down.

"Who are those men?"

"The same as those I warned you about at the market. They are Saddam's henchmen."

Elle slowly peeked back through the window, but the car was gone. The woman and two children kneeled on the dusty road outside, rocking and crying, as the crowd ignored them and went about their day. Elle thought about the compelling video it would make, the effect it would have in telling the story of the people. No one could possibly watch this back home and not feel for the plight of these families.

"Will they talk?" she asked Faiza.

"Who, them?" Faiza asked, pointing to the crying family.

Elle nodded.

Faiza shook her head. "Do you want to see them dragged away, too?"

"Will they kill that man?"

"Yes. Don't you see? Everyone is at risk. So many of our people have already been killed. He's even killed people in his own family who are not loyal." She looked up to where the hotel clerk stood watching. "We must go."

They rode in silence for a few minutes. Elle had to ask, "How do you know that man will be killed?"

"They are always killed."

Elle squinted in thought. "Why? What have they done?"

"They have spoken out."

"How does Hussein find out?"

"People. Weak people."

"What does that mean?" asked Elle.

"Saddam offers ransoms. Most of the people on the list go into hiding. Sometimes, people are so desperate for money, they turn in their own neighbors just for the reward."

"That's awful," Elle said. But the story could be compelling, more amazing than anything she ever dreamed of. Getting the video was crucial, and unless she knew in advance that someone was to be kidnapped and taken away, it was useless. Elle sat silent for a while as the cab lumbered on. "Are you at risk for talking to me?"

Faiza turned to her. "It's possible."

"Then why put yourself at risk?"

"If the stories aren't told, then it will continue. I have no choice. If I don't work, my family will starve. I've seen too many old women die while working in laundries and being forced to work as slaves because their husbands and sons have been killed. My grandmother is eighty-six. She may be killed only because she is a burden."

Elle felt a mix of fear and sadness. She turned away. Oddly, Elle found her thoughts turning to Kate. She thought about her ailing aunt and hoped that she was doing well.

She wondered if the nurse she hired was caring for her properly. She missed Rory, too.

"Can we go to your home?"

Faiza nodded.

At the home, Gali seemed surprised to see them. Elle soon relaxed and began to enjoy watching Gali fuss around the kitchen, and Houda sit and sew.

Gali's head was uncovered. For the first time, Elle was able to see her hair and face in full view. She was striking and strong, with Faiza's dark eyes and brilliant smile, but a nose that was sharper and wisdom that was whittled deeply into her weathered forehead.

"You all have such beautiful skin and hair. How do you keep it that way being in such a dry climate?" Elle asked, looking at Gali.

"Being covered keeps us out of the sun," Faiza said. She looked to her mother. "I do have good genes."

Houda walked through the room on her way to the kitchen.

"That goes for you too, Grandma," Elle teased.

Houda huffed and walked away. Elle looked at Faiza and they both broke out in muffled laughs. "She is so gruff sometimes, she reminds me of Aunt Kate."

Faiza's eyes lit up. "Who is she? You've never said anything about your family. Tell me about them."

Gali came to the table and took a seat, obviously interested.

Elle began. "There isn't much to say. My mother lives in Southern California. Aunt Kate is ornery and caustic, but I like the fact that she's honest and pulls no punches."

"Where does she live?" asked Faiza.

"On the family farm in Pennsylvania."

"I thought you said your mother was in California."

"She is, but that's not where we're from originally. I was actually born on the farm where my aunt lives. We lived there until I was about eight and then we moved to San Diego. I hadn't been back to the farm until about two months ago."

Faiza looked pained. "That must have been hard not seeing your aunt. You obviously love her very much."

Elle sat up, surprised at the comment. She thought for a moment about her time with Kate and then felt her eyes sting. She swallowed hard and smiled. "I do. She's a pretty great lady." She was able to keep her emotions from spilling over and continued. "What's weird is that I hadn't even talked to her or seen her until these last couple months."

Faiza and Gali both gave her sympathetic looks.

"It's all fine. I like my job and I love living in Washington. It's exactly the way I want things."

"Do you have brothers or sisters?" asked Faiza.

Elle squirmed and looked away. "No."

Faiza started to speak, but Elle interrupted. "I did. I had a sister, but she died when I was young. She was only five."

"I'm sorry," Faiza said softly. "How did she die?"

"Cancer," Elle lied. It was hard enough talking about her family and personal life. She didn't want to open herself up to the sorrow that surrounded Suzie's death.

"What about your father?" Faiza asked.

Elle was surprised at Faiza's forwardness. "You should be a reporter with all these questions. What about him?"

"Where is he?"

"I'll tell you about my father," she said. Elle then tipped her head to the side in a sly grin. "But you have to tell me about yours first."

Faiza raised her eyebrows, realizing that Elle had asked about him before and she had avoided the question."

"Is he still alive?" Elle asked.

Faiza shook her head sadly. "No, he was killed about eight years ago."

"That's awful. How was he killed?"

Gali stood up and stared at Elle.

"It's okay, Mother," Faiza reassured her. She turned back to Elle. "My father was murdered."

Houda, who had been sitting quietly the entire time, let out a small cry.

Faiza continued. "He was killed along with many other of our people by Saddam Hussein."

"He was one of the ones you were telling me about in Dujail."

Faiza nodded. "Over one hundred men were executed. Saddam claimed my father was one of the men who tried to assassinate him. We spent almost four years in a desert camp, before we were freed. It wasn't until we went back to our home that we realized he was dead and that our home was burned."

Elle looked around to each of the three generations of women. "I'm so sorry."

"Nothing will stop the killing. Anyone who speaks out or who is Kurd often just disappears."

"Why do you stay here?" asked Elle. "You could get a great job in Washington and then—"

Faiza stopped her. "I can't leave."

"But why? Why do you want to stay here?"

Faiza looked up at her mother. "My family is here."

"Take them with you. Get political asylum. Then you'd all be safe."

Faiza looked at the floor. "It's not that easy."

"I can help you. I can talk to some of the senators back home. I know these people and they would help."

Faiza shook her head. "You don't understand. This is my home. I can never leave."

"But you said that Dujail was your home."

Faiza nodded. "It was my home until the military took it over."

"I don't understand why you want to stay. You may be killed."

"There are things far worse than death."

Gali returned to the table with another cup and saucer. She handed it to Elle. "It's tea," she said. She had obviously noticed that Elle's coffee cup was still full. She put a motherly hand on Faiza's shoulder.

Elle smiled. "Thank you."

Faiza leaned forward and grinned. "It's your turn. I told you about my father. I want to hear about yours."

Gali returned to her seat and even Houda turned facing them in the other room. Elle starting talking about the man she thought about often but never mentioned to anyone. "My father was killed in a plane crash in 1971."

All three women wore looks of sorrow.

Elle shook her head. "It's been so long, I hardly remember him. According to my mother he wasn't the most upstanding guy. He was a schemer, always trying to get rich quick. When I was really little, I remember he left Pennsylvania quickly. I don't know for sure. It's something, my mom doesn't talk about much, but I remember there was a lot of yelling and crying.

"Mom says he hated the farm because of all the work. She said he felt that if he had the right plan, he would hit it big. He sold everything we owned to buy an old van and he moved to California. He lost everything on a business selling brushes door to door. I remember visiting him and having to live in that van for a while. Then he got some money somehow and left my mom and me to go to Alaska because of a gold scheme. The plane he was on crashed. Over one hundred people were killed."

Faiza spoke. "How old were you?"

"Ten. It's been twenty years. My mom remarried about a month later and that was just the first of many step-dads in my life. I hardly remember my father, just bits and pieces. I remember playing hide and go seek with him on the Pennsylvania farm. I loved that. There were so many places to hide and so much space." Elle stopped. A pain shot through her heart. She put a hand to her mouth, trying to control her emotions. But memories began to flood back.

"What is it, dear?" Gali asked, concerned.

Elle felt the tears form and her breathing become erratic.

"Are you okay, Elle?" asked Faiza, putting a hand on her shoulder.

Elle bit her lip. She covered her face with her hands and let the past invade her mind for the first time in years...

ഏഅ

Scenes flashed in front of her, the barn, and her father counting down the time before he came to find her. Elle pulled at the large metal handle on the door of the barn, trying to close it before he got to the number twenty, knowing inside there would be dozens of nooks and crannies for her to slither into and disappear.

When the heavy door was finally shut, she stood

breathless, as she tried to hear if he was coming close. Elle heard creaking and felt something hovering above her. It was bare feet. It didn't scare her at first. Then she saw it turn slowly. A blue face with a protruded tongue stared down at her. All she remembered was her own piercing scream. She struggled to pull open the barn door. It wouldn't budge. She was sure the monster with the bulging eyes and puffy discolored face would get her before her father could reach her. Elle yanked the handle loose and ended up knocking herself out with it.

She remembered anger and yelling that followed and a terrible sensation of being covered in blood. After that, she could never get the ghastly blue monster out of her mind. Her parents brushed her story aside, telling her it was just a dream, but Elle knew what lived in that barn and was afraid of it ever since.

∾∾∾

Elle put her hand to her forehead and felt the thin line of a scar. She looked up and found Faiza, Gali and Houda all staring at her. She rubbed her eyes and then sat up in the chair. "I'm okay."

"Are you sure?" asked Faiza.

"Yes." Elle was exhausted. "It must be the heat."

Faiza was unconvinced.

Elle swallowed hard. "There are reasons why I haven't wanted to go back to the farm in Pennsylvania."

"But I thought you loved your aunt."

"I do. But there is more. I think I've forgotten a lot, but then there are times I see things. There are so many secrets with my family. No wonder I've never wanted to be around them. I swear they are all crazy."

Faiza was puzzled.

"I know you don't understand. Here you are, willing

to give up everything you have for your family, when I don't even want to spend ten minutes with mine. It's different cultures, I guess."

Faiza shook her head. "It's different priorities."

"Whatever. All I know is that I've been perfectly fine with the way things are. I have no desire to live close to my mother."

"What about a family. Don't you want that?"

Elle imagined herself with a houseful of kids. "No. I don't need that in my life."

"You don't need a home and family?"

Elle thought a moment. "My home is a well-worn suitcase. I don't think that would be fair to a family."

"Is that fair to you?"

"Faiza, not all women have to fit into the stereotype of wife and mother."

"No, but humans need family. You can't go through life without that connection. You need to feel love, and pain, and happiness to live."

Elle shook her head. "I have seen it all. I have a career in which I tell the stories of people all over the world. I've met amazing people and have seen wonderful and terrible things."

Faiza raised an eyebrow. "Those are other people's lives. What about yours?"

CHAPTER 16

That night at dinner, Matt excused himself early. "I got a big day tomorrow. Dan, we're leaving around seven."

Dan nodded, but kept his attention on his food.

Elle waited until Matt was gone, then she leaned closer to Dan and talked quietly. "I saw something today that was awful. A man was dragged from his house and taken away because he was considered a dissenter."

Dan looked up. Elle described the scene of the kidnapping she witnessed that morning and how it played into the war. "It's like a secret society. These men lost fathers and brothers. Now they have to hide out because they're being targeted for use in the army. When Saddam's men find them, they use them as human shields. If they resist, they kill them."

Dan lifted an eyebrow.

"A video of it happening would be amazing, and maybe we can save some lives and send us back to the network as news heroes."

Dan smiled. "Zev talked about it some. Do you know when there will there be more?"

Elle nodded. "Faiza told me there are ransoms for these people. Their own neighbors get so desperate for money that they turn them in. There has to be a way to get a list and then seek out the families. We can warn them, and if we fail, perhaps we can capture the kidnapping on camera and show the world what's going on. It sounds callous, doesn't it?"

Dan thought for moment. "Somehow, we have to find the bounty hunters and get them to talk. They'll know who's on the list and whether or not they've been found."

"How do you contact someone like that?"

Dan shrugged. "There has to be a reason for them to tip us off. We'd have to pay them. If they have no conscience in turning in their neighbors, then they'll have no problem taking money from us."

Elle clutched Dan's hand. "This could be huge for us—a Peabody. We can try to warn the people then take video of the soldiers' frustrations in not finding them, burning their homes. And if they do find them…well…"

Dan smiled. "It could be big money. The Trimbaugh award is at a hundred grand this year."

Elle lowered her brow.

"Come on, Elle. You don't really look at this as just a great story that everyone pats you on the back for. I certainly don't. This is a job and this could be the big payoff we've been waiting for. You know as well as I do that a statue sitting on your shelf means nothing. This could mean security for us."

"I guess." She thought about what he said and realized it was partly true. It could be the glue that secured her position with the network. "I want you to keep this between you and me—no Matt, understand? He'll let it out for sure, and we'll end up saving no one and getting no footage, good news or bad. "

Dan nodded. "I have to go with Matt tomorrow morning. I've already agreed to shoot the b-roll for his package on humanitarian aid."

Elle dismissed what he was saying. "That's fine. I have a lot to dig up on this. It will be a lot of research."

"Will Faiza help you?"

Elle contemplated the question, but didn't answer.

Dan thought for a moment. "I will try to get what I can from Zev."

"No. I don't trust him. And he'll tell Matt."

"Elle, this isn't junior high. Zev doesn't give a hoot about any of us and that's fine. He's working for the money and if it means helping us, over Mat, he won't think twice. Besides, we need a low life to find a low life. You haven't got a thing from Faiza. Why are you still wasting your time with her?"

Elle was defensive, but knew she had no argument.

"Let me get Zev on this. The sooner the better."

Elle reluctantly agreed then felt a sickening surge come over her. She knew that she had set in motion the machine that would deliver the life her waning career desperately needed. Quite possibly it would save the life of another human being or see one come to a violent and premature end if she failed to warn them in time.

"We'll meet and talk when we can," Dan said. "Try to act as though we're still doing what we've done the last couple weeks."

Elle agreed.

"Keep Faiza out of the loop. I don't want anyone tipping someone off that any of this is going down."

"Okay."

For the next week, a pattern began. Dan and Matt were off early each morning with Zev, headed to the embassy or some other diplomatic headquarters. Faiza and Elle headed back to the small towns and villages that dotted the dusty Iraqi countryside. Each morning they stopped at Faiza's home and had pastries and thick coffee.

"You finished it," Gali said, smiling at Elle and holding her small cup.

Elle gave her a sheepish grin. "It has grown on me."

Faiza was in a back room and came out with a broad smile. Following behind was Houda, holding a large folded black drape. She went to Elle and handed her the material.

Elle took it and looked at Faiza, questioning. She unfolded part of it and realized it was a burqa.

Houda smiled for the first time since Elle had met her. Seeing her pride, Elle softened and accepted the gift. "Thank you." She sighed and looked around. "So where do I try this on?"

Faiza pointed to a back room.

Elle closed the door behind her. In the room was a full sized bed and a small nightstand. A large dresser sat against the far wall. On top were porcelain figurines of birds amongst delicate white doilies. Elle continued to unfold the dark cotton fabric. She put it on and as she adjusted the headpiece, she heard a commotion in the kitchen. Faiza's voice sounded high pitched and urgent. Elle couldn't figure out how to secure the veil around her chin and went out to the kitchen to ask for help.

She rounded the corner as she spoke, "I'm going to need help with this…."

In the kitchen the three women stood paralyzed. Then from behind the sitting room wall a tall man stepped from hiding. He was dressed in jeans, a long sleeved cotton shirt, and was clean-shaven. A white headpiece hid most of his face, but Elle could see his eyes and they stared through her like daggers.

CHAPTER 17

His eyes suddenly turned dark and pleading, as he stood surrounded by the three women.

"Who are you?" Elle asked.

Faiza stepped forward. "Elle, please don't—"

The man took Faiza by the arm and pulled her close. He looked at Elle and put a hand up to quiet Gali and Houda. When the women calmed, he spoke up. "I am Raziq. I am Faiza's husband."

Elle shook her head. "Why didn't you tell me you were married?"

Faiza looked to her husband for guidance. He nodded, giving her the okay to explain. "Raziq was teaching at the university and Saddam put him on the list for speaking out against the Bath party. He is now in hiding."

He's on the list. Elle thought, with a mixture of intrigue and horror. "Where do you hide?" Elle asked.

Raziq shot Faiza a look of fear, but Faiza continued. "He has to stay on the move. He comes home when he can, but it's a risk. You saw what happens to those who are found."

Elle nodded. "How can you live like this? Why don't

you escape and go somewhere safe?"

Faiza said, "We would, but it's more dangerous for us to leave right now. We have family outside of Iraq, but we have to be careful or we will put them at risk, too. Besides, they have people watching the borders. We can't leave, unless we have money to pay our way through."

Raziq spoke up. "This is our country. If we leave, then he wins. We have to do our work in hiding."

Faiza took a step toward Elle. "If word gets out that he's here—"

Elle interrupted, "I would never…"

Raziq still held Faiza's hand, tenderly.

Elle turned to Faiza. "I'll find a taxi back."

"I will take you," she insisted.

"No," Elle protested. "You should be here with your husband. I'll find a taxi back. I should be able to blend in better now." She motioned to her new apparel.

Faiza wouldn't take no and called for the cab. "We can't do anything that looks abnormal. Raziq will be here when I return."

Faiza pulled her veil around her face and directed Elle out the door. Once inside the cab, Faiza and Elle both sat quietly. Elle had a million questions, but knew that talking about what had just happened would be something they had to do in complete privacy. The drive dragged on, as the two women sat staring out opposite windows.

When they arrived back at the hotel, Matt, Dan, and Zev stood on the sidewalk out front. Dan stayed apart from the other two. When Elle stepped out of the cab, Zev looked uncomfortable and walked to the other end of the sidewalk. Both Dan and Matt chuckled, as Elle stood in front of them in full burqa.

"Grow up," she snapped. She bent down to the cab and asked Faiza when she was to meet with her again.

Faiza told her to plan on tomorrow, and Elle nodded. The cab pulled away and Elle turned back to Dan and Matt. "When in Rome," she said and walked into the hotel.

Matt followed her. "So what is up with Faiza? It looks like you're becoming pretty close friends. What's her story?"

Elle turned back to him and noticed Zev standing behind him. "No story. She takes me around and shows me the area."

Matt was unconvinced. "Come clean, Elle. What info does she have? I know you've got something cookin', and she's the one who's helping you. We're supposed to be a team here. So, what is it?"

Elle felt a combination of anger and fear rise within her. She turned on him. "If you're worried that I'm beating you secretly, you're wrong. You're winning, Matt. I have one story and so far nothing else. Happy now?"

"Not so, Elle. I know you're not telling me something. If you want to play like that, fine. I know as well as you do, there is one job and we're both fighting for it. You think it's in the bag, but you're wrong. You may be the golden child of Hal Norland, but this is a whole new ballgame."

"Ha, so you're not the idiot pretty boy everyone claims you are. You know as well as I do that this whole trip was to pit you and me against each other for that job in London. So, don't be giving me this team business. Faiza doesn't have anything, and I wouldn't tell you if she did."

For the first time in days, Elle realized that it wasn't just a war she was covering for the network. It was literally a battle for the only thing she had in life—her job. She walked away and refused to look back. Elle knew Matt would see the fear in her face and know that he had her running scared.

Once in her room, she flung the burqa onto the bed. At the window, she took several deep breaths, trying to clear her mind.

Outside she noticed Zev talking to a man on the street and motioning to the hotel. A knock at the door startled her and she turned away from the window and went to it. She peeked through the peephole. It was Dan. She cracked the door and he pushed his way in and closed the door behind him.

"I think I've struck gold," he said, pulling a chair out from the table. He took a seat and leaned forward.

Elle sat on the bed, facing him.

"Zev knows about the list and says he can find a way to get us our story."

Elle looked toward the window. "Are you sure we can we trust him? He seems so shady."

Dan smiled and nodded. "How else do you think we're going to get to these people? If you're kidnapping and killing people, you don't normally hang out with the upper crust of society."

Elle felt uneasy. "Did he say when he might have something? I want this story, bad." She thought about the confrontation with Matt and knew the story may be her only chance at keeping her position at the network.

Dan smiled. "Just when I think you're losing your fight, you come through."

Elle rolled her eyes. "There's more to this battle than throwing punches. I heard that Stacy Quinn at United News was asking questions about the human shields, but I don't think a lot of people know there are Iraqis being kidnapped. Most of what we've heard about the human shields has been with the Western citizens. But I don't think we have a lot of time. They'll catch on soon."

"There is no way I'm letting them break this before we do." He leaned back. "We need money."

"For what?"

"Zev. I told him we'd pay for—"

"What? I'm not paying for stories!"

"Elle, we'll get nothing if we don't. Do you really think he's going to give us this stuff for free?"

"We're paying him to guide."

"Then we'll slip him a little more for good info. Like a commission."

Elle shook her head in disgust.

"At least he's getting us stories. Faiza isn't doing anything for us."

"That's not true. She's the one who told me about the list and what the kidnappings were all about. Her family lived through all the kidnappings and killings in Dujail. She is scared to talk and I didn't have to pay her anything for that." Elle bit her lip, worried that she had said too much.

Dan stood up. "I'm not losing this. I can taste it and it's what I've been waiting on for twenty years. It's what I thought you wanted, too."

"I do. But it's people's lives. We'd be paying for people's lives."

"That's not so, Elle. We're not changing the course of anything here. This stuff will happen whether we film it or not. You're not hurting or helping anyone by covering this. You know that. We are just the messengers. We don't do anything that makes a difference. Save that for the Red Cross."

"That's not what I meant." She sat and thought. She felt exhausted and wondered if she even cared any more. "If we pay Zev, who's to say what he'll do to continue getting paid?"

Dan gave her a defeated and frustrated glower. "Not my problem. Elle, if you don't want a part of this, I'll take Matt. I know he'll be all over it."

"Don't threaten me."

"It's not a threat, Elle. I've told you before, there is nothing standing in the way of me finding a way out of this business. The money is everywhere, and I'm retiring no matter what it takes." He walked to the door. "You in or out?"

Elle refused to look him in the eye, but just nodded and gave a thumbs up.

When he closed the door behind him, Elle lay back on the bed and stared at the ceiling. She imagined the pain Faiza, Gali, and Houda would feel seeing Raziq being led away. She couldn't let that happen. It wasn't nameless faces any more.

She closed her eyes hard and scolded herself. It was her job to stay separate, objective, and callous. However, Elle's stomach ached from the torment in her mind. But why? This is what she had dreamed about all her life. Elle closed her eyes hard. Or was it?

The scenes and memories of her childhood on the farm began to rush back again. The hills, the clear expanse of sky, and the warmth of the people she felt a part of. Why wasn't this in her life until now? What had happened to make her push those memories from her mind, and why did they hurt so much now? Was her life a lie? Had she concocted ideas and recollections that didn't even exist?

She continued to let the past invade her and saw a person she hadn't remembered before. It was a boy, older than her but still young, playing and smiling on the fence posts of the corral. He captivated her, but soon the spirited, happy smile turned dark, just like all the memories she conjured.

And then there was the sense of death. It was dripping down her face, and along with it came the noise, so much pain, so much yelling. Elle sat up and looked at her hands again. She walked to the bathroom and under the lights she studied the scars. They told her she had at least tried. Elle had fought fiercely to save Suzie. The scars were her medals of honor, but they did nothing to sooth the guilt.

She wanted desperately to call her mother and get more of the story, but she knew that it would be almost impossible to call her from Iraq, and more importantly she knew that Rose would lie. She didn't know why, but she knew that up to that point in her life there was little that Rose had told her that was true. It angered Elle, but also ignited her determination to know more. What could possibly have happened that made her entire family sweep the past away?

The next two days, Elle and Dan went about their normal routines. Faiza escorted Elle every day, since Matt seemed happier with Zev. They had been in Iraq just over two weeks and Matt was turning stories regularly. Usually they were prearranged news conferences or other scheduled events, but he was able to secure several key interviews that Elle found aggravating.

Both Elle and Dan knew that their explosive story was brewing and soon they would get their big break. Elle was anxious, knowing that without it she had nothing, not even a back-up plan.

Almost every day Elle and Faiza started their morning at Faiza's home.

Muki often waited near the door and Elle kept pennies in her pockets to make him smile.

"Does he go to school?" Elle asked, wondering what he did all day.

"No," Faiza answered. "His mother needs his help."

"Where is his father?"

Faiza stared at her expressionless. "Gone."

"Where?"

Faiza looked off. "No one knows. Sometimes they just disappear."

"Kidnapped?" Elle asked, cautiously.

Faiza turned to her, but didn't answer. She pursed her mouth in thought. "He was either taken away or is in hiding. We don't know. We don't talk about it. It's better to be quiet and hopeful."

"What will happen to the boy?"

Faiza looked tired. "His age makes him a target. If you are male, and a Kurd, you're at risk. Many of the young boys turn to crime. Muki is smart and that makes him even more of a risk. His anger about losing his father scares me, because he doesn't understand that he will be eliminated without a second thought if he is caught doing anything unacceptable. We tell him to stay quiet and stay low, but I see him running in the streets all the time. His uncles try to help, but they are scared, too."

"But he's so young. He can't be more than eight or nine."

Faiza nodded and sighed. "He's almost fourteen. He doesn't eat much, but at least he has family. Many of these children don't have anyone. They just live on the streets. They are used like animals, because no one cares if they live or die."

෬๏෬

That night Elle couldn't sleep. She lay in bed listening to the clock ticking and thinking about the life of Muki and other Iraqi children. It was a strange topic for her, because she rarely thought about children. She knew they were great fodder for stories. It was a journalistic mantra—critters and kids. It was great TV.

The long nights with no television enabled her too much thinking time, and she felt like she was losing her mind. As she drifted off, she saw Muki laughing and playing on the Pennsylvania farm. He seemed at ease, and the green hills and vibrant countryside were a complete dissimilarity from the dust and concrete of the life he was living now. His bright smile made the scene even more serene, but again the blood came, just like every other time Elle allowed herself to go back. It made her wonder if she were dreaming or subconsciously letting her mind wander about what she saw in the future for the boy.

The stark clang of the phone startled her.

"We've got one!" Dan's voice was breathless on the other end of the phone line.

Elle rubbed her eyes and she sat up and looked at the clock. It was just after midnight, so she had only been asleep about an hour.

"Hurry, we just got word. It's in an area just outside the city. The car is on its way."

Elle scrambled and pulled on her jeans and T-shirt. She didn't bother with the burqa because it was dark and she doubted she would even make it out of the car. In the lobby, Dan carefully stacked tapes in his bag and checked the levels on his battery.

"Let's go," Elle urged, worrying that the noise might wake Matt or the others and give away their ploy. "We have to get there and warn them."

"We'll be fine. Zev is on his way with the car."

Just then the horn blew and both Elle and Dan looked up. Dan gathered his gear and they rushed out to the waiting car. Zev nodded then looked back at Elle and shot Dan a look of concern.

"She's fine," Dan assured.

Once inside the car, Zev pulled out and headed for the long road out of town. Dan sat quietly.

"How did you hear of this one?" Elle asked, in a whisper.

"Zev has sources."

Elle normally admired anyone who had information that Zev seemed to possess. But that night she knew where they were going. What they would see would either be a frustrated army, missing its prey and burning a home, or a scene that would make her ill.

"I have great news," said Dan and he adjusted the battery belt around his waist. "I got word last night; the satellite truck will be here tomorrow. Ethan Owen is flying in tonight, so we'll be able to edit and feed. The timing couldn't be better."

Elle raised an eyebrow. "Let's hope we have something to feed."

The car arrived to its destination quickly. It was a back street and completely dark. Zev turned to the back seat and put his hand up. "We will walk. No talking."

Dan nodded and the three crept out of the car and walked swiftly down a quiet, narrow alley. The air was still and crisp enough for Elle to wish she had worn more than a T-shirt. They continued walking fast until the alley opened up toward a street. Zev leaned back against the wall of one of the tall uniformly shaped buildings. He peeked around the corner and then pulled back and put his hand up. His eyes were huge. He pointed and then swallowed hard. Dan stayed back and Elle carefully leaned over to take a look.

"Oh, no. We may be too late," she said.

In the silent street were three cars and at least ten men. They were draped and carrying large semi-automatic rifles. Then she saw him. The same tall dark man that was on the street several days before, during the first kidnapping she had witnessed. He looked up at one of the windows of the building. Then she heard men's voices yelling and the wail of women and children screaming in the night.

"Step back," Dan demanded. "There's nothing you can do."

Elle could hardly move, but leaned back enough to let Dan get around and get his camera in position. Within seconds, the door of the large apartment building crashed open and two men carried a struggling and screaming man toward the cars.

The tall man stood defiant and poised, as the man was led up to him. He spoke something in Arabic, as the hostage hung helplessly by his arms, in front of him. The man then stepped aside and opened the car door.

The two men holding him began to push him into the car, but he leaned back and propped one of his feet against the jam of the door. Then from behind, a boy of about sixteen pushed the tall man aside and grabbed one of the captors. It allowed the hostage a free arm and he swung around, hitting the other man holding him. He yelled out at the boy as he continued to fight.

Soon the man was completely free from the grips of his captors. He ran to the aid of the boy who was in a tangle with several of the men. Then a thump. The entire group stood silent, as the man who they were sent to take away fell on the pavement. The boy who was being held cried out in despair seeing his father lay stunned in front of him.

Then the tall man walked casually over to where he was being detained, lifted the rifle butt to the boy's forehead, and knocked him senseless. They loaded him into the car, along with his father.

Dan pulled around to the side of the building and tried to control his breathing. Elle barely made out his face in the dark, but she could tell he was as shocked as she was. Then she looked for Zev, but he was gone. Dan saw her searching the dark alley for him, and simply motioned her to follow.

They crept back to the waiting car at the other end of the alley, and there was Zev, pacing. Quietly they climbed back into the car, and Zev cautiously steered back to the hotel. It wasn't until they were less than a block away that either of them spoke a word.

Dan turned to Elle, took a deep breath, and whispered. "That was news."

"That was awful."

"Awfully good news."

Elle turned away and wondered how much longer she could remain in the cab without vomiting.

At the hotel, Elle practically ran to her room. The smell of violence lingered on her clothes and in her mind. She stripped and quickly stepped into the shower. As the water poured over her head, she felt the choking grip of horror fill her. She had to kneel into the tub to keep from losing her balance as the images in her head overwhelmed her.

As she dried herself with rough towels, she had the terrible feeling that somehow Zev had betrayed the family. She couldn't prove it, but she knew that if they continued to rely on him to save people, they'd always arrive "too late." One too late was enough. She vowed to keep trying.

CHAPTER 18

The next morning, Elle found Dan, Ethan, and Matt in the satellite truck parked on the street on the side of the hotel. They were huddled around the monitor. When Elle stepped in, Matt ignored her and turned away. Elle held her breath as she anticipated what Dan had caught on tape the night before. When the clip began, it showed everything—the noise, the men dragging their hostage from the building, the fight, and the double kidnapping. When the scene ended, Ethan turned to Dan and gave him a high five. Elle turned and started to walk back into the hotel. Matt followed.

"Pretty sneaky. Did you have to tiptoe past my room?" he said, loudly over the hustle of the street noise.

"This isn't about you, Matt."

Matt stopped following her and stood near the front door. "Are you still holding our break up against me?"

Elle stopped dead in her tracks. The comment hit as though she had been smacked on the back of her head with a brick. She swung around and she glared at him. "You've got to be joking."

"What else could it be? I'm no competition to you. Hal decided before we even came out here that you would be the one. This is all just a show. To make it look like you earned it."

"I have earned it. For ten years I've been earning it." Matt refused to break his stare.

Elle reached for the hotel door and before she could grasp it, it flew open. Alley Nixon, one of the producers for United News gave a shocked reaction and then tried to compose herself.

"There you are, Elle. I..." She paused and looked confused and sad.

"What?" asked Elle, still annoyed by her discussion with Matt.

"I feel terrible being the one to tell you this." She handed Elle a folded piece of yellow legal pad paper. "They got a call at the front desk for you and they gave me the message for you. They said there was a death in your family. I'm so sorry."

"Oh God," Elle gasped. She held the folded yellow note close to her heart. "Kate." A wave of sickening salty ice water hit her straight on. She slipped the note into her sweater pocket. The same soft cardigan she had been given by the aunt she had now lost.

"I'm so sorry, Elle," said Matt, still standing by the door.

Alley put an awkward hand on Elle's upper arm. "I know that the network has a fixed wing waiting in Jordan. You can fly back tomorrow."

"I'll arrange for a car to take you there. Go pack and it will be ready in an hour," said Matt, trying to save the day.

Elle gave them both a numb nod. Everything else that was said was muffled as she made her up to her room to quickly pack. Elle crumbled on the bed. The promise she had made to Kate was broken and now she would never again see her aunt. Elle felt robbed and devastated.

Her coworkers and some of the other journalists stood solemnly in the hotel foyer when she returned. She hardly looked at anyone and headed to the door with suitcase in tow.

Dan tried to reach her before she was outside. "Elle, wait," he called.

Elle turned back with tear soaked eyes.

"I'll feed back what we have. I'll make sure that it gets in the way you planned."

With a tired and sorrowful nod, she followed Matt outside. At the airport, the van drove directly out to the tarmac. Two men, both Americans, met her and helped her onto the small plane. Once inside the plane, Elle settled into a seat near the back, and stared out the window until they were airborne. She thought about how short her time was with Kate and how odd it was that she was going to miss her so much, having hardly known her.

After about an hour, the copilot walked back to her row. He handed her a cordless phone. "We should be able to get phone service now. I'm sure you'll want to call home."

Elle nodded, but felt the sting of the word. Home. Elle formulated the words in her head, not wanting to sound phony or sappy, yet making sure Rory knew she, too, was affected by the loss.

When Rory answered the phone at the farmhouse, Elle's stomach jumped.

"Rory, it's Elle."

His voice was low and soft. "Hello."

"I'm so sorry."

He paused. "For what?"

Elle was stunned. "For Kate."

He paused. "What do you mean?"

Then she heard a familiar voice in the background. "Who is that?" she asked.

He chuckled. "It's Kate."

She felt her heart leap. "What?"

"Elle, are you okay?"

"How can that be? They told me she died."

Rory laughed. "Who told you that?"

Elle sat up straight and shook her head as if the situation would all clear up. "A message came. The call came to my hotel in Baghdad and they told me that there was a death in my…" Oh God, thought Elle. They never said it was Kate. They just said a death in the family. Then she remembered the paper she was handed. Elle hadn't looked at it because she had assumed it was Kate. She looked down to her sweater and pulled out the crumpled yellow note from the pocket. She unfolded it and gasped.

"Elle, what is it?" asked Rory, loudly.

There in dark ink were the words: Hal Norland, dead. "Oh God, it's Hal," she whispered.

"Who's Hal?" asked Rory.

"My boss. I've got to go."

"Elle, are you all right?"

"No." She said, and hung up the phone.

Elle spent the rest of the flight thinking and sleeping. When she arrived back in Washington, she called the station and was horrified to learn that Hal had been dead for days. He wasn't found until the people at the station realized that he wasn't at his desk. Hal had been divorced for decades and never had children. That is why Elle got the call. She was stunned to learn that she was his emergency contact.

No wonder the message made it sound as though she had lost a family member. Elle was his family. What saddened her even more was the fact that she didn't know Hal was even sick. He died alone in bed in his apartment and no one cared or even knew for almost three days.

When Elle got back to her apartment, she thought about unpacking her suitcase, but decided against it. She wouldn't be there long. Just enough time for the funeral, then she would head back.

She went into work the next day. People at the station stole careful glances, as if wondering whether to speak, or act as though she wasn't there. Jim Cowly, Vice President of news for the network, greeted her. Instead of condolences for Hal, he congratulated her on the work she was doing in the Middle East.

"An amazing story. Our overnights were huge and that was with only a prior day's worth of promotion. Keep it up over there," he said and then continued his obligatory sweep of the newsroom.

Elle smiled politely and walked to her desk. Without thought, she found herself looking at where Hal had sat for as long as she had been with the network. She turned away quickly before tears could come. She went through some mail and then the phone rang. It was one of the network assistants wanting to know what the plans were for Hal's funeral.

The assistant was a young woman who talked like a typewriter, each syllable snapping out sharply. She explained to Elle that the network managers and board officers needed to know when the service would be. Elle felt overwhelmed and then looked up and saw Holly Rand. She told the woman she would get back with her and signaled Holly to her desk.

Holly came running and gave Elle a genuine hug.

"I need your help," Elle said, explaining that she needed to plan the service. "You're good at these things and I'm not."

Holly smiled and nodded. "Sure."

That night at Elle's apartment, Holly organized everything from where to hold the service to what the inspirational quote should be on the programs. Elle was relieved to find that Hal had already made arrangements through his will as to how and where he was to be buried.

"So, Thanksgiving is this Thursday. It's just two days after the funeral. Do you want to come to my parents' house in Maryland?" Holly asked.

Elle sighed. She hadn't even realized what day of the week it was, let alone what holiday approached. "I'm hoping to get back as soon as I can. Thanks for the invite anyway."

Holly nodded. "There is a bit of a problem. My mother is allergic and so the cat will have to go to the boarding kennel."

Elle shrugged. "No problem."

"Well, it's just that…"

"What?" Elle asked, impatient.

"I leave tomorrow. Can you take it for me?"

"Holly, it's my cat."

Holly smiled. "If you keep it at your apartment until you go back to Iraq, it will save you about a hundred bucks."

Elle nodded. "I'll keep him here. I really missed the little guy. Wait, what about the funeral? Aren't you going?"

Holly shook her head. "I need to get home. I liked Hal, but I don't want to lose my vacation days. I haven't seen my mother in months. And I only have a week."

Elle couldn't blame her. It wasn't as though Hal would know who was there and who wasn't. But Hal was much more to Elle than just another face at work. Hal was her boss, her mentor, and her friend, but even more, he was the father she never had.

It truly was like losing a member of her family. She was so sad that her heart literally ached inside her chest.

CHAPTER 19

Outside the small chapel Elle saw a familiar form in a dark suit walking toward her. She started to squint and then surprisingly felt relieved to see a familiar face. It was Kevin Marcus.

"What are you doing here?" Elle asked.

"I heard what happened and figured you'd be back for the funeral. Can we talk?"

Elle sighed. "I'm about to give the eulogy. Can it wait an hour?"

Kevin gave her an apologetic nod and they walked into the chapel.

The pews were splattered with faces from Hal's past. When it was time for Elle to speak, she walked to the front of the chapel and held tightly to the lectern. She glanced out at the mourners. Most were old and looked to her as if hoping she'd say the words that made Hal's life make sense and make a difference. Elle felt that anything she was about to say wouldn't be enough to truly honor him. She stalled and cleared her throat.

"I don't really know who any of you are, but I knew Hal well. Hal Norland was one of the most important people in my life. He was my boss, but he was also the person who gave me a chance and taught me what I know. He was like a father to me and I will miss him dearly, every day for the rest of my life." She continued to speak off her notes about Hal's life and accomplishments. When she was done, she stepped from behind the pulpit and walked back to her seat. After the ceremony, she accepted kind words from the people attending and then walked out to her car with Kevin.

Elle turned to him. "Please tell me you aren't going to talk about how I'm trying to get my aunt's money and land."

Kevin shrugged. "Not really, but eventually we need to get the papers signed. Elle, the real reason I'm here is to see you. I still feel like we need to start over and do this right. I love you and I really think that with everything going on in your life, you can see how important having a family is. You've changed, Elle. I can see it. There's something different about the way you look and the way you are. Besides, little K.J. misses his daddy."

Elle grumbled, remembering how irritating his baby talk and wimpy demeanor grated on her. "Kevin, I have so much going on right now. I shouldn't even be here. I should be in Baghdad."

Kevin assumed his sulky, puppy dog look.

Elle looked away. Then remembered her predicament with the cat. "Speaking of K.J., can you take him for a while? Holly can't and I need to find the next flight back to Iraq."

"You're going back?"

"Of course. Why not?"

Kevin shuffled. "I just thought maybe there was a reason for you to stay."

Elle took the keys from her purse. "Sounds to me like I'll do fine whether I'm here or not. You have everything ready to go, right?"

Kevin nodded.

Elle knew what he was getting at and she had no desire to discuss a relationship, especially one that had been over months ago. With Hal gone, she had something else that needed her attention and nothing was going to stand in her way.

"So can you take him?" she asked.

"When?"

"Today."

"No, I am going to my folks place for the holidays. My mom is allergic."

She left Kevin standing in the parking lot and drove directly to the station. From her desk she would call a boarding kennel and then get booked on the first transport back to Iraq.

With Matt already there, and knowing Hal was gone, she had no room to relax.

As she drove, she pondered what she was sure everyone was thinking, that without Hal, her career would surely falter. Her thoughts lingered on the old suitcase, sitting packed and ready to go. If I'm going to London, I may need to upgrade, she thought.

When she arrived at the station, she was given guilty looks from some of her coworkers. She brushed by them and went directly to the assignment desk. Richard was on the phone. His chin sat on his chest and he nodded as though wanting her to wait.

The newsroom was like a ghost town, but Elle was used to that this time of year. As her colleagues headed out to visit family for the holidays, Elle was usually hard at it. She actually liked the solitude. It was quiet and she was able to not only get her work done, but also had time to clean off her desk and get her New Year calendar in order. Aside from a few guilt filled phone calls from Rose, it was her happiest time of year.

"There are no flights out until after the holidays," said Richard, with a shrug.

"What? That can't be. I've got to get back there."

"Unless you plan on stowing away somewhere, you're stuck here until…" He checked over his panning calendar. "December twenty-seventh."

Elle growled, "What am I supposed to do until then?"

"Dan fed down some new video already today. Why not take the time to write your story? You can do that just as well here as there."

Elle was frantic but defeated. She knew everything Richard said was true, but without being in Baghdad, she had no control over what was going on, and she knew that Matt would be honing in on her stories. She wondered about who they had saved and who they had not.

She went to her desk and threw down her purse and papers, then walked to the edit bays. "Can you cue up the feed that came down from Dan today?" she asked the editor.

He nodded. The tape rolled and again the scene played out like a rehearsed tragedy. It was another kidnapping, and another failed attempt at rescue. A man ripped from his home and the family wailing, as he was dragged off. Then Elle leaned in closer to the monitor.

"Stop the tape." She watched closely as she ordered the editor to rewind and play the clip over and over. Elle put her hand to her mouth. "That's Muki," she said pointing to the crying boy on the screen.

Richard overheard their conversation and walked over. "What's wrong, Elle?"

"It's a boy I know. Our guide lives next door to him. He's a street urchin. I was told his father was gone." She signaled the editor to rewind the tape. "This guy they're taking away must be a relative."

Richard nodded. "Like I said, Elle, amazing stuff."

Elle still stared at the crying boy on the screen. Then she noticed something else, and leaned in closer. "Oh my God," she whispered. There on the side of the stilled image was someone she recognized as well. It was Zev. Although covered in robes and with a scarf around his face, Elle recognized the cockeyed birthmark above his eyebrow.

Dan had taken this film and was clueless as to Zev's motives.

That was why he had disappeared during the first rescue attempt. Elle was right about her fears. Zev wasn't a bystander, he was a participant. Elle reeled back. "He's one of them." Then she stood up and shook her head. "That is how he knows this stuff." She took a seat just outside the edit bay.

"What do you want me to do with this tape, Elle?"

Elle was still in a state of stunned disappointment. "Leave it. I'll get with you later." She sighed. *That murderous criminal is the reason I have my story,* she thought. *If I didn't have blood on my hands before, I certainly do now. No wonder Faiza was so horrified when Dan and Zev were at her home. She had to know. I may have single-handedly sealed her fate. I've got to warn her.*

Was it too late? With the time difference, the video she just watched was already a day old.

She went to Richard. "I need to call Dan."

Richard shook his head. "No can do right now. I just talked to him about thirty minutes ago and they were just heading out on something."

"Who are *they?*"

"Dan and Ethan. Matt's still at the hotel, you can call him. What's up?"

Elle took the hotel number to her desk. She found Matt groggy from sleep. "You must warn Dan, Ethan and Faiza about Zev."

"What?" asked Matt. "Why?"

"Because he's one of the henchmen. I saw the video they shot. I recognized him in the tape. He's tipping off the army every time we go in for a rescue. If he hangs around Faiza, it will put her family at risk."

"Why? What's wrong with her family?"

Elle became even more frantic. "It doesn't matter. Please just do what I say, but do it discreetly so Zev doesn't know."

"Faiza isn't around. When you left, Dan told her we didn't need her anymore."

"He fired her?"

"Not exactly. He just told her that she wasn't needed until you come back."

Elle was angry but also relieved. "Where did Dan and Ethan go?"

Matt was angry. "They're gone? That's just great! Why does everyone find it necessary to sneak off and leave me out of the loop?"

Elle voice rose with her panic. "Please, please tell Dan what I told you. Zev isn't what he claims to be."

Matt agreed, but Elle wondered if he even heard what she said. When she hung up, she leaned back and wondered if Dan wasn't more involved than just shooting video.

Vanessa Morris, one of the interns, called to Elle as she held up the phone, "It's some guy named Kevin Marcus. He says he knows you."

"Good grief," said Elle. "I left him an hour ago. Transfer it to my desk."

The intern nodded.

Elle picked up the line. "What is it, Kevin?"

"Meet me for dinner tonight. I want to see you before you head out."

"I'm not going back for a while. There are no flights until the end of December."

"Great. Come with me to Virginia for Thanksgiving. My mom will be thrilled."

"No. I…" Elle cringed at the thought of him knowing she was available. "I have to get a lot of work done."

"You have almost a month. You can't stay here by yourself for Thanksgiving. You can take a weekend off. I can't stand the thought of you sitting here alone. I won't have it."

Elle thought desperately for a reason to say no. "I won't be alone. I'm going to Pennsylvania to see Kate."

"Oh."

"It will be good for several reasons."

"Great. I'll go with you."

"No. I mean, it would be better if I were there alone with her."

Kevin was silent.

"Family time. You know."

"Sure. So when will you be back? Can I at least see you before you go back to Iraq?"

Elle squirmed. "I'll give you a call after Thanksgiving and I'll see what's happening. It's been crazy busy here at the station—"

"I understand," said Kevin, defeated. "All you want me for is my law degree. I see how it is." He was sappy and pouty and Elle hated it.

His wimpy, needy manner made her skin crawl. She hadn't seen it coming when they first started dating. He was a powerful attorney, with broad shoulders and a string of suits that were each worth more than the car Elle drove. It was only a couple months until she saw the strong façade melt away and the childish underbelly become exposed. But the cat was the last straw. What type of man gives his girlfriend a cat and then treats it like it's their baby? Besides K.J. was *her* cat.

Elle gathered up the pile of notes she had taken while in Iraq. She needed a shower and she had to feed the cuddly fur ball waiting patiently at home. The day had been long and draining. Her thoughts again returned to Hal. She missed his gruff and gregarious nature. She gathered up her things and walked out of the newsroom. She would get more done at home.

Her car wasn't just dead but decomposing. She piled her papers into her tote and headed for the train station. Once on the metro, she glanced at the photographs in the newspaper a man was reading across from her. It showed two older Middle Eastern women crying next to a draped body. She sat and let her mind wander.

She thought about how much the women looked like Gali and Houda and how easily it could be them crying for the loss of their husband or son. Then she thought about Faiza and Raziq. Such a life of uncertainty and fear, it seemed only a matter of time before he was discovered and taken away like the others. Elle cringed at the thought.

When she arrived at her apartment, the cat was waiting and it gave Elle a sense of home. She stroked the cat as it leaned into her. Elle poured cat food into a bowl and then cleared her kitchen table. K.J. was a messy eater, but she found herself enjoying the crunching sounds he made as he ate his dinner. She spread the notes and other documents evenly on top.

Elle's stomach screamed out after being ignored all day. She opened the fridge to find nothing edible and most items unrecognizable. She laughed to herself. *Thanksgiving is this week*, she thought, and the cat is eating better than I am. Elle found some crackers, a can of minestrone soup, and a bottle of ginger ale. As she started up the can opener the phone rang.

"Elle darling, I'm glad I caught you." It was Rose. "Kate has no idea you're coming up there."

"What? Mother, I'm not going up there. Who told you that?"

"Kevin. He said you were going to Kate's. I called up there to talk to you and Kate said she didn't even know you were coming."

Elle couldn't believe what she heard. She wanted to scream. She wanted to cry. Instead she slumped down onto the kitchen chair and laughed.

"Elle, Kate said that she was alone and that she hadn't really planned a dinner. Why don't you pick something up on your way? I told her you had that funeral and all and that you probably just forgot to call her."

"I didn't forget. I wasn't planning on going. I told Kevin that so he'd leave me alone."

"Why did you do that? Now they'll both feel terrible. You have to go. This could ruin everything."

Elle looked at the mountain of work laid in front of her. "Mother, I have an hour long special to write. I can't be visiting family. I need quiet."

"Elle, you have to go. Besides, if you want boring solitude, there's no better place than that desolate old farm."

Elle started to argue and then smiled. She marveled at the insanity of it, and realized Rose was probably right. She would be free of distractions at the farm. It may give her a chance to learn more about the skeletons that not only lurked in the crevices of that old house, but also filled her mind and memories.

CHAPTER 20

The trip to the farm was a bigger hassle than Elle had expected. Since her car was dead, she had to rent one and all they had available on a holiday weekend were convertibles. Then there was K.J. With no one willing to take him, and no way to find a kennel at that hour, Elle was forced to take the little guy along.

The first hour of the trip, K. J. cried. Elle tried to ignore him, but eventually turned up the radio in an attempt to drown him out. It didn't work. She finally pulled over and looked through the bars of the cat carrier.

"What is wrong?" Elle asked. The cat stretched a paw forward and mewed sweetly. "Are you kidding me? What do you want?" She sat back and took a deep breath. The cat called for her. Elle leaned over again. "If I release you, will you mellow out?" She opened the carrier and the cat carefully peeked out.

"You silly goose. You're getting your way." K.J. walked out and looked around the car.

Elle pulled the car back on the road. Within a few minutes, the cat had made its way from the passenger seat into Elle's lap and had Elle hugging the road ahead, contemplating the weekend that was before her. As she drove, she played the events of her last visit over in her mind.

She wondered where Rory had gone and why he left Kate alone on a holiday. Without realizing it, she found herself petting the cat and daydreaming about the man with a history of scandal, and yet she had felt safe in his arms.

When Elle arrived at Kate's house, it was already starting to get dark. The lights were on inside, giving the entire home a warm and welcoming glow. She picked up K.J. from her lap and went to put him back in the kennel. He refused and squirmed free, jumping to the back of the seat and then to the floor behind. Elle twisted in her seat and turned toward the back. She could see the animal hiding below and reached over the seat to retrieve it. It crawled under the seat.

"You dumb kitty. Fine! Stay in here!" She turned back around to find Rory standing at her window. She was startled and then became irritated with his obvious enjoyment of her toil. She opened the door. "What are you doing here? I thought Kate was alone."

"Nice to see you, too," he said, with a grin.

Elle's book bag tipped out of the car and her papers spilled out. She quickly reached for them, but they began to scatter. "Darn!" Then the cat sprang from the open door. Elle was on her knees, trying to keep the papers from blowing away. K.J. looked shaken and ready to dart. "No, kitty. Stay!" she screamed.

Elle's yell startled the cat even more and it lurched toward the road. Elle stood up quickly and ran to it. It bolted into the street just as a small car rounded the bend. Elle couldn't watch and threw her hands over her eyes and screamed.

The sound was sickening, a combination of thumps

and skids. When she looked, the cat was gone. The car had stopped, and Rory was running into the field on the other side of the road.

"Omigod!" yelled a young woman, as she ran from the car back to where Elle was standing. "I didn't see it. Is it dead?"

Kate spoke up and startled Elle, who was unaware that she was even there. "I don't think so. It wasn't your fault. Go on before someone rounds the bend and runs into you."

The girl nodded and started to go to her car. She turned back and pleaded. "I'm so sorry."

Elle saw Rory walking back toward them with K.J. in his arms. The cat was wrapped in an old towel Rory had pulled from his truck.

Elle moaned and ran to him.

"He'll live but he's hurt pretty bad…"

"Give me him!" Elle screamed.

Kate spoke up. "Elle, the cat will die if Rory doesn't help…"

Elle turned on Kate. "I don't need his help. I'll do it myself. It needs a doctor."

Kate continued calmly. "Rory can take it to the clinic."

"What clinic? Where?" she asked, going to her car.

"Elle, you can't drive and hold the cat. Let Rory take you. The cat will die without his help."

"We don't need his help. We need a doctor, a vet."

Rory, who was standing back and staying quiet, stepped forward. "I am not going to let your stubbornness be the death of this poor cat. Get in my truck and let's go."

Elle watched him walk determinedly to the waiting truck. She turned to Kate, who had started to pick up the papers on the ground.

"Go help your cat. You can finish being angry with all of us later," she said.

Elle walked to the truck and gave Rory a hateful glare.

He pulled another towel from behind the seat. "Keep him warm so he doesn't go into shock."

Elle slid onto the seat of the truck and looked down at K. J. He was breathing hard with weak cries every time Elle moved him. She grabbed the towel and carefully tried to wrap him, as Rory pulled the truck quickly onto the road.

"He'll live," he said.

"How would you know?" Elle snapped.

Rory smiled.

"Why do you think this is funny? Do you hate animals?"

Rory shook his head. "I work on a farm, for heaven's sake. You are really clueless. I thought you were a journalist."

"What are you talking about?"

Rory clenched his jaw and continued driving. He took several quick turns and then turned onto a deserted two-lane road. It was dark and seemed to be going to nowhere.

"How long before we get there?" Elle asked, staring down at the cat.

"Another twenty minutes."

"Where is this place? Are you telling me there is no vet back there at all?"

"No."

Elle scoffed. "That is ridiculous. There should be something closer."

"Yes, there should."

Rory pulled the truck into a small parking lot with a

sign that read, "Animal Medical Clinic." Elle saw the lights were off and the business obviously closed.

Rory parked the truck and opened the door.

"What are you doing? The clinic is closed. We don't have time. Go to the next town or go to a hospital or something."

He ignored her and walked up to the door. He rattled through his keys and put one in the keyhole and opened the front door.

Elle watched surprised. "Why do you have a key?" she called from the truck.

He waved her in.

She carefully stepped out of the truck and walked into the building. Rory flipped on a light. Elle stepped around a small reception desk in a badly paneled room with worn linoleum floors.

Rory pushed through a swinging door and directed her to the back.

"What are you doing?" she said, following him.

In the back was a shining metal table in a small room with a large light hanging from the ceiling. "Put him down here," he said.

"What are you going to do?"

"I'm going to examine him."

She held the cat closer to her. "What? No."

"Elle, I know what I'm doing."

"No you don't. We're wasting time. We need to find a vet!"

Rory clenched his fists and stared her down. "I am a vet. This is my clinic. Now give me the blasted cat!"

"What?"

Rory turned around and pulled a framed certificate from the table behind him. He shoved it toward Elle. Elle was wild-eyed as she read, Roland Andrew Beau, DVM.

"Roland?" she asked with a salty grin.

"Are we going to save your cat, or are you going to make fun of my name?"

Elle carefully set K. J. on the table. "You're a vet. Wait, I thought you were—"

"There is a lot you don't know," he interrupted. Rory turned the cat on its side. "I need to shoot some films. Help hold him since my techs aren't here."

Elle nodded, still trying to absorb what was going on and what she had just learned about him. He wasn't the uneducated country boy she thought he was. So, if he was a veterinarian, why did he work for Kate on her farm? She continued to think as he directed her to hold the cat on the table. K. J. moaned and tried to move. When Rory was finished, he wrapped the cat back into the towel and handed him to Elle. He walked into another room, leaving her to sit and stare at the animal health posters on the wall and a wood carving of Roland Andrew Beau, DVM.

He came back and leaned against the silver table. "He's lucky he has no internal injuries, however, his leg is shattered and it will have to come off."

Elle heard what he said, but squinted her eyes trying to make sense of it. "Come off?"

"Yes. I'll call one of my employees to assist me, but it will take her at least an hour to get here. If you think you're up to it, you can hold the mask over his face while I operate. Then we can help him quicker."

"You can't cut off his leg. How will he walk?"

Rory smiled. "Animals are a lot more resilient than people. It's something I have to do often. He'll be fine."

"You cut off animals legs often. What kind of a vet is that?"

Rory bristled. "Does anything but sarcasm ever come out of your mouth?"

Elle shrugged.

"Do you want to help me save your cat or not?"

Elle relented.

"Good. So what is his name?"

Elle began to answer then looked at the floor.

Rory chuckled. "You don't know what his name is?"

Elle looked up. "Yes. It's K.J.," she snapped.

"K.J. Hmm. What is it with you and the alphabet?"

"What?"

"You're Elle. Your cat is K.J. I supposed you have a dog named ABC and fish named LMNO?" He laughed to himself.

"Oh yes, that's hilarious."

Rory used drapes to cover the cat and put a rubber mask connected to a pump around its face. He directed Elle what to do and what to look for on the gauge. She held the mask where he directed and watched the cat drift off. Rory took a scalpel from a tray. Elle felt the lights start to buzz and the room go from blurry to dark.

CHAPTER 21

It wasn't words but a groan that Elle awoke to. She blinked, trying to focus. All she could see was the bright glare of fluorescent lights. She heard movement, but it sounded more like rustling than walking. She closed her eyes and tried to sort out what was happening in her head. It started coming back to her. *The cat. The clinic. Rory is an animal doctor.*

Her eyes shot open, and she realized she was lying on a table in a small room. A snort came from her side. She turned her head slowly to find a large black dog lying in a cage next to her. Another dog, small with long black ears, slept in the kennel below. Elle sat up and put her hand to her head. She jerked back when she touched a sore spot on her forehead. The swinging door opened and in stepped an older woman with short curly hair and large breasts that seemed to fill the room.

"How you feeling?" she asked with a genuine smile. "Dr. Beau called me first thing and I came over to assist."

"Why am I on this table?" Elle asked.

The lady put a hand on Elle's leg and stood close. "He said you saw the blood and just tipped over. He caught you before you hit the floor, but he says you hit your head on the table. You have a little knot on your forehead, but he doesn't think you have a concussion."

"How would he know? He's not a real doctor."

"Oh, that's not true, dear. Dr. Beau is a doctor. He graduated from the University in Pittsburgh. He's one of the best vets in the country."

Rory walked into the room and put a hand up to silence the woman. "Don't waste your breath, Norma. She made up her mind about me a long time ago."

Norma gave Elle a questioning and disappointed look and exited with a huff.

Elle started to climb down from the table.

"Take it slow," Rory cautioned.

Elle ignored him and then felt her head begin to spin. She put a hand down to brace herself, but missed the table and started to fall. Rory reached over and caught her.

"Why are you so stubborn?" he asked. "You'd rather fall on the floor than listen to me."

She tried to push him away, but he pulled her closer. Finally she relented and lay back against his arm. "I don't feel well."

"You'll be fine, if you rest. There are a lot of people who don't like the sight of blood."

She looked up at him with heavy eyes and shook her head. "No, it's…I don't feel…" she said and fainted in his arms.

⁋⁋⁋

Elle woke up in a hospital bed. Rory sat in a chair against the wall and a nurse checked a monitor at her side. When Rory noticed that she was awake, he scooted the chair over to her.

She looked at him wearily. "Now where am I?"

"You're in a hospital."

"Why?"

Rory smiled. "I'm not sure yet. I'll let the *real* doctor tell us."

Elle turned away from him.

Rory sat silent. Elle stayed looking away and then wondered what he was doing. After a while he spoke softly. "I am sure there are reasons for hating me, but it would be nice to know exactly why."

Elle turned back toward him and looked him in the eye.

"Really," he continued. "I know there is a lot of pain in the past. But we hardly know each other. So, why are you so angry?"

Elle was stunned at his candid honesty. She wanted to answer, but didn't have an explanation. There was definitely something about him that made her feel heated. Was it his ability to fire back at her sarcasm, or was it that she actually found him attractive and that made her feel vulnerable?

After several moments without a word, he stood up and walked to the door. "I'll see where the doctor is."

She began to stop him, but lay there, feeling weak and miserable. Her heart ached. Elle fidgeted with her hands and wondered when he would be coming back. She had the urge to look in a mirror, but there wasn't one close by. She knew if she even sat up straight, she would get light headed again.

The door cracked open and she turned to it, anxiously. In stepped a thin older man in a white coat. He held a clipboard and looked over to her through small glasses.

"So, young lady, what's going on here?"

"I don't know. I just feel dizzy."

He walked around to the other side of the bed and

checked her neck and made her open her mouth. "Any chance you could be pregnant?"

"No."

He recoiled. "No?"

Elle gave a disgusted huff. "If you really must know, I couldn't possibly be pregnant because I've been basically celi—I mean I haven't—" She stopped and felt herself blush.

The doctor looked amused. Then he stood up straight and looked past her. "Dr. Beau?" he said, surprised.

Elle looked back, embarrassed, as Rory walked to the bed. *When did he come in? Did he hear what I said?* Elle felt her face heat up.

The doctor walked around the bed and shook Rory's hand. "I was just talking with the wife about you the other day. We have a new colt that I need you to look at. Also, Olivia said something about a problem you're having with building your new clinic. She said some big city relative of Kate's was out prodding around and threatened to steal the place out from under you. Is that true?"

Rory sighed uncomfortably. "Well." He looked over to Elle. "She is a gruff old hag, but I think I'm wearing her down." He winked at Elle.

Elle rolled her eyes.

Rory turned back to the doctor. "I'll get it worked out. If I don't build the clinic there, I'll figure out something."

"I really hope you're not planning on leaving us," said the doctor. "We've been without a good vet around here for years. It sure would be a shame."

"Don't worry, I'm not leaving."

The doctor turned back to Elle. "So are you with this young lady?" he asked Rory with a smile.

"Yes, I am. I was a bit worried because she passed

out when she was at my clinic and hasn't seemed to recover."

The doctor nodded. "We'll do some blood tests and make sure you're not anemic. How much do you think you weigh?"

"I don't know, about one ten."

"Hmm," the doctor mused. "That's awfully thin for your height. Have you been sick lately?"

Elle shook her head. "No, that's my normal weight."

The doctor gave her a scowl. "That may be your normal weight, but that's not normal." He looked at Rory. "You need to take better care of her." He turned back to Elle. "We'll run the blood tests, but I can predict that you are probably anemic. You need to gain some weight and start taking care of yourself or tipping over at the sight of a little blood will be the least of your worries." He reached out to Rory again and took his hand. "It was nice seeing you and good luck with the fight to build your clinic. We'll be pulling for you." He left the room.

Rory stood silent and Elle stared straight ahead. "Why didn't you tell him I was the wicked hag he was talking about?"

He put his hand on her head and she felt a warm sensation travel down her body. "I know the truth, so will he someday."

"Speaking of the truth, why didn't you tell me you're a vet? You let me go on like a crazy woman on that drive and didn't say anything."

"I thought you knew. I have no idea what people have told you. You obviously hate me for some reason."

She hung her head and spoke softly. "I don't hate you."

He chuckled.

"What?" she snapped back.

"I'd be scared to see how you treat someone you do hate."

She thought about what the doctor had said about building a clinic. "Why am I being blamed for you not being able to build a vet clinic?"

"It's not you. It's this whole thing with the will and what you grandfather did years ago. He was angry and now it has come back to haunt us."

"What did he do?"

"You don't know?"

Elle shook her head.

Rory laughed. "You don't know."

"What's so funny?"

"When your mom heard that Kate had cancer, she started trying to get her share of the land. Then when I started building the clinic, Cynthia and John got with your mom and boom, within a week, you were here. By that time Kate had the attorney get the will. And that's when everything blew up. If you didn't know all this, why did you come out here?"

"I'm not really sure. My mother talked me into it. What was wrong with the will?"

Rory laughed to himself. "It really isn't funny. But when they read it, they realized that he cut both his children out. He left everything to his only granddaughter— you."

"Me. Why? I hardly knew him."

"There was a big family fight years ago. It happened when your parents were still living here."

"I remember that. I was young, but I remember all the yelling."

"There was a lot that happened. Secrets came out, and according to the will, your grandfather decided that Kate didn't deserve it. When your mother turned her back on the family and moved, your grandfather decided to punish both. He left it to the one person he felt was family, but who wouldn't disappoint him. He died about a month after he wrote it. No one knew what he had done with the will until now."

Elle looked at him. "That explains a lot. I wondered why my mother forced me out here." She paused and thought. "But it doesn't explain why he cut them out. There are all these secrets surrounding Kate and your dad. What happened?" She started to feel the room begin to sway again and put her hand to her head.

Rory patted her shoulder. "It makes my head hurt, too. Rest and we'll talk more about it later. If you think your head is spinning now, just wait."

Elle nodded and then looked up at him. "Thank you."

Rory tilted his head to the side. "For what?"

"For taking care of me."

"I didn't do much. But if you ever need a leg removed, I'm your man."

CHAPTER 22

There was nothing wrong with Elle that couldn't be taken care of with simple rest. Stress and lack of proper diet was what the doctor officially diagnosed. Rory drove Elle back to Kate's house the following day and helped her inside. Kate waited at the stairs.

"This is awful," said Elle. "I should be taking care of you."

"You don't need a lot, just some good food and rest."

"So, you plan on torturing me."

"I'm an old woman. What else do I have to live for?"

Rory shook his head. "Are you two planning on taking this on the road? It's hard to believe you weren't raised here." He lifted an eyebrow at Elle.

Elle went down to her area of the house where Kate had already laid out her suitcase. A neat stack of papers sat on a small table by the bed. Rory followed.

"Looks like I'll have some time to get my stories put together," said Elle.

Rory looked at Elle's ragged suitcase. "You must travel a lot."

Elle nodded. "It's what I do."

"Do you enjoy it?"

She smiled. "I get to see all kinds of wonderful and interesting places."

"That didn't answer my question. So when do you plan on settling down?"

Elle shot him a glare. "What do you mean?"

"You can't run around the world all your life. Don't you want to have a home and family?"

She laughed. "You sound like Faiza."

"Who?"

"She's a woman I met in Iraq. She acted like I had no life unless I was settled down."

Rory looked at the suitcase and then back at Elle. "It doesn't look like that is what you have planned."

"No."

"Are you happy with that choice?"

"Yes."

"Are you sure?"

Elle became irritated. "Yes, I'm sure. If you are so pro-family, why aren't you married with kids?"

Rory lifted an eyebrow. "I haven't found the right one."

"Really now. You sure?"

"Actually, I'm not sure. She may be right in front of me and I don't even know it. Regardless, I'm not afraid of making that move."

Elle huffed. "I'm not afraid."

Rory grinned.

Elle threw up her hands. "Why do you do that? You try to get my goat, don't you?"

Rory lifted his shoulders in defense. "I didn't accuse you of anything. You asked me about family and I answered."

"Yeah, but you eluded."

He smiled. "Eluded that you are afraid of commitment."

"Yes."

"So you are afraid."

"*No!*"

Rory laughed. "Could there be some truth to it?"

"No. I'm not scared of commitment or family or whatever."

"So, you think wedding vows are pointless?"

Elle scoffed. "No, but I see that they didn't mean much to my mother. It seems to me that marriage is mostly for convenience."

Rory looked at her. "It seems like you have premeditated everything you've ever done. Do you leave any room for life?"

"What are you talking about? I have a great life. I travel and tell stories of people all over the world. It's wonderful." Elle emphasized the word.

"Have you ever been in love?"

"Yes."

"Are you sure?"

"Yes. It didn't work out."

"Why?"

"I'm not going to discuss this with you."

"So, it was inconvenient for you."

Elle folded her arms.

"Are you going to plan and calculate that too, Ellie?"

"What do you care?"

"I do care." Rory got down on one knee and tried to take Elle's hand.

She drew it back self-consciously. "What are you doing?"

"I'm asking you to marry me."

"Get up."

"I'm serious, Ellie. Marry me."

"Why are you trying to drive me crazy?"

"That will come with the marriage. Right now, just agree."

Elle pushed him to the side. "Knock it off."

"You said it was for convenience. If we are married then I'm considered family and I can build my clinic on the land. Of course then it will be our clinic."

Elle closed her eyes. "So, this is for money, not for love?" She smiled, playing along.

"You're the one who said marriage was for convenience."

"What do I get out of it?"

"I'm a great cook."

Elle groaned.

"Yep, practice eating now. I'm a *really* great cook."

She punched him in the arm. "You're nuts. Get up and leave me alone. I'm supposed to be resting."

"I want an answer." He pulled her toward him.

Elle felt her face heat up just from being close to him. Rory looked deep into her eyes. Elle tried to drop her gaze, but couldn't. Her eyes smiled into his.

"Let's shake on it," he said.

"We're going to shake on marriage?"

He smiled.

Elle laughed. "If I shake, will you let me get some rest?"

"I will."

She shook his hand and leaned back against the pillows on the bed.

"It's a gentlemen's promise." He gently let her go and went to the base of the stairs.

"Then I have nothing to worry about."

Rory turned back to her. "I'm glad you're back. I've missed you, Ellie."

Elle watched him as an odd sense of comfort and

confusion fell over her. The way he said he missed her
sounded more than just her being back from her month in
Iraq. Elle sat and pondered what he said. *Missed me.
Glad I'm back.* He was someone she knew before as a
child. Or was she making things up in her mind?

What just happened? She slumped back against the
pillows on the soft mattress and closed her eyes. He mys-
tified her and made her feel things she had never experienced. There was something dark and disturbing that surrounded him, and Elle wondered if she should pursue the
reasons why or run like blazes.

That afternoon Elle helped Kate and Rory put together a small but superb meal for Thanksgiving. It was
two days late, but it still felt like a holiday. Rory directed
Elle on how to baste and even taught her how to mash
potatoes with fresh chives and real butter. He really was a
great cook. The house smelled divine, and Elle couldn't
remember the last time she anticipated a meal so much.

When all was done, Rory left to tend to his patients.
Elle went downstairs and released her hair from its ponytail. She combed through it and then touched up her eye
make-up and changed into a light blue blouse. Later she
heard a truck pull up outside and smiled knowing it was
Rory returning. A subtle tingle went through her shoulders when she heard his voice in the kitchen. Elle took
another look into the dresser mirror then walked up stairs
trying to act unfazed.

As she entered the room, Rory looked over and
beamed. "It sure smells wonderful." He was freshly
showered and shaved.

Elle smiled and nodded.

Rory noticed her attempts to primp. "It looks pretty
good, too."

She blushed and then almost laughed aloud at the sil-
liness of her feelings. She literally felt like a teenager.

Kate placed silverware on the table. "Rory, can you reach the wine glasses in that cupboard above the fridge? I put the bottle in the fridge about an hour ago, hopefully it will be cold," said Kate, directing Elle.

Elle went to the fridge and watched Rory's shirt rise as he reached for the glasses. She couldn't help admire his shoulders and the curve of his lower back. When he moved by her, Elle smelled a hint of cologne. She smiled to herself, hoping he had made an effort, like she had. In the fridge was a bottle of red wine. Elle smiled to herself as she pulled it out, knowing that you didn't chill red wine. Rory must have noticed and leaned down.

"She won't learn, I've tried to tell her, but she likes her wine cold."

Elle was surprised by his comment and also intrigued. Rory opened the bottle and poured her a glass. He poured himself one and then raised the glass. "To us."

Elle sipped the wine and even cold, it tasted good. A warm and comfortable feeling surrounded her.

The three sat around the small table and spent the evening eating and getting acquainted. It was bittersweet for Elle, as the mixture of memories and new stories filled her mind. So many experiences she missed and so many things she wished she could have learned from.

Kate looked straight at Elle. "So, have you decided what you're going to do with the land once I'm dead?"

"Kate!" Elle exclaimed. "Don't talk like that."

"I want to know."

Rory spoke up. "Kate, you don't worry. It's going to family just like you wanted. It doesn't matter what she does with it."

"Yes it does," Kate insisted.

Elle couldn't help but let out a surprised giggle.

Rory shook his head. "This is why I got good grades. Imagine this showing up at your parent teacher conference," he said, pointing a thumb to Kate.

Elle looked at him oddly. "Kate went to your parent teacher conferences?"

"Every one of them."

Elle gave a "Hmm," and then thought for a moment. "So what happened to your parents?"

Rory looked over to Kate solemnly. "They're both dead."

"That's terrible," said Elle.

Rory nodded.

Elle looked at Kate. "So why didn't you ever marry Rory's father? Then you would have legally been able to give Rory the land. This whole thing with the will wouldn't have happened."

"It's not that simple."

Rory's beeper buzzed and he looked at the number display. "I need to take this," he said, going for the phone.

Elle looked at the floor and felt her heart ache. "I feel like I have missed out on so much. I feel like I've been in a coma and now I'm awake, but I don't know what's happened or who anyone is. I feel lost."

Kate stood up from the table and gathered the dishes. "We've all been shortchanged. I feel you two are the ones most hurt. That is why I want you both to have the land. You deserve it. I always wanted you to come home, El-lie."

Elle smiled. "That's nice, but after what happened to my sister, I don't know if I could ever really feel good here."

"What happened was terrible, but it was an accident. You can't let it ruin your life," said Kate, as she stacked the dishes in the sink.

Rory came back to the table.

Elle felt her eyes begin to tear, and she put her hand

to her mouth. "Even though it's been this long, I still feel so much guilt."

Rory put his hand on her back.

"Guilt?" Kate asked, as she took her seat again. "For what? You didn't do anything."

Rory shifted in his seat. "Why do you feel you're to blame?"

Elle swallowed hard and wondered why she was about to tell her guilty secret.

Rory moved closer.

Elle's eyes spilled over as she began to talk. "I don't remember a lot about being here as a child, but I know I never liked that barn. I have nightmares still about a..." She stopped and shook her head. "It sounds ridiculous, but I see a blue-faced monster flying around in it. I know it sounds like a ghost story a kid would make up, but I remember something that happened when I was really young in that barn and it feels so real."

Rory and Kate both looked at each other warily.

Elle continued. "I loved to play hide and seek, but I'd never go in there because of it. One day I had some of my friends here, and Suzie kept trying to hang around with us. I told her that we would let her play with us, if she dared to stay in the barn for one hour. She was only five years old. Once she went inside, I closed the barn door, knowing that it was too heavy for her to open. My friends and I went into the house and downstairs to play with our Barbie dolls. That's when I heard my dad yelling that the barn was on fire."

Kate shook her head. "Elle, that wasn't your fault."

"I'm not done. I didn't tell them right away about Suzie being in there. I was afraid to get in trouble. I ran to the barn and tried to go get her myself. When I went to pull on the handle, it burned my hands." She looked down at the rippled scars on her palms. "It wasn't until then that I told them Suzie was in there. If I had told them sooner, then maybe she would have lived. I didn't want her to bug me, and I ended up losing my only sister."

Kate wrapped a weak and withered arm around Elle's shoulders and leaned down to her. "You poor child. All these years you've carried that around." She brushed Elle's bangs from her face and looked her in the eye. "You were just a child, and it was an accident. The smoke had taken Suzie long before anyone even realized the barn was on fire. Even if you had said something, it wouldn't have mattered. You loved her. That is all that matters."

Elle sighed. "How do you know she was already dead?"

Kate gave Elle a troubled look. "She wasn't burned. She was hiding in one of the storage cupboards near the stalls. It wasn't even close to where the fire started. The smoke killed her long before there were any flames. She must have been dead for a while."

"No one ever told me. In fact, for years I felt that it was the monster that killed her. At least that is what I used to see in my dreams."

"Elle, you were a child, and it was a long time ago. Let it go."

"That's hard to do, especially when I keep finding out that I never really knew what happened."

CHAPTER 23

Kate cleared the table and shooed Elle and Rory out of the house for an after dinner walk, knowing it would help Elle clear her mind. They walked a short way up the dirt path toward the stables. Rory looked out to the field. The barn stood out like a drop of blood on a white shirt. Elle looked at it, too.

"We can go another way, if you like," said Rory, as he stopped walking.

Elle slowed but didn't stop until she was up far enough to see the charred backside. Everywhere she went on that farm, she could see the barn.

"I'm okay," Elle answered. "In fact, I feel relieved and liberated. I can't believe I spent my entire life thinking it was my fault. I don't think I'll ever forgive myself for making her go in there, but at least I didn't—"

Rory put his arms around Elle. "No, you didn't."

The gesture surprised Elle, but the weight of his arms and the warmth of his body against the cold breeze made it easy for her to lean back against his chest. They stood looking out across the fields and holding each other. She felt invigorated, but also a bit exposed. It wasn't like Elle to let her emotions go. She closed her eyes and sighed long and deep, with a sense of right that filled her entire being. Rory leaned down to her neck and gently kissed it. It made Elle shiver, and she smiled.

"Are you cold?" he asked.

"A little."

"Let's go inside," he said, slowly releasing his grip from her.

Elle started to walk back toward the house.

"Where are you going?" he asked.

Elle motioned toward the house. "I thought you wanted to go back."

Rory grinned and shook his head. "For someone who is so smart, you can be pretty clueless."

"What?" she asked, wide-eyed.

He turned toward the small farmhouse and then winked back at her. "Do I have to do everything in this engagement?"

She came to him, realizing what he had in mind and playfully slapped his arm. "Don't you think you are assuming quite a bit?"

Rory grabbed her hand and then picked her up and carried her into the cozy little home. As soon as the door closed, he was kissing her.

Elle felt dizzy, but safe and sure in his arms. She wanted to be closer to him than she had ever been to anyone. Her heart and mind were full of love for him, and she felt her soul being lifted off the ground and carried away. Rory sat her gently on the sofa and tenderly held her head in his hands. He kissed her lips and softly kissed her neck and shoulders.

She loved him and every touch, every kiss. He was warm and strong and made the small of her back tingle and her breathing quicken. She searched for his lips. Rory's kisses were soft but intense and Elle held onto

him, feeling each curve and muscle in his broad back.
She drew her hand softly down the length of his spine
and he shuddered from her touch, giving a deep sigh.

It was all new to Elle and her heart throbbed so in-
tensely the rush of emotion brought tears to her eyes. She
clung to Rory and swallowed back the desire to weep
with pure joy. She loved him.

They stopped and held each other in a quiet, dream-
like reverie. Rory brushed a strand of hair from her face
and told her he felt the same. Not in words, but with a
simple look. He kissed her again softly and then looked
into her eyes. Elle's head cradled in his arm and she
looked back at him with warmth he hadn't seen. "Close
your eyes," he said.

"Why?" she answered.

"I want you to trust me. Close your eyes. I'm not going anywhere."

She closed her eyes and he kissed her again. When
he stopped, she opened her eyes and found him smiling at
her.

"You're stubborn, Ellie," he said with a smile. "One
day, I will get you to let go and just be with me."

Elle kissed him and then nuzzled into his neck. "We
should get back. I'm sure Kate is wondering where we
are."

"It was a really long walk."

Elle giggled.

"I have something I want to show you before we
head back."

Elle closed her eyes. Contentment flowed through
her and she was awash in tranquility. He gathered her up
and then with purpose directed her to follow him. She
took his hand, elated. At the top of the ridge looking
down toward the road were a large concrete pad and the
skeleton of a building taking shape.

Rory paused and studied it.

"What is it?" asked Elle.

Rory looked at the ground and gave a weary sigh.

"Oh," she said. "Is it that darn diner?"

"No. It's that darn clinic."

Elle looked back at the construction site, with her mouth agape. "Your vet clinic," she whispered.

Rory just nodded.

"That's the clinic the doctor was talking about. The construction was stopped…because of me."

"I didn't bring you up here to give you a guilt trip, Elle. I brought you because you are part of this. This is my dream, but I want it to be ours."

She looked at him, stunned. Their dream? She was filled with a mix of excitement and confusion. How could a veterinary clinic be her dream? And why after one afternoon of kisses and cuddling was she now contemplating a life with a man she hardly knew? It was crazy.

"Let's go back," he said, taking her hand again.

Elle held his hand and wished he could stay with her always. When Rory released her hand, he smiled. "I'm holding you to that marriage thing."

Elle raised an eyebrow. "Really now?"

"You shook on it."

Elle smiled. "I'm keeping my last name."

"Oh, so you're that type."

Elle shook her head. "No, I just can't imagine going through life with the name Elle Beau."

Rory gave a hearty laugh. "Hey, I think it's original." Then he paused. "Ah hah! So, you have been thinking about it."

She smiled but wanted so badly to talk more. Was it all just a big wonderful tantalizing tease, or did he really feel for her? Elle was doing exactly what she promised herself would never happen. She was falling for him, without control. She had no idea what he felt or what his intentions really were, and it scared her more than any war or any group of kidnapping henchmen. Without knowing, she was hanging her heart out there, waiting for him to toss it aside or drop kick it across that expansive oat field. Should she pull back? The feeling was like a drug, she knew it would end up hurting her, and yet it felt so good at that moment, she didn't care.

❧❧❧

Kate was sitting in the small study watching an archaic black and white television. Elle was drawn to it like a moth. The news of a deadline by the UN Security Council was all Elle picked up from the broadcast until the static took over.

"Your beeper went off again," Kate said to Rory.

He checked it and went to the phone. After several minutes, he came back into the room. "I need to go. A Labrador I'm treating isn't responding well to the meds. I need to meet them at the clinic."

Elle was sad to see him go and she couldn't hide it.

"Ellie, do you want to come by tomorrow and see K.J.?" Rory asked.

"Yes," said Elle, still in a daze from their earlier escapade.

When Rory left, Elle stood at the window and watched him drive away. She sighed, as she thought about their lovely afternoon and how he held her and loved her. "I love him," she whispered softly. She said it because she wanted to hear the words and know that she meant it. Even if no one else heard it, she wanted to say it and it felt good. Elle heard Kate come into the room and she turned to find her standing and holding a large box.

"Let's talk about some things," Kate said.

"Okay," said Elle, as she followed her into the kitchen. Kate set the box on the table. It was similar to the boxes Elle had found in the closet downstairs. Kate opened it and it was filled with pictures, just like the other boxes.

Kate pulled out several pictures and placed them on the table. "This is Daddy," she said pointing to an older man. "Mother died when Rose and I were teenagers. This here is your mother and that is me."

Elle smiled sadly as she traced the full head of dirty blonde curls that fell around her mother's face in the photograph. Rose was now platinum and there wasn't a hint of wave in her harsh sleek bob. Elle put a hand to her own head full of curls and felt the cold sting of her mother's words hit her as though she were fourteen again. The constant attempts at ridding Elle of her curls and the quips about her full hips and enlarging chest were as fresh in her mind today as if Rose were standing beside her.

Rose loved to point out how slim and healthy the pencil-thin, sleek-haired women in the magazines and on the television appeared. "And even when the lens adds at least ten pounds you know."

A rush of disgust fell over Elle. From the time she was twelve years old, she couldn't remember ever not being on a diet or obsessing about something, from her ankles to her eyebrows. It was always Rose's voice that goaded her on, keeping Elle on a continual treadmill of not living up to what Rose wanted but would never be.

Now Elle sat with an aunt she barely knew, feeling elated and beautiful for the first time in her life. Her weight was up and her hair was down and she was happier than she ever remembered. It made her wish her mother could experience the same sense of contentment but knew that would never be.

Kate continued to pull pictures from the box and tell Elle who was who. Most were of Rose and Kate, and some were of Elle and her sister Suzie. It was hard for Elle at first to see the pictures of her sister, but she felt safe with Kate and soon enjoyed it.

After a while, Elle stopped studying the pictures and looked up at Kate.

"What was it you needed to talk to me about?"

Kate shifted in her seat and gave her a knowing nod. She pulled out an envelope with pictures separate from the others and pushed them across the table towards Elle. "This is also my family."

Elle carefully placed some of the pictures on the table. There was a red-haired woman and a small red-haired boy. Elle recognized the lady from the paintings and pictures. "Who are they?"

Kate pointed to the woman with a strong but bony finger. "That is Roxanne, and that is Rory."

Elle looked at the picture and smiled. Rory's hair had darkened to auburn, now, but she saw the same bright smile in the boy as she had seen many times in the man. "Is Roxanne Rory's mother?"

"Yes."

Elle gestured to the walls. "Did you paint all of these pictures of her?"

"Yes."

Elle looked through some of the other photos. "Where is Rory's father?"

"He died years before these were taken."

"That doesn't make sense. I thought Rory's mother died before his father."

"No. Rory's mother died about five years ago."

Elle reeled back. "But I thought you said you raised Rory."

"I did."

"Why did his mother let you raise her son? Didn't she know you loved her husband?"

Kate paused and looked off to the side. She turned to Elle. "I didn't love Rory's *father*."

Elle waited for something to make sense, then it hit her.

Kate nodded. "Roxanne and I were together for almost thirty years. Rory's father killed himself when Rory was very young. He left a note blaming it on me. It was a cop out. He had left Roxanne two years after Rory was born and came back when it was convenient."

"How did you meet?"

"Rory's father worked for Daddy for about five years. When Roxanne got pregnant, he didn't like the idea and used it as an excuse to run around. He was gone so much, Roxanne and I ended up spending a lot of time together, and it just happened. After he killed himself, we became a family. However, Daddy and your mother weren't exactly accepting. Your parents moved away, and I still think your mother blames Daddy's death on the stress. It was only a month after everything came out in the open that he died."

Elle thought about what Kate said. "I remember fights and yelling. I also remember driving all the way back here for the funeral. That's when Suzie died. I don't think my mother has ever been back here."

Kate shook her head. "No. In fact, your mother and I have only spoken briefly by phone ever since then."

"That's been over twenty years. Why?"

"I don't know. I'm sure that the person I chose to love was a reason to blame me for what happened. I'm sure she blames Rory, too."

Elle was angry. She couldn't believe that her mother shunned her own sister just because she was gay. And then to blame her and a child for the things that went bad was even worse. "That's crazy. I can't believe the way she is sometimes."

"Elle, I've been dealing with this for most of my life. Don't be angry with your mother. I worry most about you and the burden you have had to bear with all this. I also worry about Rory. He's already been through so much, and all I want is for him to be happy. He's a good man with a good heart. He deserves to be happy."

Elle nodded. "It's hard not to be angry."

"If you don't learn to forgive, you'll never have the ability to love."

Elle turned to Kate, whose voice seemed slow and slurred. "Are you okay?"

Kate steadied herself. "I need to lie down."

Elle helped her to her room and tucked her into bed. She sat on the edge thinking and watching Kate's face, as she finally began to relax. She started to stand, but Kate began to talk.

"Ellie?"

"Yes, I'm here."

"Be good to Rory. He loves you so," she mumbled groggily.

"Rory?" Elle whispered. She stared at Kate and wondered just how much she knew.

Kate took a deep breath and then slipped into sleep.

Elle stood up and quietly left the room. She went back to the table in the kitchen and again looked through the pictures. She began to see the farm and land, not as a commodity to sell to the highest bidder, but as part of the family, as part of her history and soul. How could her mother have no feelings or connection to this place? Even though her sister died on that farm, Elle couldn't help remembering the joy and fun they had experienced.

If she sold the land to Cynthia and John, what would become of it? The fact that Suzie had died there didn't make it an evil place. She knew that Suzie had loved being there more than anything. It was their childhood home. Elle refused to see it scarred and ravaged by anyone. She quietly went downstairs and got ready for bed. In the morning, she would call Rose and tell her the deal was off, and then she would go to Rory and show him what a handshake really meant.

CHAPTER 24

Elle didn't sleep much. She kept wondering if Rory would show up at the house. With every turn in the sheets, she still caught a light hint of his scent on her. His touch lingered on her skin and brought deep longing with every memory. She played the day over and over again in her mind, each time ending with a shiver and a smile.

She giggled to herself at how overwhelmed and in love she was. Elle believed her desire for him would never wane. It was so intense, her need to hold him, love him. She wondered if Rory was awake and thinking of her, too.

Elle felt hopeful and excited about what may lie ahead with him. She caught herself smiling as she pictured his face and his incredible smile. She also spent time playing over in her head the conversation she planned to have with her mother and the great joy she would have telling her that the wicked little scheme of selling the land to that irritating cousin was off.

When the morning sun peeked through thin curtains, Elle dressed quickly and went upstairs. She checked on

Kate and found that she was still asleep. The phone in the kitchen was the only one in the house, so she had to be quiet.

When Rose answered, Elle barely gave her time to recognize her voice. "Mother, I'm not going to sell the land to Cynthia and John. I'm letting Rory build his clinic, and I don't know what I'll do with the rest of it."

Rose raged, "I can't believe you let him suck you in. That evil little creep has done it again."

"Done what? Why are you so convinced that he is the enemy?"

"Elle, he's the reason we left the farm. And now he's getting everything he wants."

"Mother, you left the farm because you were ashamed of your sister being gay. All these years you've shunned her for it."

"What?" Rose was fuming. "Is that what she told you?"

"Mother, I know the truth now. You couldn't handle all the rumors and gossip coming from these folks you call cousins, and you deserted your family over it. No wonder your father didn't think you deserved the land."

"Ha!" Rose blurted. "I can't believe that's the story she's giving you. Poor little thing, everyone shunned her for being gay and that's the reason she should be able to give all the land to Roxanne's little boy. That's not so, Elle. That is not what this is all about."

"Really? Then enlighten me."

"Gladly. Your innocent Aunt Kate and her dear friend Roxanne were discovered. Roxanne's husband was so distraught, he killed himself. Did she tell you that?"

"Yes, but I also know he had already left his wife and child."

"I'm sure they've told you a lot of things."

"What's that supposed to mean?"

Rose continued. "What has your lovely Rory told you about your sister?"

A painful chill went through Elle. "Nothing. Why would he?"

"How convenient for him."

"Mother, what are you getting at?"

"Before you get all chummy with him, ask him about how your sister died."

"I've already talked about that with him and with Kate."

Rose scoffed. "And they both failed to tell you anything about what Rory did. Boy, that's a shock!"

Elle felt her body heat up with worry. "What happened?"

Rose forced a chuckle. "No, I want them to tell you. Let's see if they do. If you want the truth, put that little journalistic head to work for you and quit letting your heart lead you down the primrose path."

When Elle hung up with Rose, she went to Kate. She wanted answers, but when she found Kate still sleeping she knew what she had to do.

When she reached the veterinary clinic, she sat in the car and stared at the front door. Her heart was racing and she wanted so badly to hear Rory say it wasn't true. She walked in and found Norma, the same woman who was there before, filling out papers at the reception desk.

"Can I help you?" she asked, barely looking up.

"I need to see Rory."

Norma stopped writing. "Oh, it's you," she said with a smile. "He said you might be in today. Hold on and I'll bring you back." She finished writing and closed the appointment book.

Elle followed her around through the swinging doors, past the kennels, and to an exam room. Rory was bent down checking a small dog's leg. He looked up and a smile immediately spread across his face.

Elle tried to smile back, but was unsuccessful.

He closed the kennel and when Norma left the room, he walked to Elle and put an arm around her waist. "I wanted to be with you today, but I've been here with that Lab since I left you yesterday."

Elle tried to back up and Rory noticed her hesitation. "Is everything all right? Is Kate okay?"

Elle nodded. "I need to talk to you."

He looked down at her with concern. "Sure. What is it, Ellie?"

"I talked to my mother this morning. She said that you knew about my sister's death."

Rory looked uneasy. "Yes."

Elle looked at Rory. "Why didn't you say something?"

"I thought you knew everything that happened here."

Elle shook her head. "I didn't. I hardly remember anything about this place. I can still remember the fire that killed Suzy and that's about it. I have dreams, nightmares rather, about a monster in that old barn, but I always did, even before Suzanne was killed. The sight still haunts me."

Rory looked at the ground. "It haunts me, too."

"How? What do you mean?" asked Elle.

"I remember a lot more than you do."

Elle bit her lip and forced herself to press him. "My mother claims that you had something to do with my sister's death."

"Elle, it was an accident."

"Then why does she think you did something?"

Rory lowered his head. "I'm not making excuses, Elle, but when my dad died, I had nowhere to put my anger. I was so sad about what happened. I didn't know that your little sister was in the barn."

"What?"

Rory bit his lower lip and looked away.

"What do you mean, Rory? What does your dad dying have to do with my sister?" Elle stared at the ground as the memories flashed through her mind. "No, that can't be."

Rory stood silent.

"You started the fire."

Rory was red eyed, but looked at her without flinching.

"I've spent my whole life feeling like I was the one who killed her, but it was you!"

"Elle, I didn't know she was in there."

"Who cares? Why would you start a fire?"

Rory looked around as if worried that someone would overhear. "Can't we talk about this tonight?"

Elle shook her head. "I'm leaving. I'm going right back to the house and pack." She swallowed hard. "I want an answer. Why did you start the fire?"

"I was angry. The barn was the only thing I could let out my anger against."

Elle's face was red and her eyes were blurry with tears. "You killed my sister, you rotten creep. You killed my little sister."

Rory walked to her but Elle stepped back. "For twenty years I've hated myself because of what I did," said Rory, his eyes pleading.

"My mother said that you were the reason our life went bad, but I didn't believe her. I brushed her aside like a crazy old woman and stood up for you."

Rory reached out to her.

Elle stepped farther away from him.

"It was a long time ago. I don't expect you to ever forgive me, but you've got to believe me that I didn't know."

"Why should I ever forgive you? You should be in prison."

Rory paused. He began to speak, but then just nodded.

"I can't believe I allowed myself to love you. Kate knew all about this, didn't she? No wonder my mother thinks she's crazy. She's planning on giving our family's farm to a killer."

"Ellie, it's not like that. It was an accident."

"An accident? You *accidentally* set the fire?"

Rory reached for her. "Ellie, please."

"Don't call me Ellie. Don't call me anything. You stay away from me or I swear I'll call the police."

Rory put his hands up defensively. "I was hurt and trying to make it go away."

Elle stared at him with sad, red eyes and shook her head slowly. "The only thing you made go away was my sister. The hurt will never go away."

She ran out of the clinic and fumbled with her car keys. She heard him come outside and start to say something, but she jumped inside, slammed the door, and started the engine. She refused to acknowledge him. Elle could hardly see the road when she pulled away because her eyes were so full of tears.

The drive back was long and cold. She hadn't stopped to bring a jacket and found herself grappling with the heater, as tears fell off her face and onto her blouse. When she reached the house, she wiped the wet streaks from her face. Kate sat at the kitchen table looking anxious and frail. Elle stood at the door.

"What happened?" asked Kate. "You look sad and Rory called, worried."

Elle continued toward the stairs, so she could pack.

Kate called to her. "A man called earlier and wanted to know if you were here. I told him you had stepped out and that he should call back. He asked when you were leaving, and I told him I wasn't sure."

"Who was it?" asked Elle.

"He didn't say."

Elle didn't care, she just wanted to escape. She was still thinking about the fight with Rory and starting to wonder how she could have read him so wrong. "That's the secret," she mumbled. "Everyone's protecting their precious veterinarian."

She wanted to confirm everything with Kate, but could tell that she was weak and didn't want to make it worse with a bunch of questions.

Elle threw things into her suitcase. It seemed smaller than normal, and even more worn. A knot ate at her stomach. She felt her shoulders get tight, as she folded and stacked her clothes. The quilt and the down pillows called to her. Before long she found herself laying there crying, thinking about Rory, and trying to convince herself that she did what she had to do.

The phone rang upstairs and Elle heard Kate answer it. She heard Kate's feeble footsteps at the top of the stairs. Before Kate had a chance to call down to her, Elle was at the base of the stairs, "Is it for me?"

Kate nodded.

Elle wondered if it was Rory. "Who is it?"

"Someone from your work. They say it's urgent."

Elle quickly walked up the stairs and took the phone. It was Richard Prescott. His voice was serious and he cleared his throat several times, making Elle pull the phone from her ear.

"Elle, there's been a…" he searched for the word. "Problem."

"Problem? What?"

"There was a car crash. Dan and Ethan were taken to the hospital."

"Oh, God. Are they hurt badly?"

"Dan's okay, but Ethan needs surgery. They said someone sabotaged the car and caused the whole thing. They said they were robbed, too."

"How bad is Ethan? Is he going to live?"

Kate came closer and stood by Elle.

"Yes. Dan says Ethan has a lot of cuts on his face and his shoulder was mangled. They are flying him back to the states. The reason I called is so you can go back on the return flight."

Elle heard what he said, but stood dumbfounded. He hadn't called to give her word about her coworker. He hadn't called to show concern about the dangers of where they were assigned. He called because they needed her to fly back to Iraq and get to work.

"When?" she asked.

"Tomorrow. How soon can you be back here?"

"I was heading back tonight. I'll leave as soon as I get packed."

Kate walked off toward the front room. Elle's heart ached, knowing that she probably wouldn't see her aunt again. She sensed that Kate knew it, too. Elle went to her.

Kate stood at the window looking out. "Elle, your visitor is here. He's out front talking to Rory."

Elle looked out. "Great," she said wearily. She quickly went to the door and stepped out on the front porch. There stood Kevin leaning down and cooing at the cat through the bars of the cat carrier that Rory held. Rory looked up at Elle.

Elle looked down at the ground, unable to keep eye contact.

"Elle!" Kevin exclaimed. "You'll never guess. This is Rory Beau. He and I are old college buddies."

Elle looked at Rory, who shrugged.

"It's probably been ten years." Kevin bent down

again toward the cat. "And look what he did to our little
K.J. Kevin Junior is gonna be okay, isn't him," he cooed.

Rory stood pensive and obviously hurt.

Elle pulled the jacket around her, glared at him, and
went to Kevin. "Why are you here?"

He laughed. "She has always been like this. I don't
know why I've held on so long. I have the papers, silly."
He reached into a large envelope. He turned to Rory.
"Our little Elle is set to be a pretty wealthy lady. She almost lost it all to a gold-digger, but I got everything all
worked out."

Elle cringed.

Rory pitched in. "That's a good thing." He sat the
carrier on the porch. "I better head back. It was nice seeing you again, Kevin." He turned to Elle. "I've left instructions on how to care for him, in an envelope in your
car." He tried to get Elle to look at him, but turned and
left.

On instinct Elle went to say something to him, but
simply muttered "thank you" under her breath. She
watched, as he pulled out of the lane and down the road.

"So, when are you heading back? And where is this
aunt of yours?" Kevin asked, craning his neck toward the
house.

"She's inside and you're leaving."

"What?"

Elle stood her ground. "Listen to me. I appreciate
your help with all this, but we're over. I'm not your little
Elle and K.J. is my cat, not ours. I will head back when I
am ready, but you are leaving now." He tried to argue, but
Elle pointed toward his car. "Leave me alone."

"So now that you have the money, you don't need
me anymore. Is that how it is?"

Elle laughed. "I never did need you. I don't *need* anyone. Leave me alone."

Kevin scowled. "Fine. End up a lonely, old, and bitter wretch, just like that aunt of yours."

Elle brushed him off then picked up the cat and went into the house. She hid behind the curtains and watched as he swung the car around and sprayed the air with gravel as he sped off. She waited until his car was out of sight then sat the cat down and turned away from the window.

"He's wrong, you know. And so are you," Kate said, gruffly, standing in the doorway. "I'm not lonely and I'm not bitter."

"I don't care what he says."

"My life wasn't perfect, but it was good."

Elle sighed. "So, how am I wrong?"

"You're wrong when you say you don't need anyone. You *do* need someone. No one can go through life like that. You are a strong woman, Elle, but that doesn't mean you don't need love."

Elle shrugged.

"If you don't find it, it is you that will end up lonely and bitter."

"It's too much of a pain."

Kate smiled. "Is it too much of a pain? Or are you afraid of feeling pain? Nothing in life is easy. I know you hardly know me and I hardly know you, but I don't want to see you turn into your mother. If you never forgive and go through life caring about things rather than people, you'll never be happy."

Elle took a deep breath. "It's not that I don't agree with you, but I think it may be too late."

Kate huffed. "I didn't find true love until I was almost fifty. It's never too late."

A knock came at the front door and Elle wondered if Rory had come back. It was Mary. She had loaf pan with a towel placed over it. When she saw Elle come out of the kitchen she smiled with her entire face. "Elle, darling,

I didn't know you were here. How long will you be staying?"

Elle smiled back, but knew her answer would surely surprise Kate. "I'm actually leaving in about an hour."

"Oh. Did you spend the holiday here?"

"Yes."

With a cheery grin of approval, Mary handed the bread to Kate. "It's my strawberry bread. I made it for Rory. It's a peace offering, because I need his help with a sick horse, and I hate doing this when it's a holiday weekend."

Kate took the bread and peeked under the towel. "You won't be bothering him. He's already at the clinic. Give him a call and I'm sure he'll run out to your place."

Mary said, "Won't it be nice when he's closer. We can't wait. It's been almost twelve years now since old Doc Butler retired. To have a vet in town again will be heaven."

Elle felt a sharp pain in her chest, and she put her hand to her heart.

"I better run," said Mary. She touched Kate on the arm and gave Elle a quick hug. "It was wonderful to see you again." She stood back and looked at both of them. "It's so good to see you back home."

Elle tried to smile, but could only muster a half grin.

When Mary left, Kate went to the kitchen and set the bread on the counter. Elle started to walk by her toward the stairs, but Kate turned and began to speak. "I know I'm a gruff old broad who probably doesn't do a good job of talking, but Mary was right. It is good that you're here."

Elle looked up at her, shocked. Again, she felt emotions rush from her heart to her face and her eyes started to well up. She was torn between her anger at what had happened to her sister and her new found love for an aunt she barely knew. She was compelled to hug Kate, but instead uttered a muffled, "Thank you" and quickly went down stairs.

When she resurfaced with suitcase in hand, Kate was sitting in the living room.

"When will you be coming back?" Kate asked, setting aside a letter she was reading.

"I'm not sure."

"Are you going back overseas?"

Elle nodded. "I'll be careful."

"How long is the plane ride?"

"The whole trip takes about two days, if you figure in the drive."

Kate thought for a moment. "Gives a body plenty of time to think."

Elle pondered what she said and wondered if it was just a statement or a direction. "It does."

Kate struggled to get out of the chair but made it to standing. "If I don't see you, I hope you enjoy what is here. I really don't care what happens, as long as your mother, John and Cynthia don't get their hands on it. You know what is best."

"I wish you wouldn't talk like that. I will see you."

"Elle, you are one of the only people who understands the way I am. It's the way you are. Even with our metal armor, we both know what's right."

Reaching down, Elle lifted the well-traveled suitcase and went to grab the cat kennel.

Kate opened the door for her.

As Elle started to walk out, she stopped. "Kate, why didn't you tell me about Rory and the fire?"

Kate didn't blink. "There are some things you need to learn on your own. It's the only way you'll ever be able to understand what really happened."

"But how can I do that if I don't have the facts?"

Kate looked at her disappointed. "Elle, life isn't like that. When it comes to the people we love, there aren't always black and white answers. And the truth isn't always easy to find."

"Rest assured you'll have your clinic, Kate." Elle touched her shoulder. "No matter how I feel now about Rory, you'll have your clinic."

Elle knew that no matter what she said to Kate from that point on, it wouldn't matter, so she gave her a nod and leaned over and briefly touched her cheek to Kate's. She wanted to tell her she would see her soon, but instead she just smiled.

Kate watched Elle pull away and stood on the doorstep until Elle couldn't see her in her rearview mirror. When she had cleared the bend and the house was out of view, she pulled over.

As Elle looked out over the hills of her childhood home, the chilling sense of loss covered her like the snow that fell lightly around the fields. Why couldn't it have been different? She tried hard to think about her sister, laughing and playing on the farm. Elle contemplated the life she lost and what might have been.

Then she had the same thought about Rory. He, too, had lost so much of his young life. Her mind turned to Hal Norland. Elle missed him, but couldn't stop thinking of his life as empty. He ended up dying alone. She wondered if her own life would end up like his.

Elle carefully lifted the crying three-legged cat from the carrier and placed him gently in her lap. She stroked its head for a moment to calm him. "You are no longer Kevin Junior. You are now Hal. I should probably call you tripod, but that would be cruel." The cat rubbed its head against Elle's hand.

"Okay, Hal it is. Have a good visit with Holly. She put him back in the kennel. I'll be back as soon as I can."

When Elle returned home, she immediately withdrew the complaint papers and arranged for construction to re-start on the veterinary clinic.

CHAPTER 25

December, 1990:

Elle was relieved that she was back in the same hotel room at the Al-Rashid. She looked out over the street and wondered how her life had become so complex in just a few short months. It was now December and the warm Iraqi nights had turned cold.

Kate was right about the plane trip. Elle spent the hours doing nothing but thinking. She thought about the car crash and wondered who had tried to kill her coworkers and what dangers she might be walking into herself. She knew that Ethan would survive, but wondered what it was like to know that you were a target and realize that you survived.

She thought about what Dan had said on the original plane ride to Iraq about being disposable. Elle felt like she may have thrown away her chance at making her life something more.

She spent the rest of the flight thinking about Rory. She saw his face in her mind and the tortured look he gave her when she realized he had killed her sister. She played the scene over and over in her head. She wanted so badly to make it all go away, change the past so that she could be with him, but nothing gave her the solace she needed to forgive. She wondered, too, if she could ever forgive herself. *If you don't learn to forgive, you'll never have the ability to love.*

She thought about the reasons she made Suzie go into that barn in the first place. All those years she had remembered trying to dodge her sister and keep her away from her friends, but now a new motive surfaced. There was a reason she wanted to see her sister stay in that barn, and it had nothing to do with her irritating Elle. It had to do with Elle's own fear of the place. She wanted to use her sister to prove to herself that a sinister presence wasn't lurking there ready to get her. Rose had convinced her all her life that it was just a bad dream. A soft knock at the door released her from her thoughts and she went to answer it. It was Dan.

"Welcome back," he said. "Sorry about Hal."

Elle just nodded. "I'm sorry about what happened to you and especially to Ethan. I saw him at the hospital right before I came back and he looked good. It's still so scary."

"It comes with the job."

"Who do you think did it?"

Dan averted his eyes. "I have no idea, but they knew what they were doing. The brake line was cut clean. They also stole the duffle with the money we were paying informants. They knew exactly what they were looking for."

"It was Zev," Elle said with confidence.

Dan looked skeptical.

"Dan, I saw Zev in the video that you fed down. He's one of them."

"Elle, it was his car. Why would he cut his own

brakes? Whoever did it wasn't targeting us. They were targeting him."

"How did they know about the money? He is the only one who knew."

Dan averted his eyes again. "I'm not so sure."

Elle crossed her arms. "I won't work with him anymore. I know that he's part of the henchmen. Even though he helped us get news, I can't work with someone who is doing that."

"That won't be a problem, Elle. Zev is dead."

"Dead. How?"

"They found him a couple days later lying in the street. He had a small head wound."

"Shot?"

Dan shook his head. "No. It wasn't a bullet, but whatever it was, it worked. It was on a side street not far from here. We heard a commotion, so I grabbed my gear. There were people who came out of their homes and started dancing. They acted like it was a party. When they saw me filming, they grabbed their kids and hid inside."

Elle listened and let what he said settle on her. "I guess I'd feel the same way if someone threatened my family."

Dan shrugged. "I guess." He went to the door. "I've got word that there is another kidnapping going down in the morning. It's in Saba al-Bor. Will you be ready?"

"Saba al-Bor! Faiza's village?"

"Yeah, we had one right near her when you were gone. I kept her out of the shot, even though I shouldn't have."

Elle wondered what she should ask or tell Dan. "Do you know where this next run is exactly?"

Dan scowled. "It isn't at her place. There are only a bunch of women there."

Elle looked down.

"Elle, what is it?"

"Nothing," she said, convincingly. But she knew she had to get word to Faiza and her family that they were on Zev's list.

Dan reminded her of the time and then left to put his gear together.

Elle paced her room. The grinding in her stomach was overwhelming and she knew that she couldn't wait. It was no longer a question of being objective. It was a choice between life and death for someone she considered a friend.

Elle waited for Dan to leave and then pulled her hair up, hiding it under a hat. She sat in her room and waited for her chance.

When the night had quieted, Elle slinked out of her room and through the lobby. Her breathing was loud and her heart raced. She took the car and hoped her ball cap and bulky jacket hid her enough in the dark. She drove the same path she had been driven each day for weeks, but this time the road was unusually loud and lonely. At Faiza's house, Elle gave the secret knock like she remembered.

When Faiza answered, she held the door to a crack. Then her eyes grew large, when she recognized Elle. Faiza looked both surprised and disturbed. "What are you doing here, Elle?" she asked. She looked past her and around the corner.

Elle tried to whisper. "I came alone. I must talk to you. Can I come in?"

Faiza nodded and opened the door, just enough to let Elle slip by. Once inside, Elle noticed Gali and Houda huddled in the back.

"I wanted to warn you. I know that another kidnapping is going to take place and it's supposed to happen in this village. Where is Raziq?"

Faiza shook her head. "He is not here. He is hiding somewhere far from here ever since Khalid was taken."

"Who is Khalid?"

Faiza's lip trembled. "Muki's father. Raziq's brother."

"Oh, my God."

Faiza took a seat at the table. "Let them come. There is no one left to take."

Elle just stood silent.

Faiza looked up at Elle. "Why are you warning us?"

"You're a good friend."

"So are you."

Then Elle felt her heart swell and her eyes begin to tear. She took a seat next to Faiza and started to cry.

"What is it?" asked Faiza.

Gali and Houda came close and Houda put a hand on Elle's shoulder.

This act of kindness made Elle look up at the three of them. "I learned some things when I was back at the farm. I'm really confused and sad about what I know about my family."

"Tell us," said Faiza.

Elle shook her head. "I don't want to bore you. After everything you've been through, my stupid problems are so petty."

Faiza took Elle's hand. "When it comes to caring about family, nothing's petty. Talk."

Elle told them what happened. She talked about Rory and how she thought she was in love. She told them about her aunt and the scandal surrounding whom she loved and how Rory's father had taken his life as revenge. And she talked about her sister's death and how she had blamed herself all those years, only to learn that the one man she felt she really loved had actually been the one who caused the fire.

When she finished, the three women were dumbfounded. Houda sat back in her chair. She looked over to Faiza and said something in Arabic. She talked passionately and pointed to her head. Faiza shook her head and disagreed. Houda looked at Elle sadly.

"What did she say?" asked Elle.

Faiza glanced toward Houda. "She said desperation makes children do things. Armies kill men but wound children emotionally, and that is why he wanted to burn down the barn."

Elle looked over to the old woman and felt the urge to go to her and tell her she appreciated her. It was comforting just to know that Houda cared enough to comment. She turned back to Faiza and Gali. "I wish I knew why he started the fire. Rory said it was to take away the pain. He says he didn't know my sister was in there. I believe him, but I still don't know why he had to start a fire. It makes no sense and it's disturbing."

Houda made a rude noise from the other room and then stood up. She turned to Elle. "I know why," she said in broken but clear English. "He burned the memories. Kids have no other way to remove the pain. He was burning the monster in his mind. You both have a monster in that barn."

Elle thought for a minute about what Houda had said. She was right. The monster that haunted Elle's dreams and psyche was the same monster Rory tried so desperately to eliminate from his own tortured thoughts.

Houda saw the light go on in Elle's mind and stood, silently staring at Elle, eye to eye.

❦❦❦

When Elle arrived back at the hotel, Dan didn't look happy.

"Where've you been?" he asked, sorting through his tape bag. "I checked your room and couldn't find you. The truck will be here in about an hour."

"I'll be ready."

"I really hope you didn't go and screw this up for us."

Elle wondered what he meant by that but didn't say a word.

Elle went to her room and removed the hat and jacket. She wondered how much Dan knew. She couldn't help but wonder if Raziq was really safe and hoped that Faiza would take her warning and make sure that he wasn't anywhere near the home. Elle took a seat by the window and stared out over the street. It was quiet and the buzz of streetlights filled the night sky. Was she becoming too close to the story? She had broken so many rules that day and wondered if she could ever look herself in the mirror and call herself a journalist.

A knock at the door startled her.

It was Matt. He looked beat and forlorn. "Can I come in?"

"Sure."

"Are you and Dan going out on another one?"

"Yes."

"I guess congratulations are in order."

Elle gave him a skeptical look.

"You don't know?" asked Matt.

Elle raised her shoulders, unaware.

"You won a Murrow. It looks like you're right on track for the Trimbaugh. I'm surprised Dan didn't tell you. He danced around here like a kid when the call came in."

"Hmm."

"That's it? Hmm. You are up for the biggest award we can get and all you can say is hmm."

Elle really didn't know how to respond. A year ago, she would have given him a high five and gone celebrating. Now she just felt wasted.

Matt took a seat on the bed. He looked at the ground.

"Are you okay?" she asked sincerely.

Matt smiled dimly. "No." He looked up at Elle. "My wife left me."

Elle sat next to him and patted his back. "I'm sorry."

Matt shrugged. "I expected it. You know what they say about foreign correspondents and relationships. I knew it wouldn't last."

Elle continued to sit with him while he talked about some of the assignments he had taken and what his wife's response was to his absence.

"It's hard. I know I'm feeling like I may have missed out on something," said Elle, trying to comfort him.

Matt put his hand on Elle's leg. "Thank you. You have always been able to make me feel good."

Elle patted him back.

"It all makes me realize I should have known what I had all those years ago."

She smiled and gave him an "I'm flattered" roll of the eyes.

"No, Elle. I really mean it. I loved you and I don't think I ever stopped. I was selfish back then and wanted you to follow me. I realize now, we should have never split up and it was all my fault."

"It was nobody's fault. We were both more into our jobs than anything else."

He agreed. "Yes. It makes me sick that I didn't see what we could have had."

Elle smiled and nodded.

Then he leaned into her.

Elle felt a rush of shock. Did she really win in the end? All those nights of hoping that he would see what he was missing. She relented and politely kissed him. Even being out in the dreary, dusty death filled air of Iraq, Matt smelled heavenly. His lips were soft and her mind began to wander. Then she stopped. She opened her eyes, and as she did, he opened his. He backed away.

"What's wrong?" Matt went to kiss her again and she gently pushed him away.

"I can't."

"Why?"

Dan's thunderous knock made Elle jump up from the bed. "I have to go."

Matt took her by the arms. "Elle, I love you."

Elle straightened herself. She brushed Matt's hands off of her. "Don't ever say that to me again." She opened the door and Dan, seeing Matt, just mumbled. "We're ready."

Elle left Matt, without looking back.

In the car, Dan stayed silent. Elle was convinced he was hiding something. Night slowly made its way through winding streets like a trail of smoke. Elle's heart beat quicker as the driver pulled the truck just a block away from Faiza's home.

"Where is this one?" Elle asked.

No answer.

She stayed quiet and waited. Time crept slowly and Elle wondered if the men in the family had gotten out. After at least an hour, the army truck, filled with cloaked and gun-toting men, crept by on the side street. Dan motioned her to follow. To Elle's horror, he directed her right to where Faiza's home waited. The men in the truck began chanting and one went up to the door. But it wasn't Faiza's door they began to kick. It was Muki's.

"What are they doing?" she whispered to Dan. "I thought his uncles were warned, and they already took his father. Are there other men there?"

Dan ignored her.

The door crashed in and screaming started. Several men bolted inside and then returned, not with a man, but with a young boy, screaming and thrashing about.

Elle gasped. "Why are they taking Muki? He's just a boy." She pulled on Dan. "Why are they taking a child?"

Dan pushed her away and continued to shoot.

"They can't do this," Elle yelled, going toward them.

Dan reached out and grabbed her by the collar of her shirt. He yanked her back. "Get back or you're going to get killed."

"How can you just stand here?"

"Get back, Elle."

Elle stood back, stunned and sickened as Muki's mother screamed and grabbed at the men, trying to get to her young son. Within minutes, Muki was shoved into the cab of the truck and the group sped away, leaving the mother distraught on the ground. The door to Faiza's house came open and the three women ran to her. Faiza looked up, disheveled and desperate. She saw Dan and Elle. Elle stepped back into the shadows and began to sob. Dan put his camera down and walked back to the car. Elle followed slowly, trying to catch her breath.

"Did you know it was going to be the boy?"

Dan nodded.

Elle was furious. "Why didn't you do anything? He is just a little boy."

"Elle, that little boy shot a rock into the head of our guide and cut the brake line of our car. He nearly killed Ethan. This isn't like back home. These aren't normal kids. They kill. And besides, it's not my job to do anything. I just went along with you. It's my job to shoot stories. Remember?"

Elle was shaking, as the car pulled out and headed back to the hotel. "You have proof it was him?"

Dan shrugged.

"He was just trying to protect his family."

"He could have killed both me and Ethan. He didn't care who was in the car with Zev."

"Zev is part of the henchmen who took his father."

Dan cocked his head to the side and peered at her with a furrowed brow. "You're defending him."

"You're defending them kidnapping a child."

"I'm not doing anything but getting the story. And all I know is this makes the story even better."

Elle grimaced. "He was a kid in pain. He was just trying to…" Then she stopped and stared out the window in thought. "He thought he could take away the pain."

"Whatever," Dan mumbled, as he played back the scene in his camera's viewfinder.

Elle didn't look, but heard the horrible cries and yells echo from the camera. She stared out the window as the car sped along. Elle watched the faces of the people and felt they were looking into her soul.

She knew what she had to do to make things right. She donned the burqa the next morning and went to Faiza's house early.

Faiza was still in tears, and Elle's heart ached to see her friend in pain.

"I should have known. You tried to warn us and I didn't save him," Faiza said through sniffles. "The uncles got away, but he was taken."

"Faiza, don't do this to yourself. How could you have known they would take a child?"

She looked at Elle. "Did you know?"

"No."

Gali and Houda were gone and Elle looked around the small home.

"They are with Muki's mother," said Faiza, noticing.

Elle nodded.

"We have nothing. They've taken everything. We even heard that Raziq might have already been found and captured."

Elle didn't know what to say. She just sat and listened and felt her soul shrink with every word.

"You must let people know what is happening here."

Elle nodded but felt whatever she did would be miniscule.

"Please, help us."

Elle sat with Faiza and let her talk about the pain and horrible fate that surely had befallen Muki. Such incredible pain, and it wasn't even her family, Elle thought, as she listened.

Houda and Gali returned, and Faiza said something in Arabic.

Elle stood. "I should leave you alone. I wanted to let you know how sad I am. I will be at the hotel if you want to reach me."

Faiza looked unsettled and kept throwing glances toward Gali and Houda. She took Elle by the arm and walked to the door. "I have something to tell you." She looked back and dropped her voice lower. "We are leaving."

"Where?"

"We have the funds needed for passage into Turkey. We have family there."

Elle shook her head. "But I thought you said you'd never leave."

"I will never leave my home. And my home is where my family is. I have nothing here. Raziq is supposed to meet us there…if he is still able."

Elle was confused. "What funds?"

"We needed money to pay for them to get us there safely. We now have it."

"Money? You should have asked me. I would have helped."

"Elle, this is our fight."

"How did you get it?"

Faiza dropped her eyes. "Muki…"

The reality of what had happened hit Elle hard. It *was* blood money, but she knew their desperation and understood their plight. "When are you leaving?"

"Next Tuesday. We have six days."

Elle thought a moment and then looked back at Gali and Houda who sat silently. "Talk to me."

Faiza raised her shoulders. "What do you mean?"

"On camera. That is the only thing I don't have right now. I need someone who can talk and tell their story. I can show the video of the kidnappings and tell what is going on, but I need you. I need someone whose life has been destroyed by all this."

Faiza was uncomfortable and shook her head.

"You asked for my help. This is the best way for you to help your people. No one can tell this story better than you."

"They will find me and kill all of us."

"Not if you're not here. We can hold the interview until you're gone. No one will know."

Faiza stood deep in thought. She was unsettled with the proposition. "Okay, but I will need something from you."

Elle agreed and Faiza told her what to bring and how to keep it a secret.

Dan was elated when Elle told him about the interview. "I can't believe she agreed."

Elle kept quiet about Faiza and the others going to Turkey and she swore him to secrecy that the interview was even taking place. That evening they quietly made their way out of the hotel, and over to Faiza's home.

When Faiza took a seat for the interview, Elle was taken aback by her regal and defiant stance

"You ready?" asked Dan.

Elle nodded.

Faiza looked at the camera.

"Don't look at him, talk to me," said Elle. "Relax and talk. We can edit, so don't think you have to be perfect. Talk to me like we are sitting in your kitchen having Turkish coffee."

Faiza beamed and a tranquil air came over her.

"Tell me what is going on with the kidnappings and how it has hurt your family."

Faiza, without hesitation, told what she knew. Even when she felt tears coming, she swallowed hard and kept her pace. Elle was amazed. Even in the face of unimaginable horror, Faiza was articulate and effective in explaining the nightmare of her life.

Elle listened, but also thought about how proud she was to call Faiza a friend. Elle thought about how few friends she really had, and a pang of sadness hit her at the thought she would probably never see Faiza again. "Tell me what happened to your father."

Faiza, for the first time during the interview, looked uneasy. She bit her lip and appeared as though she was going to refuse to answer.

"It's important, Faiza," urged Elle.

With red eyes she began to talk about the man he was. This surprised Elle, because she had only heard about how he died, and it made her even sadder to hear about the life he had lived.

"I saw my father's lifeless body hanging above me. I will never forget that. I love him so much and yet the last image I have of him is his body hanging above me."

Elle felt a sickening twinge surge through her. The scene flashed in her mind and became intermixed with her own memories of a horrifying fiend above her. Elle felt her head begin to spin and knew this was no time to have another episode of faintness. She held onto the bottom of the chair and told herself to stay strong and push the sights from her head. She finished the interview without incident.

As Dan packed up the gear, Elle gave both Houda and Gali long and heartfelt hugs. She handed Faiza her old suitcase. "Good luck. I hope we see each other again," said Elle, meaning every word. Faiza hugged her.

In the car Dan asked about the suitcase, but Elle just shook her head and stared out the window.

That turned out to be the last of what she needed for her project. Elle spent the next few days watching hours of tape and spilling out her experiences and sights on paper. When the edited and final series of stories fed over the satellite, Elle leaned back against the truck wall and felt exhaustion set in.

"Its gold, Elle," said Dan of the final cut. "It's the best you've ever done."

Elle stayed silent. She didn't like what he said, but she knew he was right. It had been years since she felt that elated and inspired by her work. It made her feel alive.

She had dinner with Matt that night to smooth things over and express to him her desire to be friends and move on. He was appreciative and for the first time, Elle didn't see him as a competitor but rather as a co-worker. She even talked to him briefly about Kate and how being out there had altered her feelings about a lot of things. He chuckled at the change in her and told her it made her even more attractive. She scoffed, but knew that he was sincere.

On the walk back from the tiny restaurant, Elle felt content as the warm Iraqi breeze made her burqa flutter.

"You don't have to wear that," he said, noticing how it was billowing about.

She just smiled and continued to walk.

When they reached the hotel, Dan waited anxiously. "Where've you been? Richard just called and they are moving our story to the Sunday prime time."

"What? That means, it will air in just a couple of hours," said Elle, frantically trying to figure out the time change in her head.

"That's awesome," said Matt.

"*No!* They can't. I told them it had to be Wednesday. They can't run it until Wednesday."

Dan looked at her like she was crazy. "Elle, this is the most watched night. I thought you'd be thrilled."

"We need to warn them."

Dan looked at her, confused. "Warn who?"

"Faiza and her family."

"Why?"

"So they can leave. That only gives them a couple of hours of lead-time. The only reason she agreed to talk was because they were leaving the country."

Both Dan and Matt were stunned. Dan spoke up, "We can't go now. It's past curfew. It's too dangerous. We'll have to wait until morning."

Elle knew that even though her head was spinning with worry, she knew another late night run without an escort would be trouble.

The night was sleepless and Elle paced the floor waiting for the morning to come. She tried to think about where the family could hide until their passage to free-dom took place. She hoped over and over again that her efforts to help hadn't claimed three more lives.

When morning finally came, Elle was waiting and ready. Matt and Dan were both in the lobby and gave her looks of confidence, trying to ease her fears. The drive seemed endless and Elle couldn't sit still. The burqa was smothering, but she was glad to have it on. When they reached the home, Elle opened the car door before they had come to a stop. She looked around to make sure they weren't being watched.

Elle walked quickly to the door, as Matt and Dan followed. When she knocked twice, the door creaked open. She looked back at the others with fear. The door was never left unlocked let alone left open. Elle stepped inside and called out for Faiza. The home was still and nothing looked out of place. Elle continued to call, but only silence returned. She walked around and opened the doors to each bedroom, but found nothing. In the last room, she found everything in place, and her worn suitcase sitting on the bed.

"Oh no," Elle said, walking to it.

Dan followed, "What's wrong? What's in there?"

Elle stood at the bed. "They wouldn't have left it."

"What was it?"

"It was their disguises. I gave them all my clothes."

Dan nodded sadly.

Elle lifted the suitcase and the top fell open. She looked at it and then looked to Dan and laughed out loud, relieved. The suitcase was empty, except for the familiar red duffle bag. It too was empty. Elle knew then, they had left on their own terms.

"Hey, that's the duffle bag that was stolen from the car. It had all the cash in it," said Dan, holding the empty bag. "They stole the money?"

Matt stepped forward. "It was the boy. He knew they needed it to escape. He died trying to help them."

Dan looked to her with a mixture of guilt and skepticism.

Elle gathered her ragged old piece of luggage into her arms and embraced it as she let the utter relief of its emptiness surround her. Elle had no idea where they were, but she knew in her heart that the suitcase was left for a reason. It was a sign from Faiza that they were free.

CHAPTER 26

The Peabody was Elle's and so was the job in London. In early January the secretary of state had met with Tariq Aziz, the Iraqi Foreign Minister, in Geneva to discuss a peaceful resolution to the Kuwaiti invasion, but he failed. Congress had set a deadline for use of force. Normally, something like that would have Elle all aflutter, but instead it made her weak.

Like most of the other journalists based in Iraq, Elle took the long ride back to Amman. She grabbed a seat on a double prop plane and fled the weary region. She was glad to be leaving and she felt as though she had completed her mission.

Elle had until the end of the month to wrap up her life in Washington and make the move to her new position as bureau chief in London.

She was to begin her new role effectively, having the staff know that she was a seasoned and recognized journalist.

Dan and Matt stayed behind. With Elle taking the job Matt had hoped for, he had more to prove, and Dan still hoped to get one more money shot. She worried about what they faced, but knew they were aware of the danger and had no reservations.

Just two days after arriving back in Washington, Elle had already packed up most of her apartment and secured a place in South Hampton, England, that was near the water and allowed cats. It wouldn't take much to move, even with the new job being thousands of miles away.

It was January fourteenth, and the Peabody awards dinner was that night. Elle had reserved her plane tickets to London that morning. She was to fly out exactly two weeks later. She was resolved and ready for her new assignment, and yet her inability to feel excited ate at her. It was her dream job, but now that it was hers, it felt anticlimactic and empty. She was sure that much of her feelings were due to the loss of Hal Norland. The shine of the awards ceremony would be lackluster without him.

She spent the morning in her apartment writing her speech. She dedicated her career to Hal. Hal, the cat, seemed glad to have her back and got around quite well with his three remaining legs. Every time she looked at him, she thought of Rory.

Elle's seat was reserved at the table with Ethan Owen. She saw him waiting but paused at the large windows, looking out onto the busy street along the Mayflower Hotel. She gave herself the once over in the reflection and smiled at the roundness of her hips and fluffed the curls that fell around her face and shoulders. She walked to the table and took a seat next to Ethan. He looked over to her and smiled. Elle put a hand on his arm and smiled back.

"Doesn't get much better than this, does it, Elle?" he said.

She didn't answer but contemplated his question and gave a sideways nod. She felt like royalty in her beaded gown and heavy teardrop earrings. She couldn't help but stare at the sling Ethan still wore and let her thoughts drift to Muki. What happened still hurt and when her award category was announced, it was the clip of his kidnapping that was played. It then cut to Faiza's interview and Elle stared up at the screen and watched as Faiza described seeing her father's dead body hanging above her.

Elle closed her eyes and saw the vision that she had always tried to avoid. It was the ghastly blue monster that hovered above her and filled her dreams almost every night. She tried to push it aside, but it stayed with her, watching her as if trying to tell her something. A vile sensation stuck in her throat and her stomach turned violently.

"I have to go," she said to Ethan.

He stared back at her, dumbfounded. "Where? Elle, they are calling your name."

"You go up for me. I'm leaving."

He called to her, "Elle, you can't leave!"

She made it out to the hallway, and heard the applause. She pulled at the long dress and stumbled to the front of the building and out to the street. She hailed a cab and, once inside, sank down into the seat, trying to breathe. For the first time in her life she realized the demon in her head was no monster, and it wasn't a bad dream. It was a man. She knew who he was and what happened. It made everything she questioned in her life now fit. It was that last piece that had been so elusive and yet now it was so obvious.

When she reached her apartment, she threw her purse and keys on the counter. Hal meowed, as if knowing something was up. Elle went to the phone. She picked up the receiver and went to dial but then noticed the message light blinking. She pushed the play button. It was Rose.

"Elle, it's your mother. We need to talk. I know you're upset, but now that Kate is gone, we need to talk about this—"

Elle gasped. "No." she whispered as the crushing pain struck her. Kate was gone.

The words echoed in her head. As unexpectedly as she had entered Elle's life, she had left it. Elle felt regret and sadness. She felt robbed that she hadn't had more time. Then she wondered if Kate had felt the same way. Elle wiped her eyes and smiled at the thought, knowing Kate had no regrets, and was content that even though her time with Kate was short, it was defining.

Elle scooped up her cat and loaded him into the carrier.

☙❧☙

The service was held in a church that was originally a large stable. It was rustic but elegant and it couldn't have been more fitting. There were dozens of people and Elle sneaked in and sat in the back. She looked around at the strange faces, wondering if she was at the right place. From across the room she saw Rory. He didn't see her. She watched as he shook hands with people and received long hugs from some of the older women. She longed for him, but demurred. She had something else to do first.

"Elle?" Mary tapped her gently on the shoulder.

Elle turned, surprised. Seeing a kind and somewhat familiar face was a relief and Elle smiled.

"I'm so glad you're here. Your aunt was a caring and good woman. I'll miss her so much. You should come to the front and sit with the family."

Elle shook her head. "I'd rather not. I just want to sit back here and think."

Mary gave her a knowing smile. "I know that she would be glad you're here. She was such a good woman."

Elle nodded. "I know she felt the same way about you." She looked around at all the people. Again her gaze lingered on Rory. "Mary, can I speak to you in private?" she asked. "I need to talk to someone, and I think you can help me sort out some things that I don't understand."

"I'll do what I can," said Mary, as she led Elle to an area away from the crowd.

When they reached a secluded and quiet corner, Elle took a seat on a bench near a window and directed Mary to do the same. Elle gazed outside at the rolling fields of patchwork mud and snow. "I've misjudged Rory. I accused him of some terrible things."

Mary stayed silent and let Elle continue.

"My mother told me that Rory tried to burn down the barn. I didn't believe her at first, but then I confronted him, and he admitted to it. I accused him of killing my sister. That's the last time I spoke to him." Elle's voice shuttered and she looked at Mary with red eyes. "I haven't been able to sleep or think of anything else but him. I just can't believe that he did it. There has to be a reason he started that fire, and I think I may know."

Mary bit at her bottom lip. "It was such a sad time. I was only a teenager when it all happened. I don't remember a lot, but I'll tell you what I know."

"I was going to talk to Kate, but never got the chance and I don't know what to believe from my mother. I need to know the truth."

Mary nodded.

Elle continued. "When my sister died, I was playing a game with her and dared her to go hide in the barn. I told her if she stayed there for an hour that she could play with my friends and me. The reason I told her to hide in the barn was because I was afraid of it. I still have nightmares about a horrible-looking monster in the rafters." She looked at Mary. "That monster wasn't a dream, was it?"

Mary shook her head. "No." Mary told her what had

happened in that barn. Who that monster was and why Elle had suffered the scars, not only on her hands and head, but also on her heart. When she was finished, she put a hand on Elle's leg. "It's a shame you didn't know the truth all these years. It may have changed things and brought you home sooner."

Elle felt her shoulders lighten, yet her heart was loaded down with grief and guilt. "Thank you." She stood and straightened her skirt.

Mary smiled. "Are you staying for the dinner?"

Elle shook her head. "No, I need to leave."

Mary looked distraught.

Elle tried to comfort her. "Everything is good. What you told me, I had to hear. I appreciate it." She stood and took Mary's hand. "Thank you." Then Elle left.

☙❧☙

A bitter cold breeze made the clouds circle the moon as it stood out in a black sky. The crowd of mourners had settled into small talk and some of the women began the process of cleaning up after dinner. As the group pulled on gloves and buttoned coats, a stir came from the far end of the church hall.

"There's a fire!" someone yelled across the room.

The entire crowd turned toward the wall of windows where smoke had already formed a tall white spire in the night.

Rory pushed his way through and went to the door. Outside the building, he studied the plume then turned back to Ervin Coughlin and put his hand up. "I'm going. Don't call on this."

Ervin was puzzled but agreed. He stood with several others, as Rory pulled away and drove toward the blaze.

At the farm, Elle had parked her car on the knoll and

stood in the middle of the field. She watched the fire dance and the smoke slink rhythmically into the peaceful Pennsylvania night. Down the hill she could see the freshly built walls of the clinic. She pulled her sweater tightly around her. The glow of flames lit up her face and gave her a warm blush.

Rory slid the truck to a stop, and jumped out onto the snow and slush. He quickly walked to her. "Elle, are you okay?" he asked, as he approached the fire.

Her reverie was broken. Without looking at him, she nodded. "Yes."

Rory walked closer. "What are you doing?"

She smiled dazedly. "I'm burning down the barn."

"I can see that. Why?"

Elle turned and looked into Rory's eyes with purpose. "Because it should have been done a long time ago."

Rory looked down. "When did you come back? I didn't see you at the funeral."

"I was there. I left early. It's not as though it matters to Kate now."

"Then why did you come back?"

Elle turned to him with puckered eyebrows. "Disappointed?"

"No. Never."

Elle looked back at the fire. "It's hard to believe that something so warm could be so cruel."

Rory stayed silent.

Elle continued to stare into the embers but put her hand out to him.

Rory was surprised and a rush of relief fell over his entire being. "Will you ever forgive me for what happened to your sister?"

"How can I forgive you for something that wasn't your fault? I don't blame you for what happened. You were just trying to get rid of the pain. It was your father that hung himself in that barn. That was the blue monster I saw all those years ago and kept seeing in nightmares. You were a kid who tried to forget what happened. You didn't know my sister was hiding inside. The question is, will you forgive me for blaming you?"

Rory nodded and then turned to the flames. The large beams crackled and the wood slowly disintegrated in the fire. "Thank you, Ellie."

"I did this for both of us. It feels good. Now you can finish your clinic without being in its shadow."

She held her hand just inches from his chest. "I've spent my entire life running away from the thought of family and the memories of what happened here. It's time I let them go. Burning down the barn may not make it go away, but it's a start. I feel good about this. The people need what you do and it's what should be here. This is your home."

Rory looked down and saw Elle's suitcase sitting nearby.

She noticed and motioned to it. "That is what I called home." Her mind seemed worlds away and her face went from serene to sad and back. She looked up at him with eyes that were warm and loving. She reached down and took the handle and lifted the suitcase. She took a step back. Tears rolled down her face.

"Ellie, please don't cry."

Elle walked to where the glowing cinders of the fire crackled. She took that mobile home of her life and heaved it into the fire. It crashed through the burning boards and tiny sparks danced into the black of the night.

Rory stood astounded, looking into the fire, as the suitcase disappeared into the flames. "Did that have all your clothes in it?"

She brushed her hands together in a "that's that" gesture. She patted her thighs. "It doesn't matter, they don't fit anymore."

He shook his head in amazement. "Cool. More closet space for me."

She turned and laughed then cried. "I love you, Rory, I'll love you always."

Rory reached over and pulled her close, wrapping her into his chest. He held her close and kissed her long and tenderly.

"Welcome home, Ellie. Welcome home."

About the Author

Brenda Stanley is the author of four novels—*I Am Nuchu*, *The Color of Snow*, *The Treasure of Cedar Creek,* and *Like Ravens in Winter*—and four cookbooks. She is semi-retired from her job as news anchor at NBC affiliate station KPVI in Eastern Idaho. She has been recognized by the Scripps Howard Foundation, the Hearst Journalism Awards, the Idaho Press Club, and the Society for Professional Journalists. You can reach her at her website: brendastanleybooks.com

Made in the USA
Las Vegas, NV
19 February 2021

18211558R00154